DANGEROUS GUNMAN

Spur's left hand gripped the knob on the back-door and turned it. It was not locked. He turned the handle as far as it would go, pulling forward on the knob. When he was sure the latch had cleared, he opened the door an inch so he could see inside.

It was a back bedroom. Nobody was inside. He slid past the partly open panel and closed it the same way he'd opened it, without a sound. He took cautious steps across the room to the door opposite him.

That would put him in the center of the small house. He opened the second door the same way.

Just as he moved it inward an inch, a rifle went off inside the room. He pushed the door open a foot. A man lay on the floor firing a rifle over a windowsill a foot off the braided rug. He fired again.

Spur sent a shot into the wall beside the man and bellowed.

"You move a finger and you're a dead man!"

SPUR

DENVER DARLIN'

DIRK FLETCHER

LEISURE BOOKS   NEW YORK CITY

A Leisure Book ®

October 1991

Published by

Dorchester Publishing Co., Inc.
276 Fifth Avenue
New York, NY 10001

Printed in the United States of America.

Chapter One

The naked woman lay on the hotel bed starring at the man beside her. They had just made love, but she wasn't satisfied and was still keyed up, so tense and excited she couldn't keep her hands off him.

"Oh, yes, that was wonderful. You're good, you know that, considerate and tender, you are nice! Just marvelous. You even let me have my own pleasures. My husband will never let me do that. I knew you were a special gentleman as soon as we met. Now I know it for sure. We have the rest of the night."

She twirled one long strand of black hair around her finger, moving so her breasts touched his chest again. "You have to promise never to tell my husband. He would be outraged and come after you with a gun. I'll never tell him."

Wanda Livingston reached up and kissed the man

she had met only three hours ago. Then she kissed him again. "At least twice more, darling man," she said, her voice breathy, wanting him, needing to burn out the long pent-up fires that burned in her slender body.

"I don't think we can again," the man said.

"I'll have to convince you," Wanda argued, moving her naked hips against his. "I know how to make a man want me. My . . . my husband taught me, of course." She looked at him and smiled, then tried to kiss him.

She felt only a slight sting as the ten-inch stiletto, no more than a half-inch wide at the handle, thrust upward under her ribs and with deadly accuracy plunged through both chambers of her heart.

Her brown eyes went wide, her mouth opened to tell him of her shock and surprise, but the words died on her lips as her heart refused to pump again. Her whole body spasmed once with the heart failure and she fell back on the bed, her eyes staring at the cheap wallpaper on the ceiling and her mouth forever in a silent "Oh."

The man snorted, withdrew the blade, and was surprised as usual at how small a wound it made. The puncture of her white skin did not bleed. There was no pressure internally to force blood out the puncture once the heartbeat stopped.

He dressed quickly, stared at the woman again, then pulled from his pocket a small leather coin purse. He took out two 20-cent pieces and placed them over the open eyes of the woman.

Then he picked up his carpetbag, and made sure all of his belongings were safely stowed in the bag. He checked the room again to make sure everything he brought had been removed, then went to the door.

He eased it open an inch, saw no one in the hall, and swung the door inward and stepped through. He closed the door and walked away down the hall. He would be on the evening stage. It came through just after six-thirty.

He liked the stage more than the train even though stages took longer to get to Denver. He smiled grimly, thinking of the dead woman.

That's one more who has paid the price. Damn them! One more slut who will never hurt another human being!

Spur McCoy talked with the county sheriff at Franklinville, Kansas, about two hundred miles west of Kansas City.

"Appreciate what you're trying to do, Mr. McCoy, but we've about closed that case. Yes, you're right. I can see now that the killing fits a pattern you say started in Kansas City, Missouri, and continued with the next one fifty miles from us to the east.

"But like I said, the woman is six feet into the Kansas soil right now. All I have is the report my deputy wrote up."

Spur nodded, his eyes unwavering. "I appreciate that, Sheriff Nasset. That report is how we know her murder fits the pattern. What I'm wondering is about the reputation of the lady. Was she a faithful wife, did she run around any, was she wild, did she have lovers her husband knew nothing about?"

The sheriff shifted in his chair.

"Ain't right to talk bad about the dead, Mr. McCoy."

"It might be good if it could help me stop this maniac who seems to be riding the stage west through Kansas."

Sheriff Nasset sighed. He looked out to the front of his small office and then back at Spur.

"All right! Remember that this is a small town. People do talk. Hortense was what some men call an easy woman. Her husband was gone from time to time working cattle, and she . . . well, she did have men visitors now and then."

"Did she charge them or was it just for the thrill of it?"

"She never charged, said that would make her a whore. Her husband beat her up twice, but that didn't stop her. I guess somebody finally did put an end to it. Her husband was gone at the time. Just got back a week ago."

"On the day of the killing her husband was working cattle twenty miles south of town?"

"That's right. He worked there all day. Not a chance he could have done it and ridden forty miles and not been missed. We cleared him."

"But you haven't closed the case?"

"Closed? I got duties to perform for citizens of this county, Mr. McCoy. Can't dwell on the dead."

"You said she had some things covering her eyes. Did you save the items?"

"Sure did. Right there in the envelope."

Spur shook out the envelope and two coins fell to the desk. Both were silver 20-cent pieces.

"Not your usual kind of coin, wouldn't you say, Sheriff?"

"Right. Them twenty-centers look too much like

the quarters, and I hear they might not make them much longer."

"Fact is they have been minted only this year of 1875, and they'll be made next year again. But you're right. After that they won't mint any more of them."

"Glad of that. They're a nuisance."

"Could I have one of them as evidence of how this killer marks his victims?"

"Don't rightly know," the sheriff said. He rubbed his jaw. "Reckon since you're from the government and all, it would be legal enough. You sign a receipt and return it when you through with it."

"Fine." Spur put one of the 20-cent coins on the desk, then from his pocket took out a small flat envelope and shook out four more of the same kind of coins.

"Be damned," Sheriff Nasset said.

"About the size of it. This killer leaves his trademark on every woman he kills. So far he killed a whore in Kansas City, a banker's wife about fifty miles back, and now this one."

"Why does he leave a calling card like that?"

"We don't know, but sooner or later I'll catch up with him and nail the bastard. This killing happened April 4th, you said. Today is April 24th. I'm twenty days behind him somewhere."

As Spur McCoy waited for the stagecoach to come through, he sent a telegram to the county sheriffs in the two county seats 40 and 60 miles ahead. He would much rather take the train, but the railroad was well over 150 miles north in Nebraska following the Platte River.

Early the following morning, Spur McCoy arrived in Rocky Place, Kansas. It was 60 miles from the last killing. The sheriff there had another victim of the 40-cent killer.

"Near as we can tell she died the night of April 14th," Sheriff Paulson told McCoy. He had first looked long and curiously at McCoy's identification card and the letter he carried affirming that he was a member of the United States Secret Service and was on official business. The service was not well known by many outside of Washington, D.C. It had been chartered by Congress in 1859 to protect the integrity of United States currency.

Then gradually, the duties were expanded to handle any interstate crimes against the government or that local jurisdictions couldn't take care of. Now it was dealing with almost any crime where state boundaries were crossed.

"We think she died that night," the sheriff said. "Her husband asked us to look for her the next day 'cause she wasn't home when he got there. We didn't find her until a maid went in to fix up that hotel room two days after it was rented to some traveling man."

"Her name was Wanda Livingston, the report says," Spur noted. "She was married to John. Sheriff, you've told me the woman had two coins covering her eyes when she was found. Were they silver twenty-cent pieces?"

The sheriff looked up quickly. "How in hell you know that? We didn't tell nobody that. Just the hotel maid and my deputy and me know that."

Spur took out his envelope and showed the sheriff his six twenty-cent coins.

"Evidently this killer has a supply of these rare coins and he uses them to close the woman's eyes after he kills her. Just wanted to be sure it's the same killer. Oh, how did this woman die?"

"Somebody stabbed her, one neat thrust right into her heart. She didn't bleed a bit. Must have died in a half a second."

"Strange," Spur said. "This is the fourth victim, and each one has been killed in a different way. If he didn't put those coins on the eyes I'd be at a dead end."

"Maybe the bastard is hoping somebody will catch him before he kills another woman," the sheriff said.

"Maybe. One thing we know for sure."

"What's that, McCoy?"

"This bastard must hate women with a passion."

"All women?"

"Don't know. Oh, did this Wanda have a good reputation in town? Faithful wife and all?"

Sheriff snorted. "Not hardly. She had her first baby before she got married. Got pregnant with another and then got married. First husband ran off and she got married again. Tell the truth, Wanda would flip up her skirt for almost any man who could get a hard-on."

"Well, damn. She fits the pattern. More and more I'm wondering what kind of an animal this killer must be. He hates women, for damn sure."

"You know that somebody else came through here investigating this same case," the sheriff said.

Spur glanced up, surprised. "Didn't know. Who was it?"

"Not sure. I was out on a rustling problem. I

remember one of my deputies said somebody came in and read our report, then left. Deputy didn't say who it was."

"Probably meet him down the line somewhere. Can you tell me the names of the sheriffs in the next four counties to the west?"

Spur wrote the names down, then went back over the report on the death of Wanda. It seemed she had been killed by a knife, but with just one deft stroke that must have gone upward into the heart from below her rib cage. The wound was less than half an inch long.

"Damn long pig-sticker," Spur said.

The sheriff looked up. "Back in Chicago they call that a Chicago ice pick. Deadly, and takes some practice to know how to use them that good."

"Nothing at all about the man who rented the room?" Spur asked.

"It was two days later. The clerk wasn't sure. A man, but that was about all he could say. That clerk never was one to win any awards for being smart."

Spur read the report again, made some entries in a small notebook he carried in his jacket pocket, and thanked the sheriff. He had an hour before the stage moved west. Time enough for a good meal. He tried the hotel.

Spur McCoy picked up responses to the four wires he had sent from the last town at the next one down the stage line when the rig pulled in at about eight P.M.

He was nearly 40 miles from the last Kansas town and about three quarters of the way across the state. He settled down in the telegraph office and read all four, which he had asked to be sent there.

The first two towns had no reports of murdered women, but the third did. It was well over toward Colorado. The stage was almost ready to go when McCoy ran out of the telegraph office and yelled at the driver.

"Got room for another passenger?"

It was a big Concord stage, the most comfortable of the bunch still running the side routes and feeding passengers into the rail lines. Still, it had wooden seats front and back and a bench in the middle where three people sat with no backrest—if there were that many passengers.

Spur knew it would be hours and hours of misery, even with the thick cushions he'd bought at the general store. Bouncing and jolting and rolling right through the nighttime hours. They stopped every 50 miles or so for food, and every 12 miles for fresh horses.

Sometime the next morning, after several delays, Spur McCoy arrived in Grove, Kansas. It was at the west edge of Kansas where the land continued its upward sweep into Colorado and the high country of the Rocky Mountains.

Spur talked with the sheriff, who showed him the report. It mentioned the usual terrible signature of the killer: two 20-cent pieces on the eyes. In this case the woman had been beheaded with an ax, and the naked torso found in one alley and the head in another.

Spur thanked the sheriff and then asked his usual question.

"Sheriff, what was the reputation of this woman in the community?"

"She was the Baptist preacher's wife! What would you think?" he responded.

"My guess is that she was a scarlet woman, sneaking around behind the parson's back and having her way with some of the young gay blades of the town."

The sheriff looked up quickly. "Now how in tarnation could you know that?"

"Just a guess, but it follows a pattern, Sheriff, of the kind of woman this man kills. He must think he's on some kind of a holy crusade. I've been tracking this man all the way from Missouri. Any idea what he looks like?"

A young woman who had been seated in a row of chairs in the office near the door stood and came over. She was slender, maybe four inches over five feet tall, with fire-red hair and a curious smile.

"We know a little about his description, Mr. McCoy," she said. "I couldn't help but hear what you asked the sheriff. The killer is under thirty years of age, about five-eight, medium build with dark hair, clean-shaven, and no noticeable accent."

"Miss, I'm afraid—"

"I heard you were behind me somewhere investigating these murders. You happened to catch me here. I thought perhaps we could pool our efforts and grab this killer that much faster." She held out her hand. "I'm Ruth Abigail Leggett from Kansas City, Missouri."

Spur shook the delicate hand, noticing that her fingernails had been polished and tended to and that her hand was soft. He let go and she smiled.

"You are Spur McCoy?"

"Yes, Miss Leggett, that's right."

"I'm a detective, Mr. McCoy. I've been hired by a man in Kansas City to track down this killer. My client has a personal interest in seeing the man brought to justice."

Spur checked the girl more closely. Her red hair was a fiery river down her back to her waist, her eyes a soft green, and she had a fair complexion he was sure would sunburn quickly. Her smile was delightful, and a small mouth now made it even more so as her lips parted to show even white teeth.

"Is your inspection over, and did I pass?"

"You passed. However, I always work alone."

"Oh. But consider that I might be able to help and both of us working together could—"

"Sorry, that's not possible."

"Why?"

"I work for the United States Government. This is an interstate crime and I'm not authorized to work with anyone else."

"That's ridiculous. What difference does it make who you work with or through, as long as we grab this guy before he murders half the women in the West?"

"Sorry, Miss Leggett, but that's our policy. Nothing I can do about it."

"You don't even want to hear what I know about the killer?"

"I doubt very much if you know as much as I do." Spur turned to the sheriff, thanked him, tipped his low-crowned black hat with the straight brim to the lady, and walked out. She hurried out behind him.

"Look, I've been here a day longer than you have. This is the end of the telegraph line through here. The main one goes along the railroad tracks up on the Platte River. How are you going to find the next murder victim?"

"Lots of ways," Spur said as he strode down the boardwalk.

"Yeah? Name two?"

Spur hadn't thought that far ahead. Ruth Abigail hurried to keep up with his long stride.

"All right, name one way," she said.

He stopped and she almost bumped into him.

"Look, Miss Leggett. I'm tired, I'm hungry, and I need some time to think about it."

"Good. Let me buy you supper and I'll tell you what I know about the case. You can consider it and if you think it's of no value to you, I'll leave and work the case on my own. But . . ." She tapped him on the arm.

"But if you think what I know can help you and help both of us find this killer, then you'll agree to work with me until we catch this miserable bastard."

Her eyes glinted as he looked at her quickly.

"You have a pistol?" he asked.

Spur felt her move beside him, and when he looked down, the slip of a woman drew a derringer from her reticule and pushed it into his side.

"It isn't cocked," she said.

Spur chuckled. "Fine, show me to the best eatery in town. I could eat a wall-eyed mule."

Chapter Two

They both had steak dinners at a nearby restaurant that lacked in Eastern refinements such as white tablecloths and fine china, although the steak was one of the best Spur had eaten. They talked little as they ate, and he noticed that she finished her steak and dinner as quickly as he did.

"You put away a lot of supper," Spur said.

"When I hunt down killers I need it. Now that you've had some time to think about it, how will you find the next spot where our maniac has killed another woman?"

"Two choices for transportation. I can buy a horse and ride due north to the railroad in Nebraska and take the train out to Cheyenne to the telegraph and make my inquiries. Then ride the train down to Denver. My guess is since he's on this track he's heading for Denver and then maybe on west, Salt Lake or San Francisco."

"The other choice?" Ruth Abigail asked.

"The stage goes from here on through to Denver. I checked. Not a pleasant ride, and they'll be using the rugged celerity wagons, but I can make it."

"So which one did you pick?"

"The stage. I've already sent letters on the one that left an hour ago to each of the sheriffs between here and Denver. If any of them has a murder that fits our man's style, that sheriff is supposed to send a letter to me in care of the sheriff of the next county seat east of him."

"Yeah, I figured you were smart. I planned on waiting for you here today and if you didn't show up to head on west, on the stage. Already have my ticket. So we can work together?"

"Not a chance." He grinned. "That burning bush of a head of red hair of yours is tempting, but it wouldn't work. You'd wind up doing something stupid and getting me killed. That I just can't stand, getting killed."

"I might do the job myself," Ruth Abigail said. "Seriously, I ruined a whole day waiting for you, hoping that you were smart and would see the advantage of our working as a team. I'm damn good at this trade. I've got a notch or two on my gun, and I'm no wide-eyed little girl."

"You're right about that," Spur said, grinning. "You are a well-filled-out big girl."

Ruth Abigail carefully poured the last half of her glass of water into his lap. Spur's crotch was soaked immediately, and he gasped in surprise.

"Stop talking that way, Spur McCoy!" she said sharply, her voice soft but angry. "We're talking business, not bedroom tomfoolery. If I decide to work with you, it will be on a equal basis. I might not beat you in a gunfight, not the way you have that hogleg tied low that way, but I can hit what I aim at, I can ride, I can live in the open, I can move through the woods and brush and desert like a damned Indian. What I'm offering you is a straight business deal.

"We help each other catch this savage, out-of-his-mind woman-killer. That, Mr. Spur McCoy, is all I'm offering you."

"Fine. Like I say, lady, I work alone. Now, I need to go to the hotel and get a room and change into some dry clothes."

"You brought it on yourself. My offer to work together is open until eight o'clock tonight. Then you're on your own. I'm in Room Twenty-two at the hotel. For starters, I know where the next killing happened." Ruth Abigail rose, turned, and left the table as Spur untangled his legs and tried to stand.

He snorted, took the check to the cashier and paid it, then picked up his one carpetbag, the woven kind with a firm bottom in it, and walked across to the town's one hotel, the Kansan, and booked a room. He saw two men stare at his wet pants. He glared at them and they moved on.

It was slightly after six P.M. when he settled into his room, checked his Colt .45, and laid out his shaving gear for morning. The stage would leave at nine-fifteen, or thereabouts, the ticket agent had said.

Spur thought again about the slender redhead with the surging bounty of long red hair. She would be a handful, in or out of bed, he was sure. She did seem to have a special talent for detective work, especially if she knew where the next killing had occurred. He paced his room for half an hour trying to think it through. He could waste two or three days locating the next murder.

In that time the man might hit Denver, take the spur line up to the transcontinental railroad, and be halfway to San Francisco or Chicago before he could catch him.

Spur took out the pocket notebook and reviewed all of the facts about the case he had written down. He used a pencil since it was easier when traveling, and if the pages got wet in a rainstorm, the pencil marks wouldn't smear.

What the hell, in this case she might have some insight into the women that were being killed that he didn't. He'd give it a try, maybe. He went to Room 22 down the hall. He was in 14. He knocked on the door and waited.

"Who is it?" The words came thinly through the door.

"McCoy."

He heard the door unlock, and she opened it two inches so she could see him. Her face was a thin slice of white and one soft green eye.

"So what did you decide?"

"Figured I should tell you that you're on your own. I'm moving out on that stage tomorrow and following my plan."

The slice of her face frowned. Then she lifted one

brow. "About what I figured. You better come in so we can talk about this."

"No reason to talk," he said.

She let the door open further, and he saw that she wore only a thin chemise over her chest. "Come in, we need to talk." She lifted the white chemise off over her head and one full, pink-tipped breast winked at him through the partly open door.

"Damn!" Spur whispered. "You don't play fair."

"I don't plan on playing fair, I plan on winning." She held out one hand, and he took it and stepped into the room. She closed the door and locked it, then looked up smiling, her red hair falling partly over her shoulders with the motion and covering half of her breasts.

"I told you I'm no dewy-eyed little girl. I know when something is right. In this case I know you and I can make a great team to track down this bastard killer. All you need is a little tender persuasion."

"Not fair, Abby. You're too damn beautiful with your clothes on. Now with your breasts all bare . . . goddamn!"

"Let's talk," she said. "You called me Abby. I like that. One of my uncles called me Abby. He was my favorite." She took his hand and led him to the bed and sat down. He sat beside her. She pushed her leg over so it touched his thigh, and he felt the immediate flood of warmth.

Spur wore a light tan shirt and buckskin vest. She undid the vest buttons and then the shirt fasteners and rubbed her hands on his bare chest.

"Nice, hard, muscled, no potbelly. I love a man who is slender and with firm muscles."

Spur bent and kissed her. Her mouth caught his and held it. Her lips parted then and she let his tongue dart inside.

"Yeah, oh, yeah, but I like that," she said when their lips at last parted. His hand moved up her side and soon captured one of her breasts.

"Feel me, Spur. Touch me that way. I love it. Yes! I knew you would be a good lover too. Two yards tall and a foot thick. Glorious. Bet you're hung like a wild stallion."

His hand caressed her mound, working around and around, then finally coming to the areola, so pink and perfect and pure. He hesitated, then caught the tip, the soft nipple, and toyed with it, rolling it between his thumb and finger until it sprang up and hardened and he saw it build and grow.

Her breathing picked up and her hands worked at his belt. He took off the gunbelt and laid it on the floor, then went back to her beautiful breasts. He kissed her again. Then when it ended, he trailed wet kisses down her cheek, to her neck, then lower, until he found the swell of her breast.

Abby sighed. Then her breath caught as he kissed her breast. Her eyes drifted closed and she smiled and waited for his lips to travel around her breast and reach the peak.

"Yes, love, yes! Wonderful, so sexy, makes me just warm and hot all over. Makes me want to tear off your clothes."

She had his belt opened. Now she undid the buttons and pushed back his brown town pants. Only soft cotton undergarments barred her way. They were tented out and she giggled a moment, then pulled down the cotton underwear and watched his manhood swing up.

"Oh, lordy!" she gasped, sucking in a breath. Her eyes went wide, and for just a moment she bent toward his crotch. She stopped and caught him with her hand, holding his shaft tenderly.

His lips kissed her nipple and Abby gasped. Then he licked it and sucked half of her breast into his mouth, gently chewing and sucking on it.

"Oh, damn, oh, damn, oh, damn!" she crooned. Slowly she bent forward so more of her breast hung down for him. Spur moved, then lay his head on her legs so she could lower the rest of her breast to him. He traded one for the other now, and she stretched to touch his manhood.

Spur rolled away, pushing her down on the bed on her back and stripping down her skirt and a half-petticoat. She wore only soft pink bloomers with elastic at the waist. He reached for the bloomers, but she tugged at his pants.

Spur sat up, pulled off his boots and then his pants and his short underwear, and stood before her.

"My God, you're beautiful!" Abby whispered. "So lean and hard and so trim. No belly at all!"

He kissed her again, pushing her down on her back, laying half on top of her, feeling the heat from her thighs as he pressed down. She sucked on his tongue, moaned in delight, and pumped her crotch up hard against his thighs.

Spur pushed one hand down her chest, past her flat little belly to the top of the bloomers. He worked under the band, and moved down to the start of her muff of what he'd bet was red thatch.

She moaned and nodded, and he pulled her

bloomers down a ways. Then his mouth left hers
and dropped to her belly. He kissed a hot trail down
over her slight mound to the start of her pubic hair.

"Oh, God!" she yelped. "God, that's so fine, beautiful. I could lay here for hours!"

He pulled the bloomers down as he kissed lower
into the thick tangled mass of red that hid her
treasure.

Spur pushed the silky garment down onto her
legs, and Abby squealed in delight. Her hips lifted
toward him, and then sank down and moved around
and around. With one hand he tore the bloomers
down her legs and off her feet. He never noticed
when she took off her shoes.

Now Spur poised above her, looking at her whole
naked form. Perfect slender legs, rising to her red
thatch, with a swell of her hips and the nipping in at
her waist. Then a flat belly and above on her rib cage
her perfect throbbing breasts.

"Marvelous," he said. He lay down beside her,
pulling a forest of red hair away from her breasts
and onto the bed between them. She kissed him,
then sat up and caught his rod and held it, working it
back and forth twice, watching him. Her fingers
explored the heavy pulled-up sack between his legs,
then returned to his manhood.

She bent and kissed the purpled arrowhead of
him, and Spur twitched at the touch, at the idea.
Gently her lips parted and she pushed down over his
shaft, taking half of it in her mouth, then slid off him
leaving a trail of wetness. Her eyes sparkled as she
watched him.

"I hope you liked that. There's a lot more mouth
kisses like that for him soon, but not the first time."

He cupped one of her breasts, holding it, kissing the nipple. "How the first time?"

"Standing up! I've never made love standing up. A friend of mine says it can't be done."

"Don't believe everything you hear," Spur said. He stepped off the bed and beckoned to her. "Stand against the wall," he told her. She did. "Lean your back against it, then lock your hands behind my neck. Next lift up and put your feet around my waist."

"This feels strange!" she protested.

"Not for long." Spur made sure she was safely attached. Then he slid her hips away from him a little, moved her and adjusted, and a moment later drove into her slot hard and sure until they could mortise together no more.

"My God!" Abby shrieked. "You did it! It's never felt that way before. Oh, damn, here I come!"

She shivered and pumped toward him, but she could move little. Her body spasmed and trembled. She wailed in a shimmering moan of ecstasy, and her body shook and rattled a dozen more times before she sagged against him. Sweat beaded her forehead. Her chest had turned a bright pink with the proof of her climax, and she panted.

"Oh, Lord, I have died and this must be heaven's open gate!"

"Almost," Spur said, and began stroking into her, flattening her back and buttocks against the wall as he did so, and bringing a wail of excitement from her as she built toward another satisfaction.

They worked together faster and faster, and at last Spur could hold it back no longer and yelled in release as he climaxed and pounded a dozen more times, before he wheezed and gushed out lungs full of air as he tried to replace the energy he had lost.

They both sagged against the wall. Then she let down her legs, and they parted and went to the bed and stretched out there in each other's arms as they slowly recuperated from the physical orgasm.

"Be damned," Abby said. "It can be done standing up. At least one of us was standing up." She took in several deep breaths. "Now is the time I convince you to work together on this damn murderer. Look, I'm smart, I'm good at my job, I can be a big help and carry my half of the project." She grinned and kissed the tip of his nose.

"Besides all that, remember that I fuck good and I'll want you every night that we're free."

Spur laughed softly and kissed her lips quickly. "Try to learn never to oversell. Hell, I was more than convinced as soon as I saw your big tits. But I want you to go right on and convince me the rest of the night that we should work together."

Abby grinned and leaned up on one elbow and watched him, her long red hair tumbling down past her arm. "Hey, big cock, I'll do my fucking best to convince you."

They both laughed, and began trying to figure out how to get started on number two.

It was nearly three o'clock that morning before they at last blew out the lamp and collapsed on the bed and went to sleep. Spur awoke at six A.M. as he had done for ten years, went back to sleep for an hour, then got up and kissed Abby's breasts until she stirred and came awake.

They made the stagecoach with less than five minutes to spare. Abby had brought along a snack.

She said they both knew how bad the food was at the stagecoach meal stops. It was nearly 40 miles to the next county seat, this one across the border in Colorado.

They lost a wheel and it cost them two hours to get the replacement one on from under the rig. The driver had never changed one before. Spur wound up finding the lever to lift the rig and doing most of the work. There was only one other man on board.

When they got to Mountain Dale, Colorado, Abby and Spur got off the rig. It was a meal stop and they would be there for 20 minutes. Abby had told Spur before they left on the stage that the next killing had taken place in this small town five days before. They went at once to the sheriff's office. The sheriff was an older man who didn't wear a gun and couldn't see far enough to use one anyway.

They introduced themselves, then got down to the killing.

"Sheriff Pratt, was there a report made on the murder?" Spur asked.

"Yep, always have the men write out a report. Don't say much. Her name was Muriel Lowener. She was a waitress at the Newstate Cafe. Some said she made extra money taking gents into her small house of a night, but nobody would come front and swear to it."

"How exactly was she killed, Sheriff?"

"Huh? Oh, killed. Yep. Matter of fact, she was hung. Then after she was dead her heart was cut right out of her chest. Doc Thompson, our local sawbones, says it wasn't a neat job, meat-ax kind of thing. No doctor did that."

"Sheriff, you know there's been a string of killings like this back down the stage line," Abby said.

"Heard about it in your letter, you be the one who wrote it. Fact is I got a letter for one Spur McCoy from Sheriff Petroff about three counties over, right near to Denver."

Spur held out his hand for the offered letter. He took it then showed the sheriff a 20-cent coin. "Ever see one of these, Sheriff?"

"Quarter, sure . . . no, by Jack . . . that's one of them twenty-cent pieces. Same kind as was on that murdered woman's eyes. One on each eye. Blamed coins are rare as hen's teeth these days."

"He leaves a trail like he wants somebody to follow him," Spur said. "What kind of a monster is doing this?"

"The kind of monster I don't want to meet in some brightly lit street even at midday," Abby said.

Spur grabbed her elbow. "Thanks, Sheriff. We're going to try to catch the stage before it finishes its stop. Much obliged."

They caught it with only half a minute to spare.

Chapter Three

Abby and Spur bounced along in the celerity wagon toward Denver. It was a high-clearance, rugged kind of a rig with no comfort features, more like a square box with seats and curtains for sides. There was no leather suspension system as on the big Concords that would give the rig some cushioning from the ruts and bumps of the trail-like wagon road.

Even with the lighter rig, it took a team of six to pull the celerity up the grades and switchbacks moving from four thousand feet elevation at the last stop up and up and up toward the still-unseen heart of the Rocky Mountains.

"Are we chasing a ghost we'll never catch up with?" Abby asked softly so only Spur could hear. There were three others in the coach, two women and one man.

Spur shook his head. "He's real enough, a madman who, evidently for some reason, hates whores and loose women. If we run across him we'll have to be careful."

"He must be a monster," Abby said. "So many poor women."

They sat close together in the corner of the bouncing coach.

Spur nodded. "A monster, agreed, but he probably doesn't look like one. Fact is, he could look like me or your favorite uncle or the driver up on the high seat. Most terrible, vicious criminals don't look the part."

"Which makes them that much harder to find." Abby paused, her face frowning slightly, green eyes colder now, angry. "I wonder why this man is so furious with women."

"Probably only loose women. Maybe his wife was a real slut and ran away before he could kill her, so he's taking his anger out on all the other loose women he can find."

"Then why not stick to prostitutes? Lots more of them around, and they're easy to find and hire for his butchery."

"True. This next victim was killed last night. With any luck we'll at least get a look at the body and maybe talk to some of the people who saw her last. If we're real fortunate someone might remember seeing her with a man last night."

It was dark when the celerity wagon pulled into the stage depot at Willow Bend, Colorado, about 40 miles outside of Denver. They were still on the wide, high plateau sloping up toward the Rockies beyond Denver.

They took their bags and went directly to the

small sheriff's office. One of the deputies gave them the report on the woman's death.

"Name was Lady Jane from the Roundup Saloon," the deputy told them. "She was one of the best fancy ladies at the place." He looked at Abby. "Begging your pardon, miss, but that's what she was."

Spur read the report written in pencil in labored writing.

"The report says she was strangled into unconsciousness, then both her breasts were cut off."

"Yes, sir. Doc told us she must have been unconscious but not dead when he did the cutting, 'cause she didn't scream or nothing. But if she was dead she wouldn't have bled all that much when he was cutting. He said a dead body don't bleed like one does with the heart still a-pumping."

Abby looked away and took a deep breath.

Spur thanked the deputy. "We best be talking to the head madam at the Roundup Saloon."

Abby clung to his arm as they walked out of the sheriff's office. She looked up at him, her face angry. "This beast . . . he's getting bloodier. He's a real monster. First chance I get I'm going to blow his head off with five shots!"

"Sugar and spice," Spur said.

"What?"

"Sugar and spice, that's what little girls are made of. My mother used to tell me that."

"Don't get snotty. I'm building up a real hatred for this man."

"Not good for an investigator to become emotionally involved with the case or the suspect. We must remain objective at all—"

She punched him in the shoulder and he stopped talking.

The saloon was not the best in the small town, but he'd seen lots worse. They went in the front and stopped at the front end of the bar. The apron looked up, his glance lingering on Abby for a second before moving on to Spur.

"We need to see whoever handles your fancy ladies," Spur said.

"Why?"

"Need to talk about the one who was murdered last night."

"Yeah, her office is right over here." The barkeep led the way to a door behind the far end of the stand-up bar. Inside, a woman in her forties with dance-hall makeup and clothes sat behind a small desk made of inch-thick wooden siding and two barrels.

"So?"

Spur explained.

"Yeah, real shame. Sammy Lou was best girl I had. The men liked her because she had the biggest bust I ever saw. She claimed to measure forty-seven inches, but she wouldn't let me put a tape around them."

"Did you see the man she went upstairs with the last time?" Abby asked.

"You some kind of detectives?"

"That's right," Spur said. "This same man has killed seven women now that we know about."

"I don't remember seeing him, but one of our girls did. Got a good look at him just as he went into Sammy Lou's room with him. She wrote it out. I don't read too good." She passed a paper to Spur, and he read it aloud.

"Man in his late twenties, about five-six or seven, sandy brown hair cut regular, parted on the left. Slender, maybe one hundred thirty pounds. No scars, moles. Hands looked soft. Wore town pants, shirt and tie, jacket but no vest. Brown or green eyes."

Spur copied down the details in his pocket notebook and gave the paper back to the madam.

"Had the girl ever seen this man before?" Abby asked.

"No. The other girls who saw him for just a moment agreed that he was from out of town."

"He killed her in her crib, then went out the window and got away?" Spur asked.

"Right, and it was late, so when Sammy Lou didn't come down, I figured she was on an all-nighter."

Spur thanked the madam and they left the saloon. The men in the place watched them go, but none was bold enough to make any comment about Abby with Spur striding beside her and looking grim.

"At least we have a good description of him now," Spur said once they got outside. "Does it match what you had picked up?"

"Matches, but it's more than I had." Abby sagged against him.

"Let's get to the hotel."

"One room if you like," she said. "But I'm warning you, I'm too tired even to kiss you good night, let alone . . ."

Spur nodded and picked up her suitcase and his

carpetbag, and they headed across the street to the small hotel.

The man in the black suit and string tie had lost twenty-dollars in one of the smaller gambling halls at a small town just outside of Denver, and left without a word. He'd been small potatoes in the game, and nobody would remember him or miss him. He had a knack for fading into the scenery so people didn't recall who he was or where he was.

He'd decided to stop here when the headache kept building. He'd left the stage in the middle of the afternoon. Now the pain was becoming massive. He rubbed his forehead where the torture always started. It was there again.

Damnit! Now he'd have to find another one. It always relieved the pain, somehow. He couldn't explain it, but it made the anger and the terrible fury and the agony of the knives slicing through his brain all fade away and leave him in peace.

Sometimes he had to scream. When it started two years ago he couldn't control the screaming. It had broken out at all sorts of bad times. Now he knew when it was coming, and got by himself or moved to stop it from getting so bad.

Yes! Stop it again. He searched the street and saw no one. A small cafe was serving supper. His gold pocket watch told him it was just after six-thirty P.M. Yes, some food. Perhaps he could find someone there.

Before he had tried to be discreet, secretive. He wasn't sure exactly what happened during his fits of terrible anger, but he knew the lawmen would blame him, so he had to be careful. The stronger and more devastating the headaches became, the bolder he had to become. A brothel was always his last resort, his final chance before going completely mad from the terrible pain.

The eatery was on a side street, and had only three customers when he entered. He sat at a table near the back and waited for someone to come serve him. The girl he saw moving around was about 20, he decided. Pretty in a low and common sort of way, slender enough, and with large breasts that rolled and bounced as she walked. Her white blouse buttoned up the front, and two of the fasteners had come undone, showing a V of white flesh and a drop of sweat heading downhill and out of sight.

She stopped in front of him, her pencil on a small pad of paper. She grinned, and he saw her teeth were a little crooked in front and yellow-stained.

"Hi, there. You're new in town. I know every good-looking guy within thirty miles. What can I get for you for supper?" She nodded at a hand-printed menu on the wall.

"Roast beef dinner," he said. "Oh, and coffee and some cherry pie." She nodded, and leaned over on his table to write the order on her pad. As she did, the front of her blouse fell away and he could see the nipple and more than half of one of her breasts.

She looked up and saw him watching down her blouse. "See anything else you like?" she asked softly. "If'n you do, we can work out something. I'm done here in another hour." She turned and hurried back to the kitchen, her bottom bouncing back and forth under the tight skirt.

The dinner was good, and the pie the best he had tasted in a long time, sour cherries cooked to a turn in a fine sauce of their own juices and a crust that flaked and melted in his mouth.

After he was finished, she came over and sat down beside him. The place was almost empty by that time. One man drank coffee at the small counter. She grinned up at him, and her hand came out and stroked his leg, moving inside on his thigh and up toward his crotch.

"Look, I got me a real itch that needs scratching. I know it ain't ladylike for me to do the asking, but it's all right. See, I don't meet many honest-to-God handsome men like you out here in the sticks. So just relax and let June show you some entertainment. That's the side door over there. You leave by the front and come around to the side. Dark over there. You be there in about five minutes and I'll meet you. All right?"

Her hand had worked up to his crotch. He couldn't move. Her hand rubbed his crotch three times, and she felt a swelling start.

"Hey, I figure John Henry Pecker down there just answered me. See you soon, darlin'."

She stood and went to the kitchen. He got up, the headache coming on harder now. He closed his eyes for a minute, then went to the counter and paid the 60 cents for the dinner, and went out.

He knew he would turn down the side of the cafe into the dark. He saw the door ahead and waited near it, and a moment later someone came out.

"Hey, you here?" June whispered.

He stepped up and touched her shoulder, and she

pushed against him and kissed his lips before he could react.

"Yes, I figured you'd want to see more of me." She took one of his hands and pushed it down the front of her blouse on her hot breast. "That feels good, darlin'. Now come on. You can play with my titties later. Best do it inside so we won't attract a crowd."

The small house she lived in was only two blocks from the cafe. They walked there, her arm around him, their hips touching, her breast pushing against his arm. He hadn't said a word. She chattered all the way, softly. They met no one on the walk, and she hurried him to the back door and in through the unlocked panel and into the kitchen.

June fumbled with a match as she scratched it, then lit a lamp. She pulled down the blinds, then led him into the second room, where her bed sat, the pillow a soft pink with pink sheets and the covers already turned down.

She pulled the shade on the window, then put the lamp on the dresser and walked slowly to him. "Hey, I don't even know your name. What should I call you?"

"Call me Gus," he said, his voice sounding strange to his own ears. He used a different name each time. The pain had moved from the front of his head to the sides and back and now down into his neck. He could barely stand to keep his eyes open.

June stripped off her blouse, and he marveled at the size of her breasts. They were huge, with areolas two inches wide and nipples larger around than his thumb.

She grinned. "Like my two sweet girls? Best part

of a woman to help get a man is her tits. Course then after she gets him in her bedroom, she gets down to the old pussy, but no hurry for that. Kiss my girls, Gus!"

She pushed up her breasts with one hand, and caught the back of his neck and pulled his head down to her chest.

After that he didn't even think of his headache for a while. He just gloried in those big breasts, and stripped her naked and used her hard and fast the way she wanted it.

Then the headache came back and he screamed and she looked at him. "That was good, darlin', now for the second time."

That was when he hit her. He used his fist and knocked her half across the bed. She lifted up and screamed and tried to get away, but he caught her and broke her arm over his knee.

After that, exactly what happened all became a little murky. He stopped her screaming, but he wasn't sure how. There was a lot of blood, all over the bed and the bedroom. He found the ax in the shed in back, and then went to work in earnest.

His clothes were all in a pile in the hall where he had put them to keep them clean. The blood on his naked body he could wash off, he knew. His ranch training came in handy. His pa had taught him how to use an ax, how to make the undercut, how to align the fall, how to make the top cut and put the tree within a foot of where he wanted it. Yes, he was good with an ax.

When he was done he didn't even look at her. That was when he felt in his pockets and tried to find the 20-cent pieces. He knew he was getting short. At last

he found one. He only had one left. He had to think
hard before he remembered where her head was.

At last he remembered, in the oven of the kitchen
stove. He put the one 20-cent piece in place, then
closed the oven door and washed the blood off his
body at the small table where there was a bucket
filled with pump water.

An hour later he had dressed and gone to have a
beer at one of the saloons. His headache was gone.
The blinding, battering agony was washed clean. It
took him well into his second beer to understand
that the pain was gone. He flirted a minute with one
of the whores in the saloon, then went to the town's
small hotel and up to his room.

The stage to Denver left at eight the next morning
and he planned to be on it.

As he sat on his bed that night, he reached over
and turned down the lamp, then blew it out. He
tried to remember who the girl had been. Big tits,
loved to fuck, that was about it. He didn't even
remember her name. No matter, she had served
him well. Maybe this time the debt would be paid
and the headaches wouldn't come back again.
Maybe.

He turned over and faced the wall. He didn't want
to think about it. He *wouldn't* think about it. All of
that had happened so long ago, so terribly long ago.

Tomorrow he would be back in Denver, and then
soon he would be home. It had been a three-month
trip, and he was anxious to see the place. It was his
father's operation, but he was an only son, so
someday it would all be his. He would try, really try
this time, to do what his father wanted.

The idea that he should learn each of the operations had seemed wrong at first. But now he understood. How could he manage the business if he didn't understand how it worked? Yes, he would do what his father wanted.

That was when he remembered Charlotte, sweet, innocent Charlotte. No man had ever touched her breasts, he was sure. She was 21 now and a virgin and expecting him to marry her. Charlotte was tiny and cute and talented, and smart. She lived closer to Denver than his father's place, and her father was a banker or something in the big town.

Charlotte had been through the eighth grade and to three years of "finishing school" in Denver, whatever that was. He had a tear-stained letter from her. She was still waiting for him to propose. He was 23 now. Was he too young to get married? If the headaches didn't stop it wouldn't matter. Sometime, somewhere, a lawman would grab him and they would hang him, and then for sure the headaches would stop.

First thing when he got back to Denver he would go to one of the banks and insist on getting some 20-cent pieces. He could tell them he was a coin collector and wanted ten dollars worth to look through for dates and mint marks. They would understand.

He looked at the blackness of the ceiling for a long time, and for just a moment he saw the picture of June, her wide eyes, her big breasts, and then the scream that came sometime after he had started working on her. It might have been the scream when she at last died. He wasn't sure.

He did know that she had paid. She had paid the full charges for a wanton woman, the full measure of restitution for being a slut and a whore and an easy woman. June had paid in full, and he was once more able to continue his trip home without the agony of that bastard of a headache.

Soon he went to sleep. His conscience didn't bother him, not one bit. He had no conscience.

Chapter Four

Spur and Abby hit Denver the next day about noon and took a hotel room, and while Abby had a bath, Spur checked at two Denver banks to find out if either of them had any 20-cent pieces, and if anyone had been asking for them. The vice president of the Denver Mercantile Bank shook his head.

"No, I'm afraid none of our customers use those coins. They are too easy to confuse with quarters and can lead to making the wrong change. In fact, we have a policy of keeping such coins when we take them in and not giving them out."

"What do you do with those coins?" Spur asked.

"When we get enough, we sell them back to the mint here in Denver and they melt them down and recast them. It isn't the policy of the U.S. Treasury Department, but we think it's a good plan."

The second bank, the Colorado State Bank, proved to be more helpful. A teller said yes, indeed they had some of the coins.

"Do you give them out to anyone?" Spur asked.

The young man nodded. "Of course, just like one-dollar gold pieces or double eagles, or quarters. We give out any change that the customer wants. Of course the twenty-cent coin never has been popular. Most of our merchants never use them. But some people like them. And then there are the coin collectors. In fact, we had a man in yesterday who bought ten dollars worth. He said he was a coin collector and searching for two rare coins of that type. Frankly, we're glad to get rid of them. They're a nuisance."

"Do you remember the man?"

"I didn't handle the customer, but I can take you to the person who did."

Spur followed the young man to the cashier of the bank at a desk just outside of the cages the tellers used. The two bankers talked a moment, then the older man came forward.

"You were asking about the twenty-cent pieces?"

"Yes. Was the man about twenty-eight to thirty, five feet seven, and about a hundred and thirty pounds?"

The banker was surprised. "Yes, almost exactly. How did you know?"

"I've been following him. What else do you re-member about him?"

"Strange green eyes, brown hair parted on the left, and wore town clothes. I noticed that his hands were soft, so he wasn't a rancher or a miner."

Spur thanked him and headed out of the bank. He nearly bumped into a tall man in a brown sheepskin coat just in front of him at the door. The man carried a soft leather bag that looked heavy.

Outside on the boardwalk, the man moved out at a fast walk up the street. Less than 20 feet later two men surged out of a store and knocked down the tall man, and one ran off with his leather bag.

Spur saw it happen, and in a surge chased the thief with the bag and drew his revolver at the same time. He fired once over the man's head. When the thief didn't stop, Spur fired again, this time hitting the runner in the leg and slamming him to the ground.

Spur came up warily, but the wounded man had no weapon. Spur caught up the heavy leather bag, pulled the wounded man to his feet, and marched him back across the street to where the bank customer in the sheepskin coat sat squarely in the middle of the back of the other robber.

Spur put down the case at the man's feet.

"I believe this is your property," Spur said. "And if you'll call a policeman, you can have this thief charged and jailed."

The tall man in the sheepskin coat grabbed his prisoner by the back of the neck and both stood. The man looked at Spur and smiled. "Sir, I don't know who you are, but I'm in your debt. My name is Thurlow Stanwood, and I have a ranch outside of town and some other enterprises. That case contained the payroll for my ranch and my mine. I'm much obliged to you."

"My pleasure, Mr. Stanwood. I'm Spur McCoy."

Stanwood was six feet tall and sturdy. He wore a suit with vest and a gold chain and fob. A policeman ran up, and Stanwood spoke to the man for a moment. Then the lawman took the two grab-and-run thieves off toward the jail.

Stanwood turned to Spur. "Now, my good man, I insist on some reward." He held two gold double eagles in one hand and flipped them to Spur, who caught them.

"A mere pittance, I assure you, for what you saved me today. Also, I was heading for a dinner at the Cherry Creek Restaurant, the best food in town. Would you join me?"

Spur handed the coins back. "Lunch I will accept, but I can't take any money from you, Mr. Stanwood. I did no more than any citizen would have done." He frowned a moment. "The name Stanwood sounds familiar. Are you famous? Should I know your name?"

The man laughed. "I'm afraid not, sir. No, Mr. McCoy, I'm not famous. I do have some business ventures, but they are only known locally."

"Stanwood. It *is* familiar. A long time ago." Spur stopped and stared at the man. "Yes, I remember. Captain Stanwood, in the Civil War. You were with the New York Volunteer Twenty-fourth Regiment. Right?"

Stanwood stopped on the boardwalk. "Yes. Yes, I served some time with the Twenty-fourth, but it's not a good memory. More than half of that regiment died in battle, you might recall."

They moved back against a hardware store, both lost in their memories for a moment.

"Yes, Captain Stanwood, I do remember. I was a captain and company commander of Baker. I missed that fight at the country house of Chantilly in Virginia. I was wounded the day before."

"Then you remember Colonel Harland. He should have been one of those killed the day before. He did everything wrong a regimental commander could do and not lose every man. Did you know he was killed at Chantilly? Shot from behind in a minor skirmish with a mounted patrol. But they were Yankee bullets that smashed his head to pieces that afternoon."

Spur shook his head. "I never knew. I was sent back with what was left of my company. We started with a hundred and fifteen, and by the end of the previous day we had only thirty men who could walk. Half of them were wounded."

Stanwood shook his head. "Let's have that dinner and remember better times. I haven't even thought about Colonel Harland for years now. Time heals most of our wounds."

They settled down in the restaurant and ordered.

"Are you new in town, McCoy?"

"Just arrived this morning."

"If you're looking for work I could use you in my operation. For one thing, I'd bring you along when I come to Denver for supplies and the payroll. I wasn't aware that anyone knew I carried money in that bag."

"Captain, I appreciate the offer, but I have a job."

"So quickly?"

"No, I'm here on assignment. I work for the federal government."

"Oh I see. Well at least you'll have to come out to

the ranch for a week or so. Ever seen a Western cattle operation?"

"Yes sir, I have. Put in some time as a cowhand, matter of fact. It's a tough life."

"Indeed that is right. It seems I'm on the range about half the time these days."

The food arrived then and they spent the next ten minutes working on their supper. Over coffee Stanwood became insistent.

"Mr. McCoy, I owe you a lot. I have over twenty thousand dollars in that bag. It would have been gone forever if it hadn't been for you. Now I want you to be a guest at my ranch this weekend. Relax and socialize a bit. I'm having a dozen other folks out and I'd be pleased if you would join us."

"That would be tomorrow, on Saturday and Sunday?"

"Yes. We have an outdoor barbecue planned, and even some dancing under the stars. I think you'll enjoy it. We work so hard we have to stop and enjoy ourselves once in a while."

Spur considered it a moment, then nodded. "Yes, sir, Captain Stanwood. I'd be pleased to join you at least for Saturday." He got directions to the Flying T Ranch some 15 miles west of Denver toward the mountains, and said he'd be out there about two o'clock on Saturday.

After the meal they said good-bye, and Spur went down to the sheriff's office. Denver had a county sheriff and a police chief, and he talked to both of them. The sheriff had the most information.

"Matter of fact we had another killing like that just last night outside of Denver about ten miles. One of the officers from that county rode over this morning with some other material for us and mentioned it."

"A single woman was murdered?"

"More like butchered," Sheriff Warner said. "From what the report was, the girl was a waitress and had a reputation for sleeping with everyone. She won't no more. Her body was hacked up into about twenty pieces. Somebody used an ax on her."

"My God! he's never done that before. Not an ax." Spur gave the sheriff a description of the man he was tracking and all the information they had on the series of killings.

"Not a lot of help, is it?" Sheriff Warner said. "This description fits three of my deputies and about twenty percent of the men in town." He sighed and dropped the paper on his desk. "So I see that I got me a killer going through town or maybe staying, we don't know yet. I'll damn sure keep my eyes open for him, and warn the other surrounding county sheriffs about him. Where you staying, McCoy? I'll let you know if we hear anything at all that might involve this man."

Spur told him the High Country Hotel. "Where might he go from here?"

"We've got a stage line that runs at times south to Colorado Springs. Most of the traffic is on the spur line railroad up to Cheyenne, Wyoming, and then the main tracks east and west. Our butcher boy could be partway to Chicago or San Francisco by now."

"That's not good news, Sheriff. I don't know which way to go. At least it's cut down to two directions."

A deputy came in and talked quietly to the sheriff for a minute, then left.

"My deputy tells me you foiled a sneak thief this morning on a grab-and-run. Even shot one of the culprits."

"Yeah, I just happened to come out of the bank behind the man."

"Thurlow Stanwood is one of the most important men in the state. Denver would have been chagrined if we let some outlaw make off with his payroll. The whole county thanks you," Sheriff Warner said.

Spur mumbled that he would stay in touch, and got out of there. Back at the hotel, he found Abby drying her long red hair. At first she was a little embarrassed letting him see it that way, but he kissed her and she forgot the embarrassment. He helped her dry her beautiful hair, and told her about the latest victim.

"We just don't have much to work with," Spur said, pacing the room. "The sheriff is right. Our description fits half the men of that age in Denver."

"Which direction is he heading?" Abby asked.

"North or south from here, but nobody except him knows. We'll have to sit here for a while and send out some telegrams and see what we can find out. At least we'll get fast replies."

He told her about running into the old soldier from his Civil War unit.

"He invited me out to his ranch Saturday and Sunday. I'll go out for the barbecue tomorrow and then come back."

"What am I supposed to do all day?"

"Play detective. Try to find out if the man with the

description we have took the train north or the stagecoach south. That should keep you busy most of the day."

"What about tonight?" Abby asked.

"I plan on keeping you busy tonight, at least busy enough so you won't get bored and want to go home."

Abby smiled up at him, her lips opening and moving toward his lips and a serious, wanting-more kind of kiss. "Now that sounds like a good idea. First I'm going to get my hair dry. Then I'm buying a new working dress. That could take an hour or two."

"I'll wait here. I've been thinking about that damn colonel we had in the war who caused so many of our soldiers to die needlessly."

"It must have been terrible," she said, her pretty face stained by shades of anger and fear.

"Terrible is not the right word. There may not be a right word for what the Twenty-fourth went through those three days. At times I didn't think that any of us would ever get out alive."

Her hair was dry. She bent and kissed him gently on the lips and pulled back and stared at him.

"Hey, don't dwell on that. I'm going shopping, and then I'll be back for a wild, wild night of lovemaking. I don't want you breaking into crying spells thinking about the war."

"I'll have it all thought about before you're back. Seeing Captain Stanwood just brought back a lot of memories I thought that I'd buried a long time ago. I guess I didn't."

She kissed him again, let her fingers caress his cheek, then went out the door.

Spur sat there staring out the window at the

Denver street scene. The damn war! The damn Twenty-fourth Regiment. Volunteers from the state of New York, and he had been handed a commission to lead one company of men into battle. Into battle, not into the surprise of a thunderous, murderous fire that nothing could withstand. Not into death.

Chapter Five

War is man's greatest, most satisfying, and most deadly game, Captain Spur McCoy decided as he marched along beside his Company B of the New York Volunteer Twenty-fourth Regiment. They were in and out of woods, through fertile fields, and here and there in open country with gently rolling hills.

This was Virginia somewhere. He knew that. They had been assigned to the Army of the Potomac to help protect Washington, D.C., from attack. The Capitol had been burned once in wartime, by the British in 1812. Nobody wanted it to happen again, especially by the damned Rebels!

Spur wasn't exactly sure why the New York Twenty-fourth, a part of General Joe Hooker's division, was there. For more than a week they had charged around from one spot to another as General Pope tried to get his troops massed to close in on General Stonewall Jackson and smash his troops into surrender.

Spur knew that the Army of the Potomac had the worst record of the new war. It was August 29, 1862, and Pope kept moving troops and men until half of his army was so foot-weary they could barely walk.

Most of the cavalry had less than ten horses per company that could walk, let alone carry a soldier or officer.

Captain McCoy was in the regimental headquarters as reports came in that late evening. The Texans had pulled back from the fighting scene. One report had them in full retreat. Another report said that General Jackson had left the railroad embankment where his troops had been spotted, and was marching away leaving only a small rear guard.

Colonel Rufus Harland, newly promoted colonel, pranced around the small regimental headquarters under a grove of trees. He clasped his hands behind his back and brayed to his assembled officers how they would be part of Hooker's division in the morning and would help sweep the damned Rebels and Texans back toward the south.

"We'll smash them!" Harland had crowed. "Smash them and drive them into the river!"

Captain McCoy knew that there was no river in that area. He wondered if right there and then he should shoot down the untrained colonel. The man was a popinjay, and paid more attention to his uniform and the ladies than how his troops were trained, housed, or fed. The man was a walking disaster that hadn't quite happened. Spur prayed

that their colonel's total lack of military training
would not show up in this campaign. If it did, there
would be a bloody price to pay.

So far the colonel had done little to convince his
troops he knew what he was doing. He pranced, he
shouted, he struck poses, he preened, and he took
great joy in the compliments of his junior officers
and orderlies. His regiment had yet to taste the
blood of battle in any way.

Captain McCoy waited for the end of the conference, and then went back to B Company to tell the
troops that they would be tasting battle tomorrow.
He called them together and told them what he
knew, which wasn't much.

The men reacted the way he knew they would.
Few had done any fighting before. He had a mixture
of farm boys and city men, but all were volunteers
determined to do their part. The men sprawled
wherever they could find a place to lay down in a
tangle of hardwood trees and brush. They slept,
after eating what they could find. Twice in the past
two days the regiment had out marched and lost its
supply wagons. Most of the men hadn't eaten all
day. It would be a long night. Spur got little sleep.

They were up early and formed up along the road
waiting for their place in the division. Sunrise came
early as the Twenty-fourth met the other regiments
in General Hooker's division and marched toward
the front.

By now the generals had cast their lot, had been
assigned sectors, and were moving into place. B
Company came to a clearing, and to the right were
General Pope and his other generals at his headquarters on an open knoll. Spur saw him puffing on

a big cigar, joking with his subordinates and orderlies, while more troopers held the generals' horses
farther back.

Captain McCoy had been told by Colonel Harland
that their regiment would participate in the pursuit
of the Rebel forces. They would break up the Rebels'
rear guards and pursue with all available horses,
foot troops, and artillery guns. It would be a smashing victory for the Army of the Potomac!

General McDowell was in charge of the pursuit,
and General Porter with his fresh troops would
follow the lead units. Generals Hooker and Kearny
were assigned to a parallel road two miles to the
north.

"We will press the enemy vigorously all day!"
Colonel Harland had told his officers just before
they moved out with Hooker's other units.

General Hooker's men were still moving into
position when they saw the opening attack. The
pursuit of the enemy by the Army of the Potomac
became the shortest in the history of warfare. The
long blue skirmish line of troopers combing
through meadows and valleys and groves came
under fire almost at once from the rail embankment. For a few moments it looked like it could be a
rear-guard action.

"Damnation!" Colonel Harland thundered. "Jackson isn't supposed to be there! General Pope guar-
anteed it!"

By this time General McDowell had formed his
assault troops in a solid battle line and advanced
them, troopers in blue shoulder to shoulder,
through more gullies and hillocks.

At the same time there were more shots from

Rebel artillery hitting the troopers along the Mc-
Dowell assault line. They had expected a few artillery pieces to cover the withdrawal.

Then the whole railroad embankment bristled
and glistened as sun shone off cold steel bayonets
and thousands of General Stonewall Jackson's men
lined the bank.

The two sides stood for the most part, firing at one
another at the terrible range of less than 100 yards.
Crashing volleys came one on top of another. A
sergeant next to his captain took a minié ball
through the side of the head, and he spun past his
captain screaming, with blood flying, bleating in
pain before he died.

A dozen men around the same officer fell in the
first minute. Then the captain caught a rifle bullet in
his left arm, but kept shooting at the far bank.

"We're going down to reinforce!" Colonel
Harland bellowed. "Move out, on the double!"

"Colonel, our orders were to work parallel to the
battle lines," Captain McCoy called.

"This is a battlefield decision, Captain. Get your
men moving or I'll shoot you down right here!"

"Yes sir!" Captain McCoy barked. He turned and
screeched at his men and they turned toward the
fighting. The New York Twenty-fourth double-timed
down the slope, across a small valley, and up the
other side, then straight into the battle.

Colonel Harland angled the men into a gaping
hole in the line of blue where Rebel artillery had
sent in heavy salvos of enfilade fire that had slaughtered the heavy blue line of men.

"Forward, men," Harland bellowed from his
horseback.

Captain McCoy's men were in the center of the Twenty-fourth's line, and he ordered them to drop down into a slight depression that gave them some protection.

"Down! Down! Down, you idiots! Fire from the prone position! Make as little a target of yourself as possible!"

Before McCoy's men got to the line of blue they saw the heavy pall of acrid smoke hanging over the battlefield. Harland rode up and down behind his troops and never suffered a wound.

"Forward, men! Forward. Their fire is slackening. There! They're run out of ammunition! Charge, by God!"

Captain McCoy couldn't believe it. All along the line small groups had driven forward a few yards, only to be pushed back by the deadly fire from the Rebels' protected positions. Already he could see where 30 of his men were down, dead or wounded.

Harland bellowed out his order again, and the captains and sergeants down the line repeated the commands, and the troops lifted up, fired, and ran forward and fired again.

Captain McCoy led his troops. He had one of the new Spencer rifles that could fire solid cartridges and shoot seven times without reloading. Reloading was with a tube of seven more rounds pushed through the stock of the weapon. He fired, fired again, and ran forward. Two men fell in front of him, bullets through their heads. He saw their brains splatter over the ground as he ran past.

There was a slackening of fire ahead of them. *The Rebels had run out of ammunition!* Then McCoy's men were at the top of the embankment, and steel met steel as the Rebels battled with the attackers with rocks and bayonets and pistols. Before the Yanks could overrun the Rebel line, fresh ammunition arrived and new troops ran into the void, and the Yankees were pushed back down the side of the embankment, and then driven back again with punishing fire to the low place where they threw themselves on the ground.

Half of his company was missing. Many of them lay on the embankment, the rest scattered on the unwise charge to the front and back.

Captain McCoy swore at Colonel Harland. Then the colonel rode up on his horse.

"McCoy! Damn your eyes. Get those men standing and firing salvos, man. One group fire and one load. Come on, get the men firing!"

The slaughter went on. Once more the Twenty-fourth was ordered forward. The men had to be kicked and threatened with cold steel this time to get up and run toward the enemy. The volume of fire intensified wherever a regiment attacked, and now the Twenty-fourth caught most of the fire and didn't make it halfway to the embankment. Another half of the Twenty-fourth fell before they got back to their positions.

General Hooker rode his white horse along the back of the men, saw that it was hopeless charging a fixed position such as the railroad embankment had become, and ordered a retreat.

The blue line moved back, but at first it didn't seem to move at all. Then Captain Spur McCoy realized just how many of the bluecoats had been killed that day. They lay in a long thick line where they had fallen a hundred yards from the enemy position. There was a scattering of bluecoats closer to the embankment, and some behind the line where they had been gunned down by Rebel minié balls.

All along the line regiments were retreating, fighting as rear guards as best they could, then moving out and setting up as new rear guards.

At last dusk hazed the battlefield. Troops on both sides fell down where they were and rested. Generals and colonels and captains tried to get some semblance of order.

A short time after darkness, all of the troops had retreated across the Bull Run Bridge, the final rear guard came in, and the battle was over.

Most of the troops marched during the night, and somehow everyone got back to Centerville and moved in behind their entrenchments.

Captain Spur McCoy had his casualty count. He'd started with 120 men. When the fighting was over he had only 32 left, and all but four of those were wounded. He had a rifle bullet in his left arm.

Spur shook his head in the hotel room in Denver, Colorado. That all had happened ten years ago. Why was he remembering it now? Captain Stanwood. He had bumped into Captain Stanwood on the street today.

Strange how small the world can be sometimes. Stanwood was the first man from the war that Spur had met whose name he remembered.

The next day Spur had been getting the bullet dug out of his arm when what was left of the New York Twenty-fourth marched again, this time to the country house of Chantilly.

There had been a gusty wind blowing that morning driving rain before it, and then a tremendous thunderstorm struck that blotted out the gunfire at the house. There was a short, vicious battle, and Stonewall Jackson and his men were repulsed, stopping them from slipping around to the rear of Pope's entire army.

That evidently was where Colonel Harland was cut down by Yankee bullets. Spur had only Captain Stanwood's statement about this. Still, it could have happened. Somehow now it didn't seem that important.

Spur stood and walked around the room. He rubbed his arm where the Rebel minié ball had been dug out of his flesh. It still hurt sometimes.

Thinking back, Spur couldn't remember ever hearing that Colonel Harland of the Twenty-fourth had been killed in battle. Spur had not rejoined the Twenty-fourth. He had been in the field hospital for a while and then sent back to Washington when complications developed in his arm. No wonder he hadn't heard about the colonel being shot.

It still bothered him. Captain Stanwood had been emphatic about it. None of the officers in the Twenty-fourth had liked the colonel. He'd been a civilian soldier and not good at his work.

Spur shook his head. None of that mattered now. He was still trying to find a ruthless, crazed killer. The 20-cent pieces must mean something, but for the life of him, Spur couldn't figure out what.

He took out his notebook and reviewed everything they knew about the case. Not a hell of a lot. It all depended now on where the man ran, and what he did next. They might be in Denver for two or three days, or be out tomorrow. It all depended on a wanton, vicious, maniac killer.

The telegrams. He hadn't sent them yet. He went downstairs and asked the room clerk where the telegraph office was. A branch line had been strung in from the transcontinental hookup that had been finished in 1861. At the office a block down the street, he wrote telegrams to the county seats on the spur rail line leading north to Cheyenne, Wyoming.

He wasn't sure how many there were, but the telegrapher had a map that showed them. It turned out there were only four counties up that direction. In most new states and territories, counties often were large because of low populations. As the populations grew and more services were needed, one large county might split into two or more counties.

He sent this wire to each lawman:

"Sheriff. Federal law officer in Denver tracking killer of women. Killer may be heading your way. If a woman is murdered in your county, please send wire at once to Spur McCoy, High Country Hotel, Denver."

Once the wires were sent, Spur went to the boardwalk and surveyed the street a moment. Denver had been growing. At first it was only a pair of settlements along Cherry Creek, then it consolidated, and soon was the center of two big gold rushes that turned out to be glorious fantasies. Hundreds of miners and settlers who had flocked to the area had angrily turned around and headed back east again.

Now the town was moving ahead again. The

railroad spur helped. By the time Spur worked his
way back to the High Country Hotel, it was almost
six o'clock.

Abby had returned, and had just put on her new
traveling dress. It was demurely proper, but nipped
in at the waist. She watched him come in, struck a
pose for him, then turned around, letting the floor-
length skirt swirl outward.

"Well, how do you like it?" Abby asked.

"Attractive, yet not flashy. Fits you perfectly.
Should be a fine traveling and working dress."

Her hand went down to her skirt, and in a
moment came up with a derringer pistol.

Spur chuckled. "Any more surprises in there?" he
asked.

She walked toward him, smiling. "There are a few
surprises inside the dress, but you've seen them. It
might be nice for you to take another look." She
grinned impishly and swirled her long hair around
so it swung in front of her face. She peeked through
the strands of fire red hair.

"I'm warning you, I'm not at all tired this time."

Spur caught her and lifted her off her feet, kissing
her soundly at the same time, then carried her
toward the bed.

"A lady could get in a lot of trouble that way, little
girl," Spur said ominously.

"Good Lord, I certainly hope so," she said. He sat
down on the edge of the bed holding her in his lap.

She sat up straight, her face serious. "Oh, did you
send the telegrams?"

"I did, four of them north to Cheyenne."

"Good, then we're not shirking our responsibili-
ties. All we can do now is wait and try to follow this

maniac." She leaned back against him and her hand came up the inside of his thigh. "So, we might as well get comfortable while we wait and try and figure out something to do to entertain ourselves."

"Now, there is an idea I never thought of."

"I'll bet. If you don't kiss me in about five seconds I'm going to be furious!"

Spur grinned. It was going to be a busy and exciting night.

Chapter Six

The next morning, Spur walked to the livery stables and rented a horse and saddle. He tested the animal for a block and found she could run and seemed sturdy enough. Back at the hotel, he found a hitching post on the side street, tied the horse, and went up and talked to Abby.

"I've been thinking it might be best if we each had a room," he said. "That way all of Denver wouldn't know we're sleeping together, but more important, Denver wouldn't know that you and I are working on the same case."

Abby had been combing her waist-length, fire-red hair, and turned. She hadn't put on her clothes yet. Pink-tipped breasts peeked through the long hair.

"Somehow it might help us if we aren't known as being a team on this one," he added.

"Then it's not my lovemaking you don't like?"

"Hell no! We can sleep together every night."

She grinned. Then she sobered and went on combing her long hair. "Actually, it's a good idea to have a two-pronged attack. We can work together, but in public I'll let you contact the sheriffs while I try to work around the edges, research, digging into backgrounds, checking out people."

"Great. That might be especially good if the killer has been running through those little towns until he got to Denver so he could have someplace to hide. Fact is, he might come from some big town like Kansas City or even Chicago, and feel more at home here. Denver has about fifteen thousand people now. This is a big enough town to do a lot of hiding in. Maybe he'll stay. If he does, we'll have a better chance to nail him to the boardwalk and stomp all over his fingers and toes."

"Quaint, Mr. McCoy. I'd rather shoot off his balls and then cut his pecker off a half inch at a time with a cleaver."

Spur chuckled. "You have a vicious side, sweet-faced little Ruth Abigail Leggett. I'm glad you're on my side."

She stood and walked toward him, naked as an angel and twice as seductive. "I'd lots rather have you laying on my tummy and my titties than being on your side. But we could try it that way."

He bent and kissed her lips, then pulled away. "Hey, these are working hours. We can't fool around on company time."

"Why not?"

"Because you have to get your clothes on and go down and register in another room and make like you just arrived. While you're doing that, I'll be on my way out to see Captain Stanwood at his ranch. It's a useless obligation more than anything. A wasted six or eight hours, unless the barbecue is outstanding. Then I'll get back to work.

"Oh, I checked on the way up and the room clerk said that we didn't have any telegrams waiting for us. I guess we just wait until something happens."

"I'll be busy here in town too. I've got that description of our killer now. I'll show it to every place in town where he might eat or sleep. If he comes here and stays long, he'll need to do both of them."

Spur nodded and pushed back the front of his flat-rimmed black hat. "Hey, you might pay your way on this assignment yet. Do we split your fee in the process?"

She crinkled up her nose and stuck out her tongue at him. "Only if I get half of your salary as well. Even then I'd be coming out on the short end of things. Get out of here, McCoy. I need to dress."

"I'd like to stay and watch you, but I have the Stanwood thing. I'll get out of there as fast as I can."

Spur enjoyed the 15-mile ride west to the Stanwood ranch, the Flying S. There was no road, only a wagon track that way, and according to the directions Stanwood had given him the day before, not much else had developed out in that direction.

The country was a continuation of the great prairie as it sloped up toward the Rocky Mountain spires. The mountains were a snow-capped jagged range on the far horizon. He knew that some of the peaks were over 14,000 feet high. The famous Pikes Peak was somewhere along there, or maybe more to the south.

He had no trouble finding the ranch, and rode in about eleven that morning. Thurlow Stanwood himself met Spur at the hitching rack.

"McCoy! Glad you could come. Some people here I want you to meet, and the barbecue is going to be outstanding." He called a ranch hand to take Spur's horse and unsaddle it and put it in a corral.

"Nice spread," Spur said. He meant it. There were three corrals and two big barns, evidently for winter hay and some cover for the best horses in the worst weather. A long bunkhouse must have housed up to 30 hands, and behind it there was a cookshack and a dining room to feed the men. Scattered around were three other buildings, but he couldn't figure out what they were. Maybe a blacksmith shop in one.

He saw two pump houses, and a windmill cranked away in the Colorado breeze. The ranch house was the impressive part. Two stories, built in the old style with peeled and notched logs, but with generous windows along the front facing the mountains. Spur figured there must be at least 18 rooms. There were three stone chimneys reaching out of the roof, and a big screened porch was on the front. They walked in that direction.

"Got a quarter of a steer roasting out back," Stanwood said. "Want to go that way and see the works?"

Spur nodded, and they cut around the end of the ranch house. He could smell the tempting, beef-roasting flavor of the smoke before they got there. Stanwood had constructed a stand-up barbecue pit out of stone and mortar, with a firebox four feet long.

A glowing bed of coals that could only be hardwood lay in the firebox. Steel fittings on both ends held a pair of steel rods that clamped a quarter of beef, suspending it over the coals. At each end the rods were extended to where a handle was attached. There, well out of range of the heat, stood two men turning the crank slowly to roast the beef evenly.

"Takes a little practice to get it just right," Stanwood said. He took a drag on a big brown cigar. "But then we get lots of practice. I like to have a big barbecue every week or two during the good weather."

"Lot better weather than we had at that damn railroad embankment down in Virginia," Spur said.

Stanwood shook his head and tapped off the cigar ash. "Damn near the worst day of my life. Don't know why I came out of that day without a scratch. You weren't in on the Chantilly Country House fight the next day, you said?"

"I was getting patched up in the field hospital."

"Now there was a bad day, lightning and thunder and a cloudburst and us trying to kill each other. I picked up some minié ball lead that day."

"This weather looks lots better, Stanwood," Spur said. There were about 20 people around a 15-foot-wide tent with the sides rolled up. Under the tent were chairs and a table and the rest of the dinner that would be served just as soon as the beef was done.

"Enough war stories, McCoy. Come on over here and meet my family. My wife isn't with us any longer, but I've got my son and daughter. Damn proud of them two kids. Come on over here out of the hot sun and say howdy."

As Spur and the owner walked into the tent, a small, slender girl hurried up to them. She wore a sleek flower-print blue dress that hugged her neck and wrists but tucked in well at her waist. Her black hair was cut short, and brown eyes watched Spur with delight.

"Daddy, is this the hero who saved all of our money?" she asked. Her smile was quick and sincere, and Spur liked her at once.

"Certainly is, darling. Miss Terri Stanwood, like you to meet a new friend of mine, Spur McCoy. Like you said, he's the hero who saved our money."

Terri grinned at him now, and held out her hand. He took it and they shook briefly.

"Well, Miss Stanwood. Now I know why I made the ride all the way out here. I'm pleased to meet you."

"My goodness, a man who knows how to flatter a lady. Can we keep him, Daddy? We don't have many gentlemen around Denver who know how to talk to a lady."

Stanwood laughed softly, his grin now wide enough to drive a team of six through. He showed by his every glance and gesture that this girl held a special place in his heart.

"Darling, I'm afraid Mr. McCoy already has a job, but we'll try to hire him part time. Now, how are your hostessing duties coming along? When will the beef be done?"

"To a turn in fifteen minutes. We've just about got the table all set for the walk-by."

"Good. You handle it as usual," Stanwood said. He looked around, saw a young man talking to two other men, and motioned for Spur to follow him.

They walked just outside the tent, and the young men looked up as the pair came forward.

Stanwood motioned toward the younger of the men. He was about 23, five-six or seven, Spur guessed, and thin.

"Spur McCoy, like you to meet my son. This is Leslie Stanwood, one of the key management men in my operation here. Leslie, Spur McCoy."

Leslie nodded, his smile perfunctory. His brown eyes seemed to challenge Spur for a moment, then they softened. "So, the man with the gun who saved the company payroll. We thank you for that, Mr. McCoy."

"A conditioned response, I'm afraid, Leslie. Just glad I was at the right place when the men attacked. You manage the ranch for your father?"

Leslie laughed. "No, Father does that. We have a ranch, a small mine, and a good-sized lumber and logging operation. I keep the books and oversee the two other operations."

"Sounds interesting," Spur said.

Stanwood pulled Spur away to meet the rest of the men there, about a dozen who were smoking and watching the beef turning on the spit. Spur didn't try to remember the names. He wasn't that good at it anyway, and most of them he'd never see again. This little barbecue did seem to be the social event of the week. He noticed two bankers, the owner of the biggest store in town, the mayor, and a United States Congressman in the introductions.

"Meat's done!" somebody called from the spit. At once two men ran up with a table that had a butcher block top four feet long. They set it beside the spit and men with heavy gloves took the 100-pound quarter of beef off the spit while still on the steel rods and laid it on the table. Then the rods came off, and a man with a white apron and a chef's cap on began carving.

The women motioned to the men, and they moved up to the tent where the walk-by table was loaded with all sorts of cooked vegetables, salads, breads, and deserts.

"Fill your plate here and then we'll have the barbecue ready for you up there," Terri Stanwood directed. She wore a small apron now over her dress, and seemed to delight in doing the hostess chores for her father.

Spur dutifully got in line with the other men. He hoped the meal would be worth it. He had the feeling that he shouldn't be there, he should be back in Denver working on the case. But there wasn't anything to do today, not really. If the killer had stopped in Denver to hide, he wouldn't show himself for a while. It was almost certain that he wouldn't kill another woman in town and draw the hunters there.

Just then Terri came up beside Spur.

"You be sure and take one of the big plates, Spur McCoy," she said. "Have all you want and come back for seconds, and be sure to save a place for me beside you at the long table over there where we all sit down. No, no, that's perfectly all right. You don't need to wait for me. I'll be there before you know it." She hurried away with only a quick grin over her shoulder.

She was a pixie, a sprite, about big enough to tie on the tail of a good-sized kite.

Then he came to the spread table, took one of the

large plates, and soon had it almost filled with more food than he had seen in six trail rides and a church picnic.

The Flying S Ranch did not skimp on the good things to eat when management threw a party.

He stopped at the end of the table where a big hot metal tray held just-sliced slabs of roast beef. He took one, and found a place near the end of the long table. He leaned the chair beside him up to indicate the place was saved, and looked for Terri.

A serving girl came around with mugs of coffee and iced tea.

Spur looked at the ice floating in the tea, and a man across from him smiled. He was the banker Spur had talked with earlier about the 20-cent coins.

"Mr. McCoy, the ice is safe. Our mountain streams up here are pure enough to drink. So when we take water out for our ice ponds it's pure ice. We ditch the water into ice ponds and let the water settle well before the freezing winter. Then we cut the ice in blocks and store it in ice sheds with layers of straw between the ice. Usually it lasts well into August for us, sometimes September."

"Thanks, good to know," Spur said. He tried the iced tea, and it was so cold it made his teeth ache.

Then Terri sat down beside him with a plate heaped almost as high as his was. "You did save me a chair?"

"I obey orders right well," Spur said.

"Thanks, I'm starved." She dug into her food, and Spur ate as well. There was some table talk, but mostly it was a time to put food into the mouth and chew it.

Terri and Spur went back through the line for desert, cherry pie and chocolate cake for Spur. Terri settled for a wedge of gooseberry pie and more iced tea.

"Best meal I've had since I left the East," Spur said.

Terri grinned. "I fixed up the menu, but the cook did most of the work. He has the best barbecue sauce he uses on that beef. He won't tell anybody what goes in it."

They were done then, and stood, and she caught his hand. "Want a guided tour of the home place?"

"Sure. That's part of the dinner package, I'd bet."

"Absolutely."

They toured the corrals, and she showed him her personal horse, a flashy little palomino with nearly pure white mane and tail. The little mare was a beauty.

"Here are the barns," Terri said. "We use them for storing cut hay for our horses in the winter, and if the snow gets too deep we try to bring the stock in closer and take hay out to them on sleds."

She turned around and stood directly in front of Spur. Then she reached up and pulled his face down so she could kiss him on the lips.

She let him go and watched his face. "Do you mind?" she asked.

"Mind? Not a chance." He bent and picked her up, and when she was face to face with him, he kissed her again, a more demanding kiss that left her a bit breathless.

"My goodness!" Terri said when he set her down. "That was nice. Now we better continue the tour before somebody misses us." She watched him.

"That was wonderful. Just wanted you to know that was a fine, fine kiss." She hurried then, and the tour was soon over and they were back at the barbecue tent. They shared another piece of cherry pie.

That was when the horseshoe tournament began. Actually it was a case of playing the winner of the previous match. There were four horseshoe pits set up with the dirt well sanded and spaded up for good play. The solid steel stakes were driven two feet into the hard ground and the horseshoes clanged.

They were not the kind really used on horses, but larger ones, more open on the end. Spur watched and took his turn, but was soundly thumped 21 to 4. He bowed out graciously.

Terri was beside him again. She looked up at him with curiosity, her black hair framing her face.

"Daddy said you worked for the government, the federal government. What is it you do for them?"

"Actually I'm doing a general survey of law enforcement in new states to see how they measure up. There's a movement in process to find some ways the federal government might help local lawmen, but it's just preliminary."

"Oh, that's interesting." Her brown eyes looked at his. "Then you'll be in town for a while?"

"At least a week, I'd guess."

"Good. Where are you staying, in case I decide to invite you to a party?"

"Oh, the High Country Hotel."

Thurlow Stanwood walked up and nodded. "McCoy, I need to talk to you a minute. Can you scoot off somewhere, Terri?"

"If I have to." She waved and moved away.

"Want to offer you a job, McCoy. First, you'd be

security chief for my ranch, mine, and lumber operation. Pay you double whatever the government pays you. How does that sound?"

"Sounds fine, but I have a job to get done. I can't really tell you what it is, but it's important and I just can't consider any other job, not even for five hundred a month."

Stanwood looked up quickly, and Spur chuckled. "No, I'm not even making two-fifty a month, but it was fun to watch your reaction. As it is, I better be getting back to town. I've enjoyed talking with you, meeting your family, and especially the barbecue. You throw a good party."

"You're not staying overnight?"

"No, work to get done. If I get fired, I'll sure remember your offer."

They shook hands.

"I'll have one of the hands saddle your horse and bring her around."

Spur went past the food table and had one more bite of the barbecued beef, then strolled to the front of the house, where several others were getting ready to head back toward town. Some of the men spoke to him. One man in a derby hat and a stiff white collar came up to him.

"Mr. McCoy, is that your mount? If you'd prefer you could ride back to town in our carriage. Might be more comfortable."

Spur grinned. "Now that is mighty friendly of you. Fact is, I'd appreciate a ride. Could we tie my mount on back of your rig?"

They were about halfway back to town when Spur asked the man in the carriage about Mrs. Stanwood.

"She's gone," the woman said. The couple were

Mr. and Mrs. Elroy Wilton. He ran one of the large mercantile stores in town.

"Well, yes, she's gone," Wilton said. "Quite a scandal about that. Figure you should know since you seem friendly with the family."

"Leave it alone, Elroy," his wife protested.

"Can't, Milly. Fact is, Mrs. Stanwood run away and left her family. About a year ago there was a big tragedy. Stanwood's brother, Marvin, shot and killed himself in his bedroom in Denver. Seems that Thurlow's wife, Nellie, had been having a wild affair with Marvin. He couldn't stand it anymore and told his brother, then shot himself.

"It all came out then, and Nellie took her jewelry and all the cash they had at the ranch and caught the train north. No one knows where she is now. Just gone. And good riddance. It was tough on the two kids for a while, but both of them are grown, so that made it easier. Oh, Marvin Stanwood ran the second bank in town, which made it that much worse."

"Thurlow seems to have recovered quick enough," Spur said.

"He did. He's a rock. He inherited half of the stock in the bank and the widow got the rest. She couldn't stay in town, of course, and moved to Kansas City, as I recall."

"Thurlow is an absolute saint," Mrs. Wilton said. "He came back a war hero, you know. He was a full colonel in the Civil War and got wounded, and came back and took over that ranch. He's done wonders with the place."

"You say Thurlow Stanwood was a full colonel in the war?" Spur asked.

"Oh, absolutely. He still puts on his uniform sometimes for our Fourth of July parade.

"Silver eagles on his shoulders," Wilton said. "That is the military insignia for a colonel, isn't it?"

Spur nodded. "Yep, it sure is." *Be damned, now why would Captain Stanwood turn himself into a colonel? Not a chance he could have earned the rank in the war.*

Chapter Seven

By the time Spur put the horse back in the livery and walked to the hotel it was nearly six o'clock. Abby sat on the bed in his room writing in a small notebook. She looked up at him and grinned, her soft green eyes sparkling.

"Hey, I'm glad you made it back. I've been pounding the boardwalks all day and found out almost nothing. Now I'm starved. You taking me out to supper?"

"I'm still full of cherry pie. What did you find out today?"

"Almost nothing. I talked to every hotel and half the boardinghouses in town. Nobody knows the man we're looking for. A couple of the women said he could be somebody they had seen but they couldn't be sure.

"Half the men I talked to said from my description it could be half the other men in town. So I didn't win any prize today."

"I didn't either, so we're even. Supper. I'll buy you supper and have a cup of coffee." He told her about "Colonel Stanwood" and she scowled.

"Why would he do that? Could he have been promoted to colonel in that short a time? Remember, Custer went from lieutenant to brigadier general in only a year during the Civil War."

"That was later on. Anyway, Stanwood isn't a Custer. I think he found the eagles and wore them home to impress the local folks." Spur stopped a minute and rubbed his jaw. "No, not home. He was in the New York Volunteer Twenty-fourth Regiment. Which meant he had to have been living in New York at the time. So Denver wasn't home to him. He must have come here after the war for the first time as a stranger."

"So nobody knew him and he could pass as a discharged full colonel with no trouble."

"He could, but why?"

"We could always check with William W. Belknap, the Secretary of War. With your Presidential connections you should be able to get an answer out of the secretary in a couple of days. He can review his army records and see if Stanwood was ever promoted to colonel."

"You may make it in this business yet, Leggett. Come on, Abby, let's go find the old feed bin."

They stopped at a small restaurant that wasn't fancy but bragged that it had the best steaks in town. Abby had a steak. Spur had a cup of coffee and then a slice of gooseberry pie. Over the pie he told Abby about the scandal surrounding the Stanwood clan.

"Happens even in the best of families," Abby said. "This Nellie Stanwood must have been a real wild one to fool around with her brother-in-law."

"I'll agree. It didn't seem to hurt the kids any. I met a daughter about twenty-one and a son maybe two years older, and both seemed reasonably normal."

"What about Stanwood himself?"

"Can't fault him for anything. I don't think he remembered me, but he confirmed that the Chantilly Country House fight was the day after the railroad embankment slaughter fighting Stonewall Jackson. He must have been there, or done a lot of studying on the Civil War. No, he was there. I remember seeing him now, and I heard his name at regimental officer meetings. He was even in my battalion."

"So who cares if he was a colonel or a captain?"

"I do, that's who." They finished supper and walked back to the hotel. Denver was built on the banks of Cherry Creek not far from where it drained into the South Platte River. Spur wondered if the crossroads town would ever amount to anything. The mining strikes had started it growing and kept it moving, but there had to be more than that. Timber and cattle were two good additions to an economic base. Another 50,000 people would help.

Back at the hotel, they went into Spur's room and Abby took off her small hat and fluffed out her hair, then began unbuttoning the top of her dress.

"Spur, I want to show you something."

"I've already seen them."

She laughed. "You're crazy. Not that. Some of my notes. One restaurant owner said he saw a man who somewhat resembled our description take one of his waitresses home after the restaurant closed. But the waitress came to work the next morning right on schedule. When he talked to her, she said they'd gone to her place, she'd fed him some pie and coffee, and they'd talked. Then he'd left. He'd been a perfect gentleman. She'd tried to get his name, but he wouldn't tell her."

"Interesting. What's your evaluation?"

"Jumping to conclusions, it could have been our killer, but the girl did not throw herself at him, did not become an easy woman or try to seduce him, so he didn't kill her."

"Is he getting a conscience?"

"No, not at all," Abby said. "It just happened that this woman didn't fit the pattern of his victims. So she lived. If she'd seduced him, she'd be dead by now. If she'd pulled open her blouse and danced for him, she'd be in her six-foot under-the-turf bedroom by now."

"Sounds like a good story," Spur said. "I wonder if it's true. Could be. Which really means that we're stuck here in Denver until we hear that he's killed someone up the rail line to the north or down the stagecoach line to the south."

"Or maybe right here in Denver?" Abby suggested.

"Let's hope we get that lucky."

That night in bed, Abby turned toward Spur and kissed his cheek. "Not tonight, sweetheart, I'm so tired I'm almost asleep by now. Why didn't you tell me this detective work was so damn hard?"

Sunday morning someone knocked on Spur's hotel room door at a little after six o'clock. Spur came up on one elbow, surprised that he had overslept. He was on his feet a moment later in his short underwear, and pulled the big .45 from leather as he moved soundlessly to the door. He stood beside the wall nearest to the knob and spoke.

"Who is it?"

"Deputy Trolliver. Sheriff Warner says he thinks you should come over to the office right away. We've got a woman slashed all to hell and she knows who done it. Sheriff thinks you'll want to talk to the man once we catch him."

"Be there in five minutes," Spur said. Already he was on his way to the bed and pulling on his pants. He dug out his socks, slid into them, then put on a shirt and his black hat. He didn't bother to shave.

Abby slept through it all on the far side of the bed. He slipped out the door, buckled his gunbelt in place, and hurried down the hall.

At the sheriff's office the head man told Spur what they had. They then walked down two blocks to where the man was holed up with a rifle and two revolvers.

"This whore said she was just doing her usual work when this customer went wild and pulled out a knife and started cutting her. She jumped and ran, and got two slices on her butt and another on her back before she could get away. Lucky enough he started on her arms and then one leg before she bolted. Wanda will get healed up fine, but we figured you might want to see what this guy looks like."

"Hell, yes. Only our boy hasn't ever left one alive before. Wonder why he did this time."

They came up to the white house. It sat back from

the street farther than the others, as if they planned to build the big house in front of this one someday.

There was no house on either side of the white one, and the three men crouched across the street behind a farm wagon someone had left there without a team attached.

"Think he's still in there?" the deputy asked.

A rifle shot slammed through a slightly opened double-hung window, and the slug tore into the front of the wagon.

"Yes, I'd say he's still there," Spur said with a grin. The rifleman inside fired twice more, and Spur couldn't tell if he had more than one rifle, or if it was a repeater of some kind.

"Give me some cover," Spur said. "I'm going to run to the house in back of us, then go down the alley and cross the street and come up on that house he's in from the rear. Give me six or eight shots as I'm getting to the house back here, then one every thirty or forty seconds. One fire and the other one reload. Now!"

The sheriff got off a shot from his sixgun, and Spur heard the round break glass in a window. By that time he was halfway to the two-storied house behind them. He saw a man come and look out the window, then Spur was past and running to the right. He went down four houses, then came back to the street.

Be a wonder if the gunman could see him now, Spur decided. He walked across the street as if nothing was the matter. Once beside the house on the far side of the street, he ran along the alley toward the gunman's house.

Spur stopped at the house two lots over and checked the white house. He saw a rifle poked out the front window. It fired, then withdrew.

As soon as the weapon fired, Spur raced for the white house's back door. He got there panting, having taken no angry shots from the man inside. So far he was still alive. He waited half a minute for his wind to return and his heart to settle down a little. Then he drew his sixgun, thumbed another round into the sixth empty chamber, and cocked the hammer.

Spur's left hand gripped the knob on the back door and turned it. It was not locked. He turned the handle as far as it would go, pulling forward on the knob. Then when he was sure the latch had cleared, he eased the door in an inch so he could see inside.

It was a back bedroom. He guessed only four rooms: two bedrooms, kitchen, living room. Nobody was inside. He slid past the partly open panel and closed it the same way he'd opened it, without a sound. He took cautious steps across the room to the door opposite him.

That would put him about in the center of the small house. He opened the second door the same way.

Just as he moved it inward an inch, a rifle went off inside the room. He pushed the door open a foot. A man lay on the floor firing a rifle over a windowsill a foot off the braided rug. He fired again.

Spur sent a shot into the wall beside the man and bellowed.

"You move a finger and you're a dead man!"

The man froze, and Spur took three quick steps

and kicked the rifle out of the man's hands. Spur felt two shots hit the outside of the house, and then in a small piece of silence he brayed out his message.

"Cease fire, it's all over!"

"Yeah, right!" He heard the faint call from outside.

A half hour later down at the Denver County Jail, Spur finished his talk with the slasher. The man was about 40, bald-headed, and with only half his teeth, and those were jagged black stumps.

"Not my man, Sheriff Warner. He's all yours. He's too old and too ugly. Besides that, he claims he was in town most of last week. Three days right here in your jail sobering up."

Sheriff Warner looked at his deputy.

"About the size of it, Sheriff. Old Scroggins there was drunker than a pair of mating skunks last week, so we dried him out a bit, then kicked him out two days ago."

"Which gives him about the best defense he can have. My man killed that last woman the same time this guy was drunk in your cell."

The sheriff swore softly. "Hell, I thought we'd cleaned up two problems at once here. I guess not. He'll do some time in state prison for this shenanigan, I'll tell you straight."

Spur headed back to the hotel. Abby was sitting up in bed trying to rub the sleep out of her eyes when he came in.

"Where have you been?" she asked.

"Oh, you're up. I asked you if you wanted breakfast and you said forget it."

She threw a pillow at him. He caught it.

"I did no such thing. I'll be dressed in ten minute and expect to have a big breakfast. Now, where have you been?"

He told her about the early morning call. "So he couldn't have been our man."

"Besides, our slasher, stabber, chopper never leaves anyone alive to testify against him. This must have just been some wild drunk."

"Abby, if you'd told me that an hour and a half ago, I could have saved myself a lot of trouble."

"You didn't ask me. You just sneaked out to play your big-boy games of cops and robbers. The shooting woke me up."

"Sorry. You going to get dressed?"

Abby grinned and winked at him. "That depends on you. Anything in particular you have in mind to keep me from getting dressed?"

Spur took off his hat and sat down beside her on the bed. "Woman, this is working time. What I have in mind ain't fitting and proper for working hours. And if you don't get dressed, it means my leaving you up here and not buying you breakfast!"

They were in the hotel dining room ten minutes later ordering.

After breakfast, Abby went back to the hotel and Spur walked down to the train station and checked with the telegraph operator, who shook his head. "Not a thing for you, Mr. McCoy. I keep watching, but just nothing has come in so far."

Spur went to the small stand-up desk/table and wrote a message to General Wilton D. Halleck, his boss in Washington, D.C.

"Any record of Captain Thurlow Stanwood of the

New York Twenty-fourth being promoted to colonel. Any record of his present location. Please advise soonest."

Spur sent the wire, paid for it, and walked out to the platform. The train was coming in from Cheyenne. It would discharge its passengers and freight, then back up a quarter of a mile to where the engine would disconnect and be switched onto a turnabout track. Then it would come back in front of the passenger cars and freight cars, if any. That way it could hook on to the cars again and pull them back to Cheyenne.

He watched the people getting down, then heard a strange noise and saw a freight car next to the last passenger car. When he walked up that way he was surprised to find a double-deck freight car packed full of sheep.

Strange to see that many sheep in cattle country such as this. He watched as the passengers who were going to Cheyenne got on. Then the engine backed out of town a quarter of a mile and stopped.

Spur could see the trainmen working the freight car, and soon the sheep began to run down a chute and into a nearby field where three young men and five sheepdogs quickly bunched the woolly critters into a herd as the first ones waited for the last to come from the car.

They were out of town far enough that few people noticed them. It was only the big cattle ranchers who were so dead set against sheep anyway, Spur knew. The old stories about sheep poisoning the range for cattle were all lies. Also, well-managed herds of sheep did not eat down graze to the point of killing it anymore than cows did. Spur shrugged. It was a long way from a killer of women to a sheep herd. He turned and walked back toward the hotel.

Alfonso Ortega urged the last of the reluctant sheep from the lower section of the freight car and jumped down behind them. He gave quick hand signals to his sheepdog, and it drove the 12 sheep across the open expanse and through a small field toward the rest of the flock.

Ortega was Spanish, about five feet eight inches and burned dark brown by the constant exposure to the sun with sheep over the past 35 years. He had starkly black hair, a hook nose, and steady brown eyes. He had been in America since he was a small boy, living with his father and mother and sheepherders in the far north part of this new land. He had grown up as a shepherd, learning about the animals, knowing when one was sick and what to do for most of the common problems and diseases. He also knew when a sheep had to be carried back to the main station where it might be treated, or disposed of to stop any spread of the illness that it had.

Ortega knew everything there was to know about sheep. He knew little else, except that he had worked for other Spaniards and other sheep ranchers and saved his money. He had married and started a family, and still he saved for his dream: that one day he could have a sheep ranch of his own, be a landowner!

Now it was coming true.

He signaled to the boys, and they began driving the flock of 200 ewes forward along a finger valley stretching away to the west and to the south. They had a 20-mile drive, but there was no rush.

The sheepdogs worked like small machines, out-thinking and outwitting the sheep as they moved slowly across the valley and over the small flat ridge into the next slope. About a mile out from the train, they moved alongside a small stream with some brush, and Ortega walked into the brush and a few minutes later drove out a small wagon pulled by two mules. It was a combination chuck wagon and prairie schooner.

In and on it was everything a sheepherder would need for six months with his flock. It carried a stock of dry food, tools, medicines, blanket rolls, cooking utensils, and one sixgun.

Ortega drove the wagon along beside the flock of ewes. The dogs and the three young men let the flock graze as the animals moved along.

Ortega watched the ewes as they grazed. They were the most wonderful sight in the world to him. They would be a fine addition to his flock. They would nearly double the size of his flock, and by this time next year there should be another 190 new lambs from these mothers-to-be. He grinned and kept driving ahead.

His wife Rosana would be delighted. She had worked with him side by side as they scrimped and saved, as they raised their three sons in the old traditions, yet with an eye to the current day and this new land that had become home to all of them.

Ortega saw a wolf slipping past a rocky patch 300 yards above where the sheep grazed. He shouted a warning to Jose, who looked where he pointed. Jose signaled to one of the dogs, who raced toward the spot and soon sent the lurking young coyote charging away. So it had been only a coyote and not a wolf. Ortega was not even sure if there were any wolves this low in the mountains. Higher they would find some, and farther to the north. Here he was not so sure.

Ortega waved to his sons, and they kept the sheep grazing to the west and south, heading them toward the fold and their small cabin, toward his homestead. Alfonso Ortega hummed a simple tune he had learned 30 years ago. He was pleased, he was a happy man. What else did he need but three fine sons, five working sheepdogs, a fine wife, and a homestead of his own and a flock of sheep. But even as he thought this, his steady brown eyes watched the slope of the hills and the skylines, watching for anything that could mean trouble.

Chapter Eight

Ortega, his sons, and their five sheepdogs herded the flock along slowly, letting the hungry animals graze as they went. They had them spread out so they wouldn't make a definite and easy-to-see trail across the virgin prairie and hills as they worked southwest.

Alfonso Ortega was not a stupid man. He could read and write. He had battled his father so he could learn to do both when he was young, because he had seen how his father had been held back because he could do neither.

It had been a bitter struggle when Alfonso decided to get married and go out on his own. The first years were hard, and then with a family of three boys it became even harder.

He worked for a sheep ranch in northern Kansas, and made sure that his three boys went to school.

Now all three could read and write, and he was proud of that.

Twice he had seen everything he owned lost. The first time rampaging cattle ranchers stormed through the owner's sheep spread and burned all the buildings to the ground, including the small house where Alfonso and his family lived.

Alfonso and his family escaped with only a few burns and the jackets they pulled on when the raiders rode in firing shots and stampeding the sheep out of the fold.

Starting over again, finding clothing for the family had been hard enough, but then the owner of the sheep ranch decided to give up and move on. Alfonso and two other stockmen drove his remaining sheep into the wilds of what would someday become Wyoming and tried again.

There it had taken longer, but the wild son of a big rancher had come by himself one night and shot and killed the sheep rancher and burned the barns and rousted the workers into the night.

One of the other stockmen had used his rifle and shot the cattleman's son dead. As soon as the others saw the cattleman fall, they gathered their goods and left the country any way they could. They had seen "cattlemen" justice before. Just because a cattleman killed a sheepman didn't give the herders the same right to retaliate.

Before it was over, two drovers and the sheepman's son had been hanged by vigilantes prodded on by the cattlemen.

Ortega let the past flow away from him as he rode the chuck wagon beside his sheep. *His sheep!* He had waited so long for this time. Now he would stay well away from any ranchers, and not bring their anger down on his family.

After all, this was 1875 and the times were changing. Some of the more progressive cattlemen were even raising sheep themselves now on land that would not support cattle. Perhaps this was the place where he and his family could stay forever in peace and justice and harmony with everyone. Perhaps.

One dog streaked to the right, turned a runaway ewe, and trotted with her back to the flock. They had not lost even one of the prized ewes on this drive to their ranch, and Ortega was determined not to. Five dogs were too many for a flock this size, but he wanted to be sure to get all of the animals into his land as quickly and safely as possible.

Jose Ortega was 16 and the oldest son of Alfonso. He had learned the sheep business from his father. Jose was especially good with the sick sheep. He could tell by watching them move if they were hungry or thirsty or in need of some medical care.

He handled the veterinary stores on the chuck wagon. They had everything they needed there to tend to a flock for six months.

By living right on the edge of the range that they owned, they could work the sheep in four flocks in four different directions from the cabin, and bring them back each night to protect them in the fold. There were no wild dogs here, but cougars and large bobcats and coyotes could kill several sheep in only a few seconds if the sheep were not protected.

Wolves he was not sure of. He would have to listen to the calls the next full moon night.

They worked down to a small stream, where the sheep paused and drank their fill. After the dogs had sampled the water as well, they drove the animals across the stream and up toward a narrow valley that would soon lead to the next valley. They would then be halfway home.

Ortega figured it would take them two days to move the 20 miles, but he was in no hurry. The important job was to get the sheep across the bottom of some of the land that the big Flying S Ranch claimed it controlled. There was no point in explaining to the cowboys that it was open range, not owned by anyone but the United States Government and ready to be homesteaded.

Cattle ranchers always tried to control all the land they could. They would stake their claim along a river, but make the homestead only a hundred yards wide to cover the stream, and then survey it out so the homestead stretched along the water for six or seven miles. All legal. Infuriating.

Ranchers thought they "controlled" land for a day's ride or 20 miles on each side of their legitimate homestead. They might control it, but only with guns and men. When the time came to sell the property, only that deeded to the rancher could be sold. Then the recriminations started to fly.

Alfonso Ortega wanted to stay at least 20 miles away from the Flying S. Then he'd have no trouble with them. If a small rancher moved in closer to him, he would ride down and talk to the man, and probably find him a reasonable sort. Most men were. Most big cattle ranchers weren't.

Ortega stopped the wagon as it crested the little

hill and looked back west and north. Beautiful. An untamed wilderness all the way to the towering Rocky Mountains on the horizon. He had no idea how far away the peaks were. They shone in the afternoon sun like towering ice palaces. He watched it all for a moment, then swept the surrounding land again with his penetrating stare. He could see no cows, no calves, no sign of any man. Good. The last thing he wanted right now was to tangle with the Flying S ranch hands.

A quarter of a mile away in the edge of some brush near a stream, Chad Alstair couldn't believe what he saw. The whole damn hillside was white and moving.

"Goddamn sheep!" he exploded. His first instinct was to take his rifle and start whamming away at the four men and the wagon he saw. Then he shook his head and thought it through. He was a good 15 miles from the ranch, way out on the edge of the land they controlled.

The damn sheep had crossed over part of their range, but they were moving and couldn't do a lot of damage. Hell, yes, he'd tell the foreman about it. After he did the rest of his hoorahing of these few critters down here, and pushed them back toward the better grass and where most of the rest of the south herd grazed. He was due to report back in at the home place tomorrow.

Chad was on a two-day count and one-day round-up to keep the stock close enough to the main range so they could find them come fall. Wasn't the best job on the ranch, but he'd asked for it. Now he had a night and another day before he could report back to the foreman. Chad shrugged. Hell, sometimes things just don't work out the way you'd like them to.

He eased his gray down into a small valley and found two cows and calves. He rode toward them, waved his hat, and began moving the four critters up across the small ridge and down into the better grass in the five-mile-wide valley just to the north.

He'd have to do the same maneuver 20 more times before he lost the light. Then he'd stretch out under some tree, fry some bacon and eggs, eat a half loaf of bread, and call it a day.

It rained that night, a furious thunderstorm that blew up out of nowhere from the mountains, and Chad had to pull his poncho out from under his blanket. By that time he was soaked to the skin and his fire was out.

He shivered until morning, swore at the sun, and got back to work. The rain had been harder than he realized. It was enough to wipe out any sign that there had ever been a herd of 200 or so sheep crossing the bottom of their range.

So he'd report it anyway.

He did about eight o'clock that night when he got into the main place. Thurlow Stanwood had just lit up a long brown cigar when Chad told him directly what he'd seen. The foreman stood by listening.

"You say they were heading southwest, and cut across the bottom of our land?"

"Yes, sir. But that damn rainstorm washed out every track made over there. I couldn't track a herd of buffalo after that one."

"How many did you say?"

"I figured maybe a hundred and eighty to two hundred. Hard to count them damn things."

"I heard in town somebody was going to try to raise sheep over in that area. Guess they won't bother us much. Damn creatures kill the grass, you know that?"

"Yes, sir," Chad said.

"Well, thanks for the information. We'll watch that range."

Chad and the foreman left and Stanwood looked at his son, who had also listened.

"One of these days we're going to ride over there and shear us a few damn sheep with some double-ought buck. Getting about time to discourage this gent, whoever he is. Don't you think that's the right thing to do, Leslie?"

Leslie Stanwood looked up quickly. He hadn't paid much attention to what the cowboy had said. He was waiting for his father to give him his weekly wages, $100. He earned it sometimes. Hell, he didn't know that much about keeping books anyway. That was why they had a bookkeeper do the work.

"Yeah, teach them sheepherders a lesson, Pa. That's what you always say."

"Next week. We'll wait and be sure it ain't gonna rain. Then we'll take about ten men and ride over that way until we find the damned sheep. The herder's house and wagon won't be far off. You're going with us, Leslie. About time you found out that it takes guts and determination to hold a spread like this one together. It ain't just luck and loyalty."

"No, sir," Leslie said. He watched his father count

out the ten-dollar gold pieces. Ten of them. His father made a stack of five and then put five more beside it. At last he shoved the stacks of coins across the big desk to his son.

"How things going between you and Miss Charlotte Fenton?"

"Fine."

"You going to marry her?"

"I . . . I don't know."

"Hell, why not? She's nice enough. Got big tits and wide hips. Good for birthing babies. You should have about four to help you run this place after I'm gone."

"I . . . well, I haven't asked her yet."

"You been alone with her much? I mean, you had your way with her yet? That usually makes a woman want to tie the knot."

"Oh, she wants to get married. I just don't know. I don't think so for a while."

"Hell, boy, you're twenty-three already. Time you was doing it."

"Yes, Pa. I'll think on it."

"You going somewhere?"

"Figured I'd go into town, stay a couple of days."

"You whoring around, boy?"

"No, sir. Them painted, dried-up whores just don't appeal to me. Too common."

"For damn sure there, boy. Well, you take care. You get back here and we'll go see them sheep. You ever shot a sheep, boy?"

"No, sir."

"Real sport, real sport. We'll see what we can do early next week."

Thurlow Stanwood watched his son walk out of

the den. Stanwood shook his head. He couldn't figure out for the life of him what was the matter with that boy. Done his best with the kid. Hell, he'd even taken him to a whorehouse in town that had a young girl when he was 16.

Come to think of it, after that the kid had seemed to kind of turn into himself. Stanwood slammed his fist down on the top of the desk. The kid never would be good enough to run this ranch and the rest of the operation. He was weak and scared.

Hell, he was too much like his mother. At least that whore was gone and couldn't hurt him anymore. Stanwood figured he'd done a pretty damn good job with the kids since his wife had robbed him blind and left in the middle of the night. Damn her soul!

Christopher Perry came to the door, knocked, entered, and sat down in the chair across the big desk. Perry was three inches under six feet tall, and had grown a paunch over his 52 years. He was unmarried, and headed up the logging and sawmill division of Flying S Enterprises.

Perry wore conservative clothes and had a proper haircut, with eyeglasses perched on his nose. He used them just for reading. His ruddy complexion had nothing to do with the outdoors. Most of it came directly from the small end of a whiskey cork. His stark green eyes peered at his employer.

"Figured it was about time I reported in and gave you the figures on the mill. We been doing fine. Overall board feet cut last week is up by almost ten percent. Probably because we're working on that order for timbers and the railroad ties. But a board foot is a board foot.

"Now, here is our latest statement of goods sold and income and the continuing overhead as pro-rated out over the work we get ready for market.

"Actually our cost came down about three percent last month. That's partly because our volume on the sawmill lumber production is up."

"Chris, you know that all these reasons and excuses bore the hell out of me. How much hard cold cash did we make over what we spent last week?"

"Twelve thousand four hundred and sixty dollars, from the sawmill-lumbering operation."

"Well, that's as good as a cattle drive. You can do this year round?"

"Not when it snows so hard we can't get logs out of the woods, or wagons of lumber to town or the railroad. I'm still fighting to build a spur rail line directly to the mill. Less than twenty miles, and it would quadruple the amount of lumber we can ship. That's our bottleneck now. We cut more than we can haul to town on the wagons."

"How much does a locomotive cost?"

"I had one offered to me two weeks ago for four thousand dollars."

"Damn, that much?"

"You never have to feed it hay or oats, and it won't die on you in the middle of a July afternoon."

"Yes, but the upkeep, mechanics to keep it running, laying the rails—"

"But we can sell twice as much lumber as we're selling now. And right now we cut twice as much lumber ready to sell as we can haul out."

"I see your point. I'll think it over carefully. Anything else?"

"We could use a few more good men. I'm going into town tomorrow and hire six, men who are single and can live in the barracks."

"Fine, fine. Now I really want to talk some things over with Terri. You'll stay the night and go on to town from here tomorrow?"

"That's the plan," Perry said, and stood. He left the room with a small frown showing. *Damn him! He knows I hate kowtowing to him this way. God damn him!*

Perry went to the first guest room on the second floor and threw himself on the bed. Things hadn't been this way ten years ago. Then he had been a full partner with Stanwood. Perry had been the one to come up with the idea to take over the Flying S Ranch.

He'd met Stanwood shortly after the ex-soldier left the army. Stanwood didn't know anything about ranching. Perry had done all the hard work, set up everything, and they'd gotten ownership of the ranch. A damn $15,000 ranch that didn't cost them a cent! Then just a year later he'd lost it all.

Sure, he'd gambled a little bit, but what the hell. Sure, he'd lost more than he should, but Stanwood had gone to court and paid off his gambling debts and gotten a court order that the payoff was to cover the purchase of Perry's half of the Flying S Ranch and all its properties.

Gone, goddamned gone in a blink of an eyelash, the stroke of a judge's pen! Gone and forgotten. He had been a full partner. Then suddenly he was broke and with no job.

Stanwood had made a big show of giving him a job. Set him up on the mountain and told him to start a sawmill. He'd done it, done it all from scratch. Learned a new trade, found the equipment, brought it in and set it up and ran it. Did it damn well. And he did it all for wages.

Wages! Damn it all! He still should be a fifty-fifty partner in Flying S Enterprises. One of these days he would own the whole damn thing. He'd been doing some planning of his own. It took time, and he'd had time. Another two weeks and he'd be ready.

Yeah, then this big ranch house, the ranch, the mine, and the lumber business would all be his! All his and about goddamned time!

Chris Perry pulled his clothes off and slid into bed. Just thinking about it brought a smile to his face. It would be all his, and damn soon now!

Chapter Nine

"Oh, my, no, I'm not new in Denver," the woman in her thirties said to the well-dressed young man across from her at her dining room table. He was so handsome! She could hardly believe her good fortune when he had helped her up when she had fallen on the boardwalk.

He had been so kind and courteous, and offered to walk home with her to be sure she was not injured. She had insisted then that she repay his kindness with some of her own and offered him tea. He had been gracious and said he would have time for one cup if it would make her happy.

Happy? She glowed with the thought. Six months she had been widowed, and she hadn't really thought about a man, but now with this remarkable young gentleman sitting across from her, she sensed a warmth between her legs that was spreading.

Helen Foley smiled. Why not? He was so handsome and polite. Surely he would be gentle.

"Would you like some more tea?" she asked. She looked up and her glance touched on his face. He watched her intently. A bright smile wreathed her face. She knew she was pretty. She had been careful about not getting as fat as her mother had been. She disliked fat people.

"Yes, a little more tea might be fine," he said. "You mentioned that your husband was a pharmacist?"

"Indeed. And a good one. But he fell and shattered his leg, and two days later he was gone. The doctor said some of the shattered bone chips must have penetrated into his bloodstream and been taken back to the heart, killing him before anyone knew what to do."

She lifted her brows. "But Gerald always said that life must go on. He said that to those who came for medicine that didn't work right. Life must go on."

"No children?"

"No . . . I . . . we just didn't have any."

She rose and shifted to the side so her breasts would show off to the best advantage. She had fine breasts, she knew. "Would you like to come into the parlor? The sofa there is so much more comfortable."

"Yes, Miss Helen," he said, "that would be good. You were telling me about your dreams of becoming a concert pianist."

"Oh, that. A silly girlish fantasy. I was never that good on the piano." They went to the parlor and sat on the beige sofa that was soft and with the back sloped just right. He let her sit first, and then he lowered beside her, but not too close.

"You never did tell me what you do," she said. Helen was too embarrassed to tell him that she had forgotten his name. Her mind went into the next county whenever she had the slightest thought about an intimate contact with this man. He was beautiful!

"Oh, I buy this and that, sell things at a profit. You mentioned that your husband had some of that new life insurance. You get enough money to live off from the insurance company back in New York?"

"Yes, isn't that a good system? We paid into it each month, and now with the unexpected tragedy, I'm well fixed for the rest of my life."

She reached for something on the small table in front of the sofa, and as she did, she slid toward him. Helen picked up a magazine and then put it down. Now her leg was only a piece of cloth away from his.

Helen had been nervous before, but now a calm settled over her and she turned to look at this young man. "I would guess that you are not married, right?"

"Oh, no, ma'am. I'm not married at all."

She laughed and he smiled. "Good. Would it offend you if I said I think you're one of the most attractive men I've ever seen in Denver?"

His smile broadened. "No, ma'am, that wouldn't offend me at all. It's most kind of you. I'm not sure that you mean it, but a compliment is always good to hear."

She smiled at him. "Oh, I'm sincere, and I have been out in the public quite a bit recently. I truly admire you." She leaned toward him and her thigh touched his. Helen looked at him frankly and saw that he wasn't moving away from her touch.

She felt a surge of emotion, and the warm glow in her crotch now added a dampness she could feel. Slowly she leaned toward him, her lips parted, her eyes taking on a smoky smoldering color of blue.

"I am in my own home and I do wish to be kind to you for being so helpful, but now would you be kind to me and do me the honor of kissing me . . . just once?"

Their faces were close. His arm came around her and pressed her closer, and his lips found hers. It was a soft, gentle kiss, and Helen sighed when it ended. She dropped her head to his shoulder and sighed again.

"That was just beautiful, beautiful!" She turned her head and looked up at him. "I . . . I know it would not be ladylike for me to ask you to kiss me again." She stopped, and her best smile turned her face into an appealing beauty. "But I wouldn't be honest with you if I said that I would make a big objection if you did kiss me again."

For a moment he stared at her. Then there was a hint of resignation in his eyes as he bent and found her lips for the second kiss. It lasted longer, and she pressed hard against his lips wanting to open hers, but afraid to.

When the kiss ended, she turned and lay in his lap, her head pressing on his fly. She felt no serious lump there. Her breath came in ragged gasps now. Her eyes shone. Her mouth came open and she watched his young face.

Slowly she reached upward, caught his neck, and

pulled his head down gently until he could kiss her. This time her mouth was open and his tongue swept in, dominating her, penetrating her, sealing the offer with his own positive response. It was a long kiss and they breathed gently. Her hands found one of his, and she pulled it between them so his fingers fell on her breasts.

She pressed his hand against her flattened breasts and moaned softly as the kiss continued.

When it broke she opened her eyes to see his reaction.

"I . . . we shouldn't be doing this, Miss Helen."

"I'm not Miss. I'm a widow and I have had a man in my bed for almost five years. Right now I'm missing all of that. Right now I want you to tear off my dress and carry me into the bedroom and have your way with me. *I need you to make love to me!*"

He watched her, then slowly unbuttoned the fasteners down the front of her dress. A tear came to his eye, but he brushed it away.

"You're so very much like her," he said softly.

She held his hand on her breast, and then moved it around caressing her through the cloth. "Like who? I don't understand? Like a lady friend you had who married someone else?"

His smile was strange, but he nodded. "Something like that. I should be going."

"No!" She said the word sharply and he looked at her. She sat up and finished unbuttoning the top of her dress, then pulled the garment down from her shoulders so it fell around her waist. Then she crossed her arms, caught the sides of the white cotton chemise, and pulled it over her head.

Her breasts bounced and jolted from the sudden

movement and the pull of the cloth. They were firm and high and gently pointed, with a narrow band of pink areola and tipped with flame-red nipples that were now pulsating and had already lifted and stood at their full height of sexual excitement.

"Please don't go. Please love me, make me feel like a real woman again."

He closed his eyes for a moment. His hands balled into fists as if he were fighting something. When he opened his eyes they held a glint she hadn't seen before, as if it were a look of anticipation.

The young man bent and kissed her breast, and she moaned in delight. He lifted up. "Did you like that? Tell me exactly how you feel right now and what you want me to do to you."

She frowned for a moment, then reached over and caressed the crotch and fly of his trousers until she found the swelling. Then she held it, petted it.

"What I want . . . I've never said it before. I guess I can. Yes." She unbuttoned his fly and pushed one hand inside until she found the hardness, which she caught and held.

"Yes, I can. I want you to take the rest of my clothes off. I want you to take me into the bedroom, or even right here. I want you to pet me and fondle me and kiss all over my body.

"I want you to strip off your clothes and kneel between my thighs and push your big lance right up inside me until it can't go any farther. Then I want you to chew on my titties, and suck them like a baby would and kiss me and then pound into me, poking me until you shoot your load as far up my tube as you can."

She stopped and watched him. "Then I want you to do it again and again, five or six times. I want you to put it in my other hole, and let me suck you off and do anything you've always dreamed about a woman doing to you."

She stood up, caught his hand, and pulled, and he stood beside her. It was still early afternoon. Helen led him into the bedroom, closed the door, and then pulled the dress off over her head.

"Now, beautiful man, what do you want to do to me?"

He growled and dropped to his knees and jerked the half-slips down so she could step out of them. Then he pulled down her silk-soft bloomers and threw them aside.

She was slender, full-busted, with gently curving woman's hips and long tapered legs. Beautiful. He didn't think he had ever seen a more perfect figure. He pushed forward and kissed her breasts, then chewed on them until she whimpered in pain and he eased up.

He pushed her down on her back and watched her lift her knees and part her legs, opening herself, showing him her most prized part, her best bargaining resource. It was there for free, his for the taking.

He settled between her legs and in one hard, fast stroke lanced into her slot. She was ready, and there was almost no resistance. She moaned as he slid into her, and then yelped in wonder.

"Oh, damn! Beautiful. I think I want to fuck forever! There's no feeling in the world like it!"

The young man now having his way with Helen had undressed carefully, putting his boots near the side of the bed. He pumped and ejaculated almost automatically, with little more feeling than shaking hands. He heard the woman screeching in her delirium of delight, and then it was over and they rested.

Now, he decided. But as his hand closed around the long thin Chicago ice pick knife, he changed his mind. No, not yet. She wasn't quite ready yet. This one he wanted to frighten, to scare so badly that she might die of a stopped heart! Yes. That would be as much punishment as the final thrust.

First she had to calm down, to rest and to be sharp and ready to understand terror.

As he waited, his own body returned to its normal rhythms. He thought about his mother. His eyes blinked and his face quivered with hatred when he thought of her. For a moment his body shook, but he stilled it with a surge of concentration.

"You all right, sweetheart?" Helen asked. "You just rest up a minute more and we'll do us a real wild one, okay?"

He nodded in the afternoon light coming in the window.

That reminded him of how his mother always liked to leave the window open on the second floor of the house. He didn't want to think about his mother. Then in one flash of a second he was gone, and he was 12 again, and his mother was at his door looking at him.

"Darling Boy, you don't have to be afraid of your mother. I'm here to take care of you. Have I ever hurt you?" She was soft and warm and her hair was golden, but there was something wrong with her eyes.

He shook his head. "No, Mommie, you never hurt me."

She smiled and went in his room and locked the door with a bolt behind her and watched him. He wasn't as tall as she was. She knelt down and put her arms around him. She kissed his cheek, then undid his belt.

"We're going to play a game today, Darling Boy. Remember the one last time? This one is much, much more fun. First, do you want to see what I'm hiding under my blouse?"

He nodded, knowing she wanted him to nod.

She undid the buttons slowly, letting him peek at the sides of her small breasts. Then she flipped back one side of the blouse and he saw her pink, brown-tipped breast, all of it!

He made a small noise in his throat and she smiled.

"Yes, Darling Boy, nice. Very nice. Now twice as nice." She showed him her second breast and he swallowed, his eyes wide. She had never done this before. She always let him feel them under her dress, but she never showed them to him. Breasts, tits, wow! Then she did as she always did, took his hand and put it on her breast.

"Now, play with my titties, the way I showed you. That makes Mommie feel just ever so good. Go ahead."

"What if . . ."

"Nobody is going to see us. Your pa is out on the range and your sister is having a nap. The cook is busy. Come on, Darling Boy, be nice to your mommie."

He did then, fondling her breasts, rubbing them

the way she had shown him. She breathed faster and harder, and then she put her hand down under the skirt of her dress, and a minute later she clutched him and her whole body shook and he thought he'd hurt her. But she'd said before this was what felt the best, and he was the one who made her feel that way.

When she calmed down again she told him to pet her titties again, and this time she undid his belt all the way and pulled down his trousers. He wore short underwear then, and she pulled that down as well.

"My, you're growing bigger," she said. "My, my, my, but you're going to be so long and thick when you're all grown up. The girls will go wild."

He stood still as he always did and she reached in her hand, but before she could touch him, the spell broke and he felt the live, moving woman under him, and he wiped sweat off his face.

"You have a bad dream?" Helen asked.

"Yeah, a dream. I say anything?"

"You moaned and yelped a couple of times, then your hips kept humping and humping me, like you were getting ready again. Hey, I want you to wait for me. You rested enough?"

He nodded.

She rolled over and got on her hands and knees.

"You ever do the doggie?" she asked, looking at him over her shoulder, her round, pink bottom exposed to him.

He shook his head.

"Hey, good, it's easy. You just mount me from behind the way a male dog gets into a bitch in heat. I'll be the bitch in heat. Damn, it's been a long time.

I want to wear us both out before I let you go. Can you stay all night?''

He nodded, then moved up behind her on his knees and found that it wasn't hard at all. He figured this might be the way the early men made love, taking their clues from the animals.

Before he got in place, he had reached into his boot, taken the Chicago ice pick from its special scabbard, and put it on the side of the bed.

This time he didn't even think about the woman. This time it was for him. He would do it just as he climaxed. He would remember this one. He would try to remember this one.

She worked him up fast, and screamed in joy with two of her own climaxes before he was ready. Then he felt it coming, grabbed the Chicago ice pick, and just as he climaxed drove the long thin knife upward under her chest, piercing her heart. She gagged and tried to say something, then fell forward on the bed as he drove into her the last time and spent himself, then came away and pulled the long knife out of her at the same time.

He sat on the edge of the bed, wiping off the knife. Helen was a slut. She had wanted him to do it. She had asked him! She was a slut like his mother. Why couldn't he just find his mother and kill her and it would be all over? He had to kill his mother, but until he found her he'd settle for any loose woman he found.

He hadn't planned this. It had been a chance meeting. He had been being a gentleman by helping the lady to her feet when she fell down. He had carried her packages and sipped her tea. The whole fooling around and the sex had been *her idea*. It seemed like it was always the slut's idea to have sex. He felt in his pockets of his pants on the side of the bed.

Yes, he had several of the coins. He rolled her over and closed her eyes, then put the coins over her eyes. He seemed to remember doing this before. Had he? He thought he had.

"Twenty cents, Darling Boy. That's plenty for you to spend when you go to buy candy. Remember, twenty cents, and all you have to do is let Mommie feel good. Look, I'm giving you two dimes. You like to help Mommie feel good, don't you, Darling Boy? I know you do. Maybe next time Mommie will show you something different. You're getting bigger now, growing more. Have you ever . . . has it ever got . . ." She stopped and stared at him, then put his hands back on her bare breasts.

"Oh, yes, Darling Boy, that feels so wonderful! I wish we could play games this way all day. But just once a week, I promised you. Now, you take your twenty cents and you go have some fun, buy some candy. You do whatever you want to do. You made Mommie feel so good, Darling Boy."

He shook his head. He had to dress. He had to get out of here quickly. He figured someone must be looking for him. It was a mistake to stay in Denver. But where should he go? Home? That was a laugh. How would he be any safer at home? He dressed quickly, picking up everything, making sure he left nothing behind.

He cleaned off the long thin knife on the sheet and put it away in his boot. He'd seen several men carry such weapons. They were little good in a face-to-face fight, but for a quick kill from behind they were unstoppable. He checked the room again. It was getting near dusk, and the room was in shadows now. He picked up his hat off the parlor table and left the lamp unlit as he slipped out the back door. It was just starting to get dark.

How long had he sat there on the bed remembering his mother? He had no idea. It was soon fully dark. He hurried down the street. He wasn't in the mood to do any gambling tonight. Maybe later. What he wanted was a bed and a long night's sleep without any of the dreams. Afterwards he usually didn't have the dreams. Not for at least a week.

Chapter Ten

Spur McCoy got to the telegraph office in the train station five minutes before the day man came on. It was almost eight A.M. and the night man shook his head at McCoy's question. The tall man walked the platform for ten minutes, then went back inside. The day man waved at him.

"Mr. McCoy?"

"Right?"

"Just got in a message for you, from Washington, D.C. You interested?"

Spur rushed over to the counter and the operator printed out the telegram and handed it to him. McCoy held the paper up to the light and at last went over by the window to read it.

"Spur McCoy, High Country Hotel, Denver, Colorado. Captain Thurlow S. Stanwood never ranked beyond captain. Army records show he was killed in the battle of the Chantilly Country House in Virginia, August 31, 1862. Signed: Gen. Wilton D. Halleck.''

Spur frowned and read the note again. Surely there was some mistake. He remembered Stanwood as the same officer he had seen in the New York Twenty-fourth Regiment. Stanwood knew about the Chantilly battle. He was there. But the army said Stanwood was killed in that fight. Then what was he doing here alive and well?

By the time Spur walked back to the hotel he had worked out at least two answers. One, it was a mistake, and Stanwood's identification had gotten on someone else who died that day in that battle. Possibly. Most battles were horrendously confused mixups and mistakes anyway. Probably. He didn't need to say anything to Stanwood about it.

The farther he walked the more he realized there could be another explanation. Stanwood could have planted his identification on some other man who'd died, some other officer, perhaps one who'd had his face disfigured so identification would be hard, nearly impossible. Then Stanwood had taken the other officer's identification and faked his way out of the army.

But why? Why indeed. It gave Spur a new slant on the big rancher. He had some more work to do digging into the background of Mr. Stanwood and how he had come to own such a large ranch in just ten years.

He talked it over with Abby as they had breakfast at a small restaurant near the hotel. They decided they shouldn't eat all the time at the hotel and establish a pattern.

"Why would someone want to pretend to be dead?" Abby asked.

Spur had come up with some more reasons. "Maybe he wanted to get out of a bad marriage . . . but that doesn't seem reasonable since he was married until about a year ago, and has two children who had to be the product of that marriage and were born long before the war started."

"You shot your own foot with that reason, McCoy. Another reason might be because he wanted to drop out of sight. The Twenty-fourth Regiment men all came from New York, didn't they? You did."

"The ones in 1862 certainly did. Bright, eager, and ready to die."

"So the message would have gone to his home in New York that Stanwood was dead. Then he could come West and start his fortune under a new name or his real one."

"Good try, but why would he also bring his wife and two children along? And why would he keep using his real name if he wanted to vanish and start over?"

"Beats me. I'd guess that we're going to try to find out about the good Colonel Stanwood while we're here."

"Not a lot else for us to do right now. We can look up some of the old land records. I'm wondering how he got such a big ranch put together so quickly."

"Maybe someone else started it and he latched onto it when it was a going concern?"

"Could be."

A deputy sheriff came to the cafe door and looked inside. He saw Spur and motioned to him. Their breakfast was done anyway.

"Duty calls. Maybe it's good news for a change," said Spur.

Outside, the deputy walked with them toward the county building and the jail.

"Sheriff Warner says you better come take a look. We had a woman killed yesterday or last night. A neighbor stopped over to borrow some eggs this morning and said things didn't look right." The deputy looked at Abby. "No place for a lady, if you'll beg my pardon, miss."

"Oh, I was going back to the hotel anyway." She glared at Spur and he waved at her, and the two men marched away past the sheriff's office and two blocks down the main street before they turned left down Third.

A short time later, Spur looked at the dead woman. Naked, her clothes thrown about the room. Obviously a love scene. There was almost no blood. Only a smear just under her rib cage where a thin blade had gone in. It could angle up into the heart.

"Damn Chicago ice pick," Spur said.

Sheriff Warner looked up from a chair. He had been looking at the scene. "I've been trying to make some sense of it. There evidently was a sexual encounter. Then the woman was killed with one swift stroke and the blade wiped off on the bedding."

"Twenty-cent pieces on her eyes," Spur said. "That settles it for me, Sheriff. No one else has done that. We haven't told anyone about it. Nothing has been in the newspapers. It has to be our killer. What about the woman?"

"Helen Foley, a modest little woman, early thirties, widowed less than a year ago. Lived here on a

modest stipend from some insurance firm back
East. She was quiet, don't think she had anyone
courting her. She never went out to the theater or
the concerts. Real quiet. We'll talk to the woman
who found her. She's in hysterics yet, her husband
tells us."

"Even the most reserved can kick up their heels
now and then, Sheriff. Otherwise our race would die
out. She was a widow. Maybe she encouraged our
boy. Evidently that's all it takes to set him off on his
murderous sprees. I don't see any sign of a fight or a
struggle, do you?"

"Not at all. Looks like they had tea in the dining
room. Then my guess would have been that they
moved to the couch, and from there to the bedroom. You see, we found the lady's white chemise
on the floor under the couch, like it had been kicked
there accidentally."

"Sheriff, could I ask your men to stay outside? I
want to do a complete search of these three rooms.
It will take some time, and I want to be sure that
nothing is touched or moved. Is the chemise where
it was found?"

"Yes, sir. I'll get my men out and tell them to wait
to move the body. You're sure this is another victim
of your killer?"

"Damn sure. Now I have to find something to tie
him to the scene of the crime, whoever the hell he
is."

Spur hung his jacket on the back of a chair in the
kitchen and began going over the house. He started
in the dining room. There were tea things set out on
the kitchen table. A tea strainer, a can of bulk tea
with the top left off, and a dish of some homemade

cookies that might have been forgotten and left there.

In the dining room he found two chairs out of their regular spots, as if they had been used and pushed partly back. There were two teacups and saucers and spoons, and a sugar bowl near them on the table. One cup was empty, the other half full. The china teapot sat nearby on a trivet.

He got down on his hands and knees and looked under the table, but found nothing on the polished and waxed hardwood floor. Not even dust. Helen had been a meticulous housekeeper. Everything seemed to be in its place, precisely set, waiting to be used.

A rocking chair was close to the window. A magazine lay nearby on a small table. A bag filled with knitting needles, yarn, and a partly done garment sat in the rocking chair.

He checked in the kitchen, but found nothing new. Only a dead fire in the kitchen range. He went back to the bedroom. Spur noted the position of each piece of clothing. This was not a neat person. This was passion, pulling off clothes and dropping them or throwing them.

The dress near the door, the chemise in the living room near the couch, shoes and hose beside the bed, petticoats near the head of the bed, bloomers on the bed itself near the top.

Where was something from the man? He checked the position of the body. Spots of blood on the handmade quilt showed to the right of the body. He hadn't noticed them before on the red quilt pattern. Had she been stabbed there and rolled over? Yes, about the right distance. She was stabbed when she lay facedown? Not possible. Maybe she was sitting and fell forward on her stomach, or she could have been on her hands and knees.

He lifted his brows, and went to his knees and checked around the floor again. Sticking out from under the long quilt that came nearly to the floor over the bed he saw something white.

Spur picked it up and pulled it free. A man's white linen handkerchief. An expensive one. Not the kind that most men used. He checked it for a monogram, but there was none. He folded it after seeing no bloodstains of any kind.

It was the only male item in the room. At last, perhaps, he had a clue, an item from the killer himself. It might be important, and then it might be worthless, but it was at least something.

An hour later, he gave up on his search and let the undertaker come and take away the body. There were no close relatives. There would be no church service. Spur took the two 20-cent coins and put them with the handkerchief.

Perhaps someday there would be a method of identifying someone just by testing something he had touched or handled. It certainly would come in handy in this case.

By the time he got back to the sheriff's office and reported his find, it was nearly noon. He went to the hotel room and found Abby waiting for him.

"Anything?"

He showed her the handkerchief.

"Expensive. Most of the men on the street don't carry a snot rag like that one." She grinned as she said it, and he snorted.

"True. Your job is to try to find out where it was

purchased. Can't be more than one or two places in town that would sell an expensive bit of fluff like this."

"I can do that. I also did some looking into the life and times of Helen Foley. I found out on the street she was the woman murdered. Lots of talk about. Seems Helen was a regular churchgoer, sang in the choir. Pristine in word and deed. Widowed eight months ago. No man has ever been seen calling at her house. She is not a loose woman. Gets a check from a New York insurance company from a policy on her late husband.

"Not a hint of scandal, not a drop of bad blood with anyone I talked to. She seems virginal pure and untouched by anyone since her husband departed this earth."

"That doesn't help much," Spur said. "Breaks the pattern."

Abby shook her head. "Not necessarily. I found one shopkeeper who saw her fall down on the boardwalk in front of his store yesterday afternoon. He hurried out to help her, but by the time he got to the door, a well-dressed gent had picked her up, dusted her off, and carried her packages as the two walked down the street.

"The store owner couldn't identify the man. Said he didn't even look at him that closely. He had customers and had to hurry back to his cash box. He did say the man wore a dark suit and a conservative town hat. He didn't have a walking stick, and the owner couldn't be sure if the gent helping Helen had a gold chain and watch fob or not."

"So why doesn't this break the pattern?"

"She's a widow. Say she did fall down, accidental-

ly or on purpose, and this handsome man helped
her back to her feet. He might insist on seeing that
she got home safely and walk her there. It's only
about three blocks away.

"Then, just speculating, she might insist on re-
turning his kindness and make tea for him. Were
there tea things out?"

"There were, used."

"Good. Then during or after tea, our widow
might start missing her husband, missing his lovemaking, and she might get all hot and flustered and
*at that time become the aggressor and throw herself at
him.*"

"Could be."

"You said you found her chemise in the parlor.
Somehow her dress got unbuttoned and off her
shoulders and the chemise up and off, leaving her
naked to the waist. That was on the couch in the
parlor. Helen must have been wanting him by then.
No struggle, you said, so the chances are she
showed off her breasts to him trying to seduce him."

"And that would fit into the pattern of our boy,
who then accepts the free roll in her bed and
rewards her with a quick and painless death. Damn,
you might be right. At least we know he did it. The
coins prove that. No word has been given anyone
about the seldom-used coins that the killer covers
the victims' eyes with. We still have our boy."

Spur paced the floor a moment. Then they went
downstairs and ate lunch at a different restaurant
than they had earlier. Spur took out the linen
handkerchief and looked at it.

"'Pears that we both better track down who sold

this. You take half the town and I'll take the other half."

Two hours after lunch, they both met at the Johnson Haberdashery. It was the fanciest men's clothier in town, and Mr. Johnson himself examined the handkerchief. Two merchants had told each of the searchers that Johnson's would have the item.

"Yes, yes, we sell a good number of these. I'm sure it's the ones we sell because of the pattern in the weave. It's a new pattern that we got in about six months ago. I remember because the older weave was not as soft and pliable as this one and we had some complaints."

"Can you tell us who in this area purchased handkerchiefs such as this one?"

"It would take some work. I would guess that it is terribly important?"

"Let me say that Sheriff Warner would appreciate it if you could get us the name or names as quickly as possible," Abby said. She smiled. "I would appreciate it as well."

"Of course, of course. Let me check my records. I can remember two gentlemen off hand, but I can have a complete list for you in an hour. Will that be quickly enough?"

"Splendid," Spur said.

Outside, they idled their way down to the telegraph office, but there were no messages for Spur. He had given up getting any responses from sheriffs either way along the tracks or trails. Now he knew the killer had been in Denver as late as the previous night. Would he run again, or would he try to hide in this larger town? Spur knew at once that any outlaw would have an easier time hiding in a larger town. The killer probably would stay in Denver.

They were back at the Johnson Haberdashery in 45 minutes, and Mr. Johnson presented Abby with a list of 12 names.

"I've put down the address of each, and the firms they own or run. Most of them are businessmen. There may be a few more names, but my bookkeeper has one of my set of charge books so I can't go over that one."

"This will be a fine start, thanks so much," Abby said, giving him one of her glorious smiles. She patted his hand and she and Spur went outside.

They studied the list in the bright sun as they stood there on the boardwalk.

"A banker, a big property owner, two hotel owners, as well as the mayor and two lawyers, and a bunch more," Spur said.

"So how do we handle it?"

"We talk to them gently, and ask if they were in town two and three weeks ago. If they were, they are eliminated as suspects, since our killer was a traveling man during those weeks."

They split the list and started making their calls. One of the men asked bluntly why Spur wanted to know if he was in town on those dates.

"Sir, there has been a crime committed and a handkerchief such as this connected with it. If you were in town those two weeks, and can prove it, you couldn't possibly be a suspect in the case."

"Oh, yes, I haven't had a vacation in two years. I'm here six days a week. Any of my employees and my wife can vouch for me."

Spur talked to two employees, and thanked the man and left.

Abby had a gentler time. She told them at the first that there was a problem involving a handkerchief such as they had purchased from the Johnson Haberdashery, and then inquired if they had been in Denver during the two important weeks.

They met at the same cafe where they had lunch, and now both sagged in defeat.

"Every man I talked to can prove he was in town," Abby said.

"Mine too. So that doesn't help us one hell of a lot, does it?"

"Not so it would count in a baseball game," Abby said.

"Johnson said he still might get us some more names."

"So we're at a dead end again," Abby said. "The woman herself and the man who saw the fall don't help any at all."

"We can always go back and talk to him again," Spur said.

Five minutes later they told Leon Hesacker why they were at the hardware store.

"Mr. Hesacker, what kind of a hat did the man wear? Try and remember, it's important."

"Hat . . . hat . . . yes, a gent's hat, not a derby, but not a cowboy's or a miner's. A town hat, black, low crown. About all I remember."

"His suit. What color was it?"

"Black, can say that for sure. White shirt and high starched collar. I didn't see a tie, but he must have had one."

"So it could have been a string tie."

"Might have been. Did notice that he wasn't a big man. Kind of thin as I recall, but mannered. A gentleman, I'd say."

"No look at his face?"

"Not that I remember. I couldn't pick him out in a crowd if that's what you're saying. Wish I could. Hate to think that the son of a . . ." He stopped. "Sorry, miss. Hate to think that the killer was right there and I saw him and we can't catch him."

"That might or might not have been the killer, Mr. Hesacker," Abby said smoothly. "We can't be sure."

"I'll think on it some more. You stop back."

They walked slowly toward the hotel. Some of the stores were closing up for the day.

Spur checked at the hotel in his box. There was a message. He read it and showed it to Abby.

"Mr. McCoy. I'm Terri Stanwood. We met at the barbecue at our ranch Saturday. I knew Helen Foley. Maybe I have something that might help. Could you come to our town house at 111 Third Street sometime today? I'll look forward to talking with you."

It was signed by Terri Stanwood.

"Sounds like a tough assignment," Abby said, one brow raised.

"Business," Spur said. "Maybe that Saturday barbecue wasn't a waste of time after all."

"Before or after supper?"

Spur sighed. "Decisions, decisions. After."

"Good. I could eat half a roasted grizzly bear."

Chapter Eleven

After supper that evening, Spur stopped by at his room in the High Country Hotel and shaved closely, slapped some rose water and bay rum on his face, and combed his reddish brown hair. It was still fuller around the sides and longer in back than most of the men wore it, but not anywhere near to his shoulders like the mountain men.

He put on a clean shirt and a fancy red vest and his brown jacket, and even polished his boots a little. Then he walked to 111 Third Street. The three-story house was the biggest anywhere around. It was well tended and cared for, had a rose garden along the front walk next to the street, and had a white wrought-iron fence all the way around the house.

Spur went through the gate, closed it, and moved up the concrete walkway to the front door. There wasn't much concrete in Denver. It was an unusual and expensive touch and out of the reach of most working people.

He twisted a bell on the door and heard it jangle inside. Almost at once the panel opened and Terri Stanwood grinned at him.

"Hi," Terri said, her round face with the high cheekbones beaming at him.

"Hi, yourself. Is this a good time for us to talk about Helen Foley?"

"It's a great time. Come in."

She had dressed carefully for the meeting. She was small and slender the way he remembered her, with soft black hair, brown eyes, and a cute little face. The dress she wore was cut low so the edges of her breasts showed, a formal party dress. It clung tightly to her body, showing the swell of her hips, and then hid her legs all the way to the floor. It was made of some shimmering fabric which changed colors slightly when she moved.

"I was afraid you might not come," she said.

"But you put on your dress-up dress just in case?"

She grinned. "Yes. If you came I wanted to impress you."

"You have."

She showed him into the parlor, which was down a short hall. He figured there must be 20 rooms in the little "town house" that the Stanwoods owned. It was furnished well in the solid traditions of the decade just past, tastefully yet not overdoing it. She sat on a short sofa and nodded at the place beside her.

He sat down, and found her stare steady and inquiring. He slid around it and got to the point.

"You said you knew Helen Foley and might be able to help catch the man who killed her."

Terri lifted her brows and her face almost broke. Then she controlled it. "Yes . . . yes, I knew Helen. I liked her. She was gentle and kind, soft-spoken and a good wife to her husband until he died about a year ago. Helen was teaching me to play that new game, bridge."

"You said she was a good wife to her husband. Do you know if she was ever unfaithful to him?"

"Good Lord, no! Helen was the perfect wife. She never even *thought* of fooling around with another man. She was totally dedicated to William. His death was a real shock to her."

"Since then?"

"She never went out much. We played bridge twice a week when I was in town. She always came here. One day she said she would do a year's mourning before she would even consider letting a man come courting her. She was an attractive woman, and already two or three men here in town were interested in her. But she held them off."

"Then you wouldn't call her a loose woman?"

Terri laughed, and Spur was surprised. He liked the sound of her laughter.

"Helen? I just told you, she was faithful in her marriage and in her mourning. The fact is, Helen was a bit of a prude. I don't think she even liked . . . you know, being in bed with her husband."

"If this embarrasses you, Terri, we can stop."

"No, I don't embarrass easily. It just seems strange that you're asking questions as if Helen were some kind of a loose woman. Why?"

"I shouldn't tell you this, but the man we think

killed Helen has killed nine women between here and Kansas City. He has killed prostitutes, waitresses, women he met in the street. In every case we believe the woman had loose morals. We think that may be the reason he's killing them."

"Then Helen Foley doesn't fit the pattern. I'm sorry. She just doesn't fit."

He told her what they knew about the man who helped pick her up and carried her packages home, and about the service of tea for two.

Terri pushed a little closer to him on the couch. "Spur McCoy, can I speak frankly?"

"Of course."

"I'm a woman. Helen was a woman. Now, in the same situation, it could have happened to me. I mean, Helen hasn't had a man in her bed for almost a year. In spite of what you hear, women sometimes yearn for a lover just the way men say they have to have a woman. It happens.

"Let's say this man was nice to her, extremely courteous, a real gentleman. He walks her home, and then to be courteous she invites him in for tea to repay his kindness. He is still a gentleman and handsome, and suddenly her emotions just explode and prim little Helen turns into a brazen woman who wants to be loved."

Spur frowned. "What would you say if I told you that we found Helen's chemise in the parlor under the couch?"

"That doesn't surprise me. The only logical conclusion has to be that either he or Helen took down her dress and took off her chemise. Was there a struggle?"

"None that we could determine."

"Then it's obvious to a woman. Helen had this urge to make love and enticed the man, and at last pulled down her dress and took off her chemise to let him know she wanted to make love right then."

Terri lifted her brows in surprise. "Oh, my dear sweet Helen. You picked the wrong man to ask to love you."

"So you think that Helen can fit the pattern?"

"Yes, not as a type of woman, but as a woman who at that moment wanted something more than tea." Terri touched Spur's arm. "I can well understand a woman like that, the sudden urges." She watched him carefully. "I get those special, undeniable urges sometimes myself."

Spur looked at her in surprise. "Well, I'm glad to get a woman's opinion about Helen. Evidently she did fit the pattern, if only for a few hours, but in that time it resulted in her brutal murder."

"Spur McCoy, could I speak frankly?"

"Of course, honesty in all things."

"Good. Spur McCoy, I greatly admire you. I am absolutely undone by your great handsome looks and your hard, muscular body. Am I being too forward?" She watched him closely, her face a thin mask that was ready to shatter from almost any reply.

Spur picked up her hand and held it in both of his. "Terri, you are a small, beautiful flower blooming here in the wilds of Denver, high in the mountains."

She smiled, her face glowed, and she leaned forward and kissed him gently on the lips.

"Then, Spur McCoy, why don't you pick me?"

He touched her face when her lips left his. His eyes were serious as he watched her inches away from her round face.

"Terri, some flowers should be left on the hillside to sweeten the air and brighten the scene. A flower lasts five times as long if it remains on its stem than when it is picked. Bluebells and snow daisies should remain in place."

She nodded, moving closer to him again. "But I'm not a bluebell. I'm a rose with thorns and I want to be picked and seen. I want to show you my petals and let you know my scent. But I'm warning you that I have thorns."

She kissed him again then, a demanding, serious kiss, and her arms went around him, and her body flowed against his, her breasts pushing firmly against his chest. In response his arms went around her and he felt her lips open on his. When the kiss ended she leaned back and watched him.

"See, Spur, a perfectly modest, proper lady can turn into a wanton, sexy woman after just one kiss." Her hands went around his neck and clasped together.

"Sweet Spur McCoy. That wasn't just a demonstration. I've been thinking about you ever since that quick kiss we had in the barn out at the ranch. My, that was nice, but this time it was better."

He looked around the room.

She giggled. "You don't have to worry. We have a cook and caretaker here and a gardener. The gardener is gone for the day and the cook-caretaker is finished with her work and in her room. She never comes out unless I pull a cord and call her. You're alone with me, Spur McCoy, and at my mercy."

"Might not be such a bad fate."

"Might not?"

"Prove it to me."

She kissed him again, a slow, building kiss that progressed to her open mouth and her tongue darting inside his the moment his lips parted.

Gently he eased back on the couch with her so he lay on his back and she on top of him. The kiss continued, and they were both panting for air when it finished.

"Oh, my, Mr. McCoy!"

"Oh, my, Miss Stanwood!"

"Maybe we should try that again." They did, and it worked out the same way. Now her face was flushed. Terri's breath came fast and her eyes glistened.

Spur pushed them up and they sat again. Slowly he reached his hand over to her chest and cupped one of her breasts. She let out a long sigh.

"Oh, yes, I hoped you were going to touch me there. I want you to, I need you to."

Spur had been surprised by the first kiss, then watched the girl a moment, and he could see her working herself up to an encounter. It seemed that she, much like the recently murdered Helen Foley, needed to have some incentive and then work at it to get into the mood for making love.

He kissed her the second time with some enthusiasm, and then was sure of the project. It could be interesting. His hand cupped her breast and caressed it through the soft cloth. It was larger than he had first thought. Women were always surprising him with exactly what they hid under their clothes and the size of various parts of their bodies.

He moved his hand up to the top of the dress, and

worked his fingers under the cloth and directly on her bare breast.

"Oh, my! Mr. McCoy, it does seem that you're becoming serious in this situation."

He kissed her and then smiled. "I'm as serious as you are, Terri. It might be better if we talked about it more in one of the bedrooms. What do you think?"

"What a delightful and different idea. Spur, you do have good thoughts, you know that?" She stood quickly, caught his hand, and led him up the stairs to the second floor, then to the third story. It was really only a half story, with slanted roofs for the ceiling. Each of the four small rooms had dormer windows, and each had a bed, dresser, and sofa. They probably were guest rooms.

She took him to the window and showed him the lights of the town which were now starting to come on in the streets and houses below. They could see half of Denver. She put her arm around him and drew tightly against him, then looked up.

"Denver is going to be a great city one of these days," she said. "Oh, not in our lifetime, but after that. I just wish I could see this town in a hundred years!"

"I'd be glad to see *anything in a hundred years,*" Spur said with a chuckle.

She laughed with him, and then they went over to the bed and sat down side by side, so close their thighs touched. She put her hand on his leg.

"I just don't see how a man can have all those big muscles," she said.

He put his hand on her breast. "We have them to protect the precious parts of a woman like these two." He bent and kissed her breasts through the dress, then the swelling tops of them that pushed out of the cloth.

"Oh, my, Mr. McCoy! That kind of carrying on could get a girl all upset, all undone. No way to know *what a girl might do* if you were to kiss me there again."

He bent and kissed her breasts, then pushed the fabric down and kissed them again. The cloth stretched, and she gave a soft little mewing sound. Then the dress popped loose somewhere and dropped down to reveal her breasts, large with thick soft pink areolas and red nipples that were pulsing with new blood.

"Well, now. It's my turn to say, 'Oh, my, Miss Stanwood.' Just magnificent! Sometimes I think a woman's breasts are her most beautiful feature. So sculptured, so poised and posed and perfect. Delightful. Does this bother you?"

"Sitting here half naked bother me? Not right now, not when I'm feeling this way."

"How do you feel?"

"All warm and pleased, happy, like I'm about to melt and wanting to melt faster. Like I'm going to go flying into the sky and wishing my wings would grow quicker. Like I'm going to sail on a glorious boat out into the mighty ocean and praying that the boat builders will hurry."

"You're a poet," he said. He bent toward her breast, and her hands caught his head and held it a moment. Then she pulled his mouth over one of her breasts.

At first he kissed the red areola so gently she must

not have been able to tell he had even touched it. Then again with more force, and she cried out, a surprised, joyous sound of pleasure and desire and anticipation.

"You really know how to make a girl feel all hot and gooey and like she was melting," Terri whispered. "Oh, damn, but I love it when you kiss my titties."

Spur concentrated on the beautiful breasts then, smothering them with kisses, licking them with his tongue until she shivered and lifted up and then cried out with a long wail of need. She pushed one hand down to his crotch and found the swelling there, and laughed softly and rubbed it through his pants.

"Good, good! I was hoping that you were going to be affected by all this. Oh, God, but that is fine!"

She wailed again, then pushed one of her breasts deep into his mouth until he could hold no more of her. He chewed on her white and pink flesh, working out until he nibbled on her nipple and she surged away from him, her eyes wild.

She lifted the dress off over her head and threw it on the floor, then stood there in silk bloomers that covered her but outlined exactly what was under them.

She stepped to him and knelt between his spread legs and kissed the bulge behind his fly, then opened the buttons and tugged and pulled until he yelped. He helped her, and thrust his manhood out of his fly.

"Oh, my, so marvelous. I don't see how you do it. All soft one minute, then hard as a pine tree the next. Beautiful. The most wonderful part of a man."

She bent and kissed the purpled head, then put his hands on her waist.

"I want to be naked with you, Spur McCoy," she whispered, her voice heavy with passion.

He stripped down the bloomers to find her crotch protected by a swatch of black hair. Below that angled out slender, well-shaped legs. She stood there beside the bed, her legs slightly apart, watching him.

"You next," she said. She took two steps toward him and stripped off his clothes, laying them carefully over a chair. She ran her hands down his firm, muscled chest.

"I love chest hair. It's so damn sexy. Makes me go wild."

A moment later they lay beside each other not touching, watching, waiting. Gently they reached out and kissed each other's lips, only lips touching.

"This is crazy," Terri said. "I've only met you twice. I don't know a thing about you except that you're in town working for the government. Here I am ready to make love with you."

"But this isn't your first time," Spur said.

"No, but I'm not a wild woman. I've made love with exactly three different men. No, one was a boy. He was sixteen and I was fourteen. But I know what I like."

She sat up. "McCoy, right now. Make love to me right now. I want to be on top. I've never been on top."

Spur nodded, moved to his back, and pulled his legs together. She grinned as she moved over him, straddled his legs, and then began to ease down with her hips toward him. Spur held his lance upward, and she adjusted and moved again and gave a little yelp as he entered her and drove upward as she slowly lowered herself onto him.

"Oh, God, but that feels wild!" Terri crooned. "So wonderful. Let's just stay this way."

He moved upward, then down, and she gasped.

"Wonderful! I've never felt it that way before. No pain, no pressure from above. It's marvelous!" She yelped again as he stroked, and slowly she began to counter his movements thrust for thrust.

She began to pant and to hump faster, but then the urgency passed for her and she frowned at him.

"Damn, I never can quite do it. I know something is supposed to happen, but it never quite does."

Spur moved his right hand, worked it between their bodies, and found her clit. He eased down from her for more room. Then he began to twang the small node.

"What are you doing?" she asked, looking at him, her voice sharp, demanding, yet curious.

"How does it feel?"

"Feel? feel? Oh, God, it feels . . . just . . . wonderful!" Then, before she could say anything else, she moaned and let it grow into a wail, and then her whole body shattered and she trembled and gasped for breath as one tremor after another slammed through her slender body. Her hips jerked and her shoulders rattled and she couldn't speak, just a moan of joy and delirium.

One time she almost stopped, but he twanged her clit again and she powered into another series of spasms that left her with tears spilling down her cheeks and gasping for air to feed her starved lungs.

She collapsed on top of him, and he pulled out his

hand. Through tear-swollen eyes she stared down at him. "My God, where did all of that come from?"

"You've never had an orgasm before?"

"Nothing like that. Oh, sure, I got excited, but it just faded away. This time it exploded. Nobody ever told me about that little button down there. You sure pushed it . . . damn! Oh, we forgot about you!"

She lifted up and slammed down on his lance, then again and again as Spur powered upward to meet her strokes. He had been close before, and now he soared over the top and splashed down miles and miles at sea as he erupted with a volcanic explosion that jetted his seed upward. He pounded her high eight times, then sank back down, his arms strapping her to him as they both collapsed and panted.

It was five minutes later before he could move. He let go of her, and she lifted away so she could see his face better.

"Now that's what love should be like," she said softly.

"Should be, but isn't always."

He pushed her away from him and they both sat up.

"I was hoping that you could stay here the rest of the night," she said.

"Be nice, but I've got too much to do. Work, work, work."

"I hope you find the monster who killed Helen Foley. He killed, so he should die."

"I'm trying."

They both dressed, and she walked with him to the front door.

"You think of anything else about Helen's friends,

you let me know. It could be someone from here who came back from a trip."

"I'll think about it." She paused. "You be sure and come and see me again before you ride out of town. Now that I've met you, I don't want to lose you so fast."

"Promise," Spur said, and walked out the door.

Chapter Twelve

Jose Ortega and his brother Marco, younger by one year, had worked the herd of 500 sheep slightly beyond the area where their father told them to be. The graze was good there, and they would stay there for only two or three days before they worked the flock back toward their more secluded area.

Jose was built like his father, short and sturdy with black hair and inquisitive brown eyes. He knew little but sheep, but he knew them so well his father had turned over most of the nursing and sick care to him. He was 16 this summer, and proud to be a sheepman.

He had no weapon. The only one the family could afford was his father's revolver, but he had learned to shoot it. Now he carried his favorite staff, a slender oak branch just over four feet long. It was dry and hard and little more than an inch in diameter at the small end, and barely an inch and a half at the large end. He had killed a roving mountain lion with it once when the big cat had caught a ewe and Jose had slipped up on the animal and clubbed it. He still had the skin as his trophy.

The sheep moved slowly, the two dogs they had with them obeying silent hand signals to keep the sheep bunched and to retrieve strays. The dogs knew sheepherding as well as the boys did.

Jose sat on a small rise watching the flock, and a new sound caught his attention. Living in the open, he had developed his sense of hearing and smell. He could follow wood smoke on a wind drift for miles and come right in on the fire.

Now something sounded unusual. It came from the left, toward the large valley and the cattlemen. Jose tensed. A moment later he saw the first horse and rider come across the ridge to his left.

The rider stopped, and Jose knew he could see the flock. There was nothing Jose could do. He whistled sharply, and his brother looked up and saw the riders. They both moved closer to the sheep. Jose signaled the dogs to bunch the flock, and he lifted his staff and moved toward them.

He had never confronted cattlemen before, but he knew it was not good. As he watched, three more riders came over the ridge. Now all four of them whooped and galloped toward the flock. They were less than a quarter of a mile away now. The rider in front held up his hand, and suddenly a shot snarled into the quiet clear mountain air.

Jose knew they were too far away to fear that the round might harm him or the sheep, but the fact that they had guns frightened him more than anything else. With a man, even one on a horse, he could hold his own in a contest. But in a fight against a revolver he knew he didn't stand a chance. They might each have a gun, four guns!

He hurried then and stood in front of the flock as the men rode up. He held his staff in both hands and walked toward the oncoming riders.

When they came close enough to hear he called out.

"Stop. The sheep are not used to horses."

"Ain't that one hell of a shame," the man in front snorted. "What you doing with them damn critters in here on Flying S Ranch land?"

"This is not a part of your ranch. We're twenty miles from your homestead."

"Kid has a smart mouth," the leader of the four said. "What's your name?"

"What's yours?" Jose shot back.

"Well, a real hardcase. I'm Dave Bordelon, ramrod of the Flying S, and don't you ever tell me where my ranch boundaries end or begin. Get your poisonous, filthy, wool bitches off our land. Do it now."

"You got no cause—"

A shot roared into the stillness and the bullet slammed into the ground a yard from Jose's bare feet. He jumped to the side. As they talked, the men had ridden closer, and now were only ten feet away. As soon as the shot sounded, Jose darted forward, swung the staff, and cracked it against Bordelon's right leg halfway to his knee.

Bordelon bellowed in rage, and spurred his mount forward into the sheep.

"Scatter them," Bordelon ordered. "Drive them out of here. Shoot the fucking sheep!"

Jose stood there, his mouth open in surprise, as the horsemen charged into the flock. They panicked at once, and turned and bleated and scurried out of the way of the tall horses, then scattered in every direction.

The cowboys laughed and fired their sixguns aiming at the sheep. Then two of the men chased Prince, one of the sheepdogs, firing at him until they hit him and Prince rolled and crawled under a low shrub for protection. The riders lost interest and chased more sheep, moving them south and east.

Jose bellowed in rage as he ran after the riders. Tears streamed down his face as he saw at least a dozen of his prized sheep bleating in pain or dead where they had been ridden down by the horses or shot.

He stopped and watched in anger and frustration as the cowboys drove the animals and continued to shoot at them. He had seen the dog hurt, and now ran toward where it had vanished. He found Prince a moment later, and coaxed him out of the briars. Prince had been shot in the shoulder.

Blood covered Prince's black and white fur. The dog looked up at him with sad, wondering eyes.

"You stay here, Prince. I'll be back. Stay." He gave the stay sign again and then ran back toward the sheep. Where was Marco? Before he saw Marco, he could tell that the flock had been scattered over a mile or two. It would take several days to gather them again, even with two good dogs, and now he had only one.

Jose knuckled tears out of his eyes and ran toward where he had last seen Marco.

He found him limping and waving his brown hat

trying to bring some of the sheep back into the flock. Jose ran up and caught Marco and helped him sit down.

"You hurt bad?" Jose asked.

Marco shook his head. "No. I wouldn't move and one of the horses knocked me down. Nothing broken."

The boys stood there staring at each other. They were about ten miles from the home fold and the cabin.

"What can we do now, Jose?"

The older brother stared at his scattered flock. The riders were laughing and shouting now and riding back the way they had come.

"First I tie up Prince's shoulder. The men shot him. Then I carry him back to the cabin and bring out another dog. You use Millie and start gathering the sheep into a flock again. I know it'll be hard. Do the best you can. I'll run as far as I can. It's still morning. I'll be back before dark with one of the other dogs. We better get started."

Jose ran back to the wounded dog. He ripped up his shirt to make a bandage. He couldn't tell if the bullet had come out or not, but Prince would die unless he got him some treatment and medicines back at the cabin. He stopped the bleeding, then picked up the dog and headed for the cabin.

It took Jose two hours to run and walk back to the home place. Alfonso Ortega listened to the story as he got ready. He took his revolver and put a box of shells in his pocket. Then he and Jose worked over Prince. The revolver bullet had gone through his upper shoulder and exited. It left a nasty wound, but in time, Prince would recover.

Alfonso and Jose both ate mutton and bread, then filled canteens. Alfonso saddled their one horse that could be ridden and lifted the tired Jose on board. They took two of their best sheepdogs and rode for the scattered flock.

It took them an hour and a half to cover the ten miles. The horse was winded and the dogs tired. Alfonso sat on a small rise and looked across two little valleys where he could see his sheep. He swore silently and then hurried ahead.

He only paused at the scattered flock. On the way Jose had told him everything that happened. Jose had described the leader of the group, the foreman Dave Bordelon, and the big chestnut stallion he rode. The animal had a diamond-shaped blaze on his forehead.

Marco was still limping, but when the dogs came he used two of them, and the trained dogs quickly began gathering the sheep. The animals, used to the dogs, soon quieted and moved back into a flock in the middle valley. Even with three dogs working, it would take until nightfall to get most of them, and another full day to find those that had strayed.

Marco reported that he had found 18 sheep dead and half a dozen more injured so badly they probably would die. Their father set his jaw and Jose watched him closely.

"What you going to do, Pa?"

"I'm going to take a ride over to the Flying S and have a talk with the man there, the kind of talk that he understands."

"Pa, you be careful. We can't live here without you."

Alfonso looked up, realizing that his oldest child

was growing up. He was a man already in many ways.

"I'll be careful, son. It depends how careful this man Bordelon is." He watched the flock a moment, and blinked away moisture at the number of dead sheep. Then he nodded at his boys, and rode away to the north and west, toward the Flying S Ranch.

He knew it was about 20 miles. That would give him time to make his plans. He was through being pushed around by cattlemen. They understood violence, so he would deal with them in the language that they knew. He would answer an attack with an attack. Slowly, as he rode along, he figured out what he would do.

There would be no chance that he could identify and confront this Bordelon. But he had one way to strike back at him personally.

It took him more than five hours to ride to a point where he could see the Flying S Ranch buildings. By that time it was fully dark. The Big Dipper told him that it was not yet nine o'clock. He tethered his tired horse in some brush near a creek, and lay down in the soft grass and rested for two hours.

It was just before midnight when he slipped up to the main corral and studied the animals in the soft light of a full moon. He didn't find what he wanted. He moved to a smaller corral near the barn. There were only 20 or so horses there. Quickly he found the big stallion, and saw that he was the chestnut color of deep red and with white stockings. Yes, that was the one.

Without a sound he slid through the bars of the corral and moved like a shadow around to the horses. He came up beside the big chestnut and patted his flank, then rubbed his neck. One last look showed Alfonso the white diamond blaze on the big chestnut's forehead.

Ortega acted swiftly, not allowing his sense of concern for every living animal to get in his way. His heavy knife lanced deeply across the big stallion's throat, cutting the vital arteries and bringing a gurgled scream from the animal. Ortega knew he had done the job right.

Quickly Ortega slid away from the foundering animal, and crawled through the bars and ran away from the pen into the blackness of night. He dropped to the ground and watched the buildings. He had heard no alarm. He had seen no roving guards or watchmen. The ranch was big and proud and secure. At least that was what the owner thought.

After a half hour, there was no reaction from the ranch. He moved forward to the big corral and undid the gate and swung it wide. Then he walked inside and silently drove 60 horses out the gate and headed them into the high valley. He did the same with the small corral of horses, and saw that the big chestnut was down and not moving.

With more than 80 horses free and wandering toward the range, he played his last card. The smaller of the two barns had a rear door. He entered, and found a stack of hay that was dry as tinder. He struck two matches and lit the hay in three places, then raced out the rear door and ran for his horse near the creek.

Once on the animal, he galloped toward where most of the horses were milling about 100 yards from the corral. He yahooed them, driving them in a group away from the ranch.

Now, behind him, he heard shouts, and could see the fire leaping up the outside the barn. They didn't have a chance to stop the fire. He drove the horses faster now, galloping them for as long as he could. Then he settled them down to a steady walk as he drove them farther from the ranch buildings.

After five miles, half of the herd had drifted away, but he kept pushing those he had, grouping them and driving them forward to the south and west.

Behind him, the fire had burned out to a soft glow on the horizon, and he kept driving the horses.

Nearly an hour later all but two of the mounts were gone, and he left them and turned more south and rode for his sheep ranch. Never again would Alfonso Ortega sit quietly and let a cattleman push him around! He had told them that plainly and with emphasis tonight. Now he would see what they would do next.

What he hoped was that, as with most bullies, they would back off when they were confronted. Only time would give him the answer. In the meantime he had a herd to save, and carcasses to bury after salvaging what he could of the mutton. Perhaps they could dry some of it in the warm summer sun.

Alfonso Ortega knew a fight had been begun today by the rancher, and had been continued tonight, and it could not end until one or the other of them was destroyed. He was going to do everything in his power to protect his family and his ranch.

* * *

Back at the Flying S Ranch, Dave Bordelon sat beside the big chestnut and let the tears stream down his face. When he saw that some of the horses were gone, he checked the last corral and found his mount. He had caught the big stallion on the range, and had broken him to saddle, but had never broken his spirit. The horse had been with him for seven years on three different spreads. Bordelon loved that animal more than he ever had a human being.

Who in hell would do something like this? Then he remembered the defiant fury of the little sheep-herder. No, he was only a boy. He wouldn't have the courage to do this. Then who? He shook his head in despair.

Thurlow Stanwood stood in his pants and slippers watching the roof of his smaller barn fall inward in a shower of sparks and flying embers.

"Who could have done this?" he screamed at the men around him. "Somebody hated me, hated the ranch to do something like this to me." He watched one of the barn's walls fall outward, and a dozen men scurried out of the way. "Someone said the raiders killed one horse. Which horse was it?"

Nobody knew. Stanwood walked to the corral and found his ramrod sitting by the dead animal.

"Bordelon. That your stallion?"

"Yes, sir."

"Why?"

"I don't know."

"You mentioned something about running some sheep off the far south pasture yesterday?"

"Yes, but the shepherds were just a couple of kids. Fifteen, sixteen. They couldn't do something like this."

"Kids have parents, Bordelon. You hurt either boy?"

"Not sure. Willy said one of them got knocked down when he got too close to his horse."

"Stupid bastards!" Stanwood exploded. "Did I tell you to stampede any flock of sheep? Did I tell you to try to run them away no matter where they were?"

"No, sir. But just common sense . . . I thought. . . ."

"Trouble with you, Bordelon, is you don't think. You should learn to play chess. Every move you make is followed by a move of the other side. You have to think four or five moves ahead to see if the move you want to make is really to your advantage. If you'd thought this one through you wouldn't have charged into those boys or their sheep."

"You mean some dirty sheepherder came in here and did all of this? One man?"

"Could have. Killed your stallion, opened the gates, drove out the horses, set the barn on fire, then drove the mounts out into the prairie. Well, damnit, Bordelon. Get off your ass, cowboy. Send every man we have walking out onto the prairie and the valley, and find as many of the mounts as you can. Bring them back here and saddle them, and in the morning get out there and round up the rest of our riding stock.

"This is all your fault, Bordelon. Every mount you don't bring back is coming out of your pay. So you better hope that you do a damn good job. Now, get on your feet and get moving, or pack your blanket roll and walk out of here. You don't even own a horse anymore."

Chapter Thirteen

Christopher Perry met Leslie Stanwood in the family's town house. Leslie was the only family member there that day. The two stared at each other for a moment, not in hatred, but with some emotion close to it.

"I see you've come sniveling around again, Perry," the much younger Stanwood said.

"You always did have a bad mouth on you, boy. Let's just do our business and I'll be on my way."

Leslie Stanwood scowled. He balled his fists, but he would be no match for the taller and heavier Perry even though he was 30 years younger.

"You know that I may kill you someday for doing this to me," Leslie said.

"I'm not doing anything to you, Leslie. You did it to yourself a couple of years ago. I just happened to be there and saw it. I didn't plan it, but I'm not about to forget it either. The case is still open. The sheriff would like nothing better than to convict someone of the crime."

"So I made one little mistake."

"That was not a little mistake, Leslie. That was a gigantic blunder, a criminal act, and only my family loyalty and my concern for the company keeps me from telling the sheriff."

"That and fifty dollars a week, you hypocrite!"

"Now, now, Leslie. If you want to start a name-calling contest I have some choice ones I can use with you. You really don't want to do that. Just give me the money and I'll leave you alone. I don't even want to know what you do in town so much."

"You better not." Leslie handed him five ten-dollar greenbacks, and the manager of the logging and lumbering division of Flying S Enterprises smiled. He folded the bills and pushed them in his pocket.

"Now, that's a good lad, Leslie. It's always a pleasure doing business with you. I'm off to the mill." He stared at the younger man. "Leslie, you try and stay out of trouble now, you hear me?"

Perry smiled as he walked out to his buggy and stepped on board. He had made the deposit at the bank of the company money, and signed some papers that needed to be taken care of. Then he'd arranged for a new logging lease on some government land high over their mill. It was a good day.

All the way back to the mill, a little over 20 miles slightly north and west, Perry worked on his plan. It had to be simple, it had to be swift and sure once he began. There was absolutely no room for error. If anything went wrong, he would be the one in jail or dropping through a hangman's trapdoor.

That was what he was the best at, planning. He had learned his lesson early, and for the past ten years had been working for pay, not for profit, because of it. Now was the time. Rather than a big revelation of the fraud that began it all, he decided to let the fraud stand. He would simply eliminate Thurlow Stanwood, and produce partnership papers of several years before with a clause giving the survivor total ownership of Flying S Enterprises.

His plan would work. The family would fight it, but he would win. Then he would have what he had worked toward for ten years.

Christopher Perry thought about how it all began as he drove the light rig toward the lumber mill in the near edge of the mountains.

He had met Thurlow Stanwood in Kansas City and they rode west together. Both had just left the Union fighting forces and the war, and were out to make their fortune. Stanwood had hinted at a grand plan he had, and had even changed his name to bring it off.

In Denver they put the plan into effect. Stanwood proved to be a good actor, and with a full beard and a domineering manner, he soon convinced the lawyers of his survivor's rights to the well-established Harland Cattle Company ranch situated to the west of town.

Nobody in Denver had ever seen Josiah Harland, only brother of Colonel Rufus Harland, late commander of the New York Twenty-fourth Regiment, the man who'd fallen in battle shortly after the Chantilly Country House fight.

Stanwood told Perry that he had sat with Colonel Harland in his last few hours, and the colonel had told him everything about his ranch outside of Denver and about his one brother, a wastrel who had died in the bawdy houses of New York City two years before. Stanwood had seen a glimmer of an idea, and pumped the colonel for all the family information he could get.

Colonel Harland had never married, had no other kin, and his mother and father were both dead. It was a perfect setup for a takeover, and Stanwood needed a second man to swear about his heritage.

It only took a week in Denver to complete the legal technicalities. Even as the land was being transferred, Stanwood, pretending to be the brother of the dead man, told them that he hated the West and would be selling the ranch as soon as he could find a legitimate buyer. He affected flashy clothes, a top hat and cane, and made himself out to be a fussy Easterner.

Then he returned to their hotel and waited a week. During that time, Josiah Harland ceased to exist. Stanwood shaved his full beard, bought all new clothes, range clothes, contrasting sharply with the Fancy Dan style of dress of Josiah Harland. He cut his hair differently, parted it on the other side, affected a drawl, and showed up at the county clerk's office with a bill of sale signed by Josiah Harland and Thurlow Stanwood. The ranch and all its lands and cattle and buildings now belonged to Thurlow Stanwood and his partner, Christopher Perry.

Perry had changed his appearance and name as well, and the two rode out to the ranch to see what they had stolen. It was a working ranch even then, but with little direction or control, since the owner had been gone for three years.

Stanwood and Perry charged into the breach and soon had the place operating well, and profitably. After the second year of cattle sales in the growing town of Denver, they expanded the ranch and put up a new bunkhouse and barn.

That same year a new gambling hall opened in Denver. It was staffed by attractive young women, and one in particular caught the favor of Perry. He always gambled at her table. He took her home one night and made love to her, and the next day at her table he lost over $1,000.

He took the cash he owed the gaming table from the company bank account, and went back to the ranch for two weeks. Perry knew he would return to the gambling hall. This time he and the cute little dealer made love again, and the next day he lost another $800. Again he made it up from the bank account.

For more than two weeks, Perry spent every minute he could at the gaming table run by the raven-haired little beauty with the talented, slender body.

By this time Thurlow Stanwood had heard stories about Perry and his pretty gambling lady. But when he finally tracked Perry down, a great deal more money had been withdrawn from the bank. An audit of his account showed that the gambling losses had increased to just over $12,000. The bank account was overdrawn, and Stanwood reluctantly made up the difference so his partner wouldn't land in jail.

That night at the ranch, Stanwood took Perry out behind the barn and they fought. They were about the same age, both strong and angry.

Stanwood knocked out two of Perry's teeth, broke his nose, closed both of his eyes, and then broke his arm. When Perry couldn't get out of the dirt, Stanwood told him that their partnership was finished. He had a lawyer draw up a paper, and Perry had to sign it or go to jail for theft and fraud. The paper said that Perry would sell his half of the Flying S Ranch to Stanwood for $12,000, the sum of which had already been paid to cover his gambling debts.

Stanwood knew he was in a precarious position. Perry was the one man who could ruin him by exposing the fraud by which they got control of the ranch. So he offered to let Perry stay on as an employee. He would have the job to start up and manage a new lumber mill Stanwood was bringing in to saw the timber off the mountains.

Perry sighed now, remembering. It might have been better right then to go to the sheriff and tell him everything, then run before they could charge him. That way Stanwood would be brought down.

But now he knew he had done the right thing. He'd made the sawmill into a success, and Flying S Enterprises was now worth well over $1,000,000! Half of it should have been his. But that didn't happen, so now *all of it would be his!*

Just the last few details. It would have to be an accident. They happened all too often in the woods. He would need one man as a witness. He had the man picked out, one with five children and a desperate need for his job. The man would do and say as he was told to do. No problem there.

Now for the timing. He had the legal papers all drawn up. He had been to Cheyenne last month to talk about railroad spur lines, and while there he had hired a lawyer to draw up the new agreement. For another $20 the man had dated the document four years previous to the real date. Perry had let the contract lay in the sun part of one day to brown and age it, and crumpled it about so it looked like an older document.

Yes, most of it was ready. Just the accident itself. He hadn't chosen the right one. It couldn't be anything too spectacular. Most men in the woods were hurt by falling or rolling logs. A rolling one might be just the ticket. Perry concentrated on how it would work as he continued up the long valley that ended in a draw, and then to the mill itself on the banks of the small river.

Damn! Soon all of this, all of Flying S. Enterprises, would be his! He had worked hard enough for it. He had earned it. All of this would make his $50 weekly "contribution" from Leslie Stanwood look like small pocket change.

Christopher Perry rode into the mill, gave his buggy to a workman to put away, and ran up the steps to his house.

He grinned when he saw who was waiting for him. She ran to him and kissed him passionately, one hand caressing his crotch. She pulled away, her arms still around him.

Lotti, the daughter of one of the mill workers. She was 18, and loved nothing better than a long romp in his bed when her mother was gone to town for a few days.

"You didn't tell me you'd be gone so long. I just can't wait to get your clothes off and take just real good care of you."

The room was dark now. He had pulled the blinds and made sure that no trace of light seeped past them. Then he lay down on the bed on his back, his hands under his head, and he remembered. There was no way to stop the remembering. When he did, often the bad dreams didn't come and he didn't have to hurt anyone.

He pulled the long thin blade of his Chicago ice pick from his boot, and felt of the razor-sharp edge and the stiletto point. Deadly. That was what he wanted, something deadly to hold.

His mother had not been deadly. She had been so slow and easy and subtle. It took him a lot of years before he realized what she was doing. She bathed him long after most boys took a bath by themselves, but he didn't know that.

It seemed that she had been washing him since he was a baby. That summer when he was 12 he wondered why she still was there, but he really knew. He just didn't understand it.

She watched him as he washed in the round tub. Then she had him stand on his knees in the soapy water and she washed his crotch and his privates.

"We have to be sure that you stay real clean down here," she said. "Boys can get diseases and hurt themselves if we don't watch out."

She washed him again down there just to be sure, and then helped him out of the tub and dried him.

He usually enjoyed that, but this time she concentrated on his crotch to get him dry.

"If you're damp down here it can bring on a rash, and we don't want that, do we?" She dropped the towel then and asked him the usual question.

"Do you want to see my two girls?"

He nodded the way he always did, and she opened her blouse and her big breasts came out, so round and pink and with red circles around them, and on the very end, brown nipples like the old female dog had. He knew they were tits.

"Play with them, Darling Boy. You won't break them. Mommie likes you to feel them and rub them, remember?"

He did, but he didn't like it. Somehow it seemed wrong, but there were no other boys his age to ask. Way out in the country on the ranch, he had no playmates besides his little sister, and she was only a girl.

He really didn't understand what his mother had been doing all these years, even when he was 12. But then when he was 13, she tried to give him a bath again, and he shook his head and told her he was a big boy and he could take his bath all by himself. She left reluctantly. Now he knew what she was doing and it was bad. Mothers shouldn't do that. One Sunday after church, his best friend there talked with him and they told each other things. He found out his friend's mother never touched him and didn't help with his bath.

His body felt different now too. One day he was climbing the apple tree and he felt all funny and his pecker got hard, and suddenly something shot out of it right in his pants. It had been the wildest, best feeling he ever had, but it frightened him a little too. His friend at church nodded when they talked about it. He said the same thing had happened to him about a year ago.

"You just shot your load," the other boy said. He was 14. "That's how men make babies, you dummy. The man shoots his load into the woman and she has a baby."

For a month he didn't let his mother touch him. Then she came into his room one night when he was sleeping and lay down beside him. When he woke up her hands were on him and his penis was big and hard like that day in the tree.

He pushed her away.

"I just want to talk to you," his mother said.

"No. Don't touch me there."

She opened her nightgown and put his hands on her breasts. "You can touch me here. The way you used to do, to make me feel good. Remember that, Darling Boy? You touch me and I'll give you twenty cents the way I used to. Two bright shiny dimes."

He left his hands on her warm and soft breasts for a moment. Then she pushed his hands down between her legs. "You can touch me here too, Darling Boy." She pressed his hands into her crotch, and he felt around. A few seconds later she gasped and shook and vibrated and moaned as she fell on the bed shaking and shivering.

He jumped away from her and ran into the hall. He went back when she quieted. His mother smiled at him and kissed him. She saw that he was still hard.

"Let me fix that hard old thing for you," she said, smiling. "I can make the swelling go down." He didn't move. He couldn't move. She was his mother. Her hands went down to him where he stood and stroked him three times, and he yelled in surprise and his hips pounded forward and it felt wonderful, just the way it had in the apple tree the time before.

After that they played "games," as his mother called them, two times a week. Each time he got 20 cents because he "won" the game.

"You must promise that this is our little secret," his mother told him. "Don't ever tell anybody. They might not understand."

So he didn't. Then he grew to be 14 and then 15, and his mother found more interesting ways to "take care" of his erections. Each time he got the two bright dimes, sometimes a half-dozen dimes, but he always thought of them as 20 cents. He knew it wasn't right, but what could he do?

When he was 16 and taller than his mother, he pushed her away one night and told her never to come to his room at night again.

She laughed at him. "If you don't want to help your very own mother, I know where I can get some help, some release. Lord knows your father is too busy to bother with a mere wife anymore."

That was when she started going out during the day, and sometimes at night. He heard talk in the town about her. Not a lot, but enough. His mother had turned into a slut and he hated her.

Then one day he planned how he would kill her. She was too evil to live. She had made him into a freak. He didn't know how to talk to girls his own age. They laughed at him and he ran to get away from them. He still wanted to kill his mother, but he didn't know how to kill anyone.

One day, watching the men butchering two pigs and a steer, he figured out how he could do it.

Before he had the chance, his mother left home and never came back. Their father told them she was on a trip to see her sick mother, but he and his sister knew better. She was gone, and people all over town were calling her a slut and a whore.

That very day was when he made a vow that he would find this woman who had abused him, and she would pay for what she had done. He would make her suffer. Then he would kill her. He could do it with a knife. He'd watched more butcherings since the first, and it seemed easy for a knife to cut the throat or stab into the heart. Either way. But first he had to find her.

For five years he thought of little else. But he still hadn't found his mother. He was grown now, 21, and slender but with a stern resolve about his purpose in life. He had to find his mother and kill her.

He took trips looking for her. One to California on the train. One to Kansas City. Everywhere he went he looked for his mother. The headaches came on his first trip, and it was so bad he cried. No one saw him. That was when the woman came to him in his hotel room and offered herself for only a dollar. He had been mesmerized. He couldn't say no to a woman.

She went into his hotel room and took off all of her clothes, and then removed his, and showed him some things his mother hadn't told him about the female of the species.

They made love three times, and she charged him three dollars. Then he killed her. It had been easy. A quick slash across the throat, and then jump back out of the way of the blood.

He left the room and signed in at another hotel. Women were always getting killed in Sacramento. The next day he took the train back toward Denver, and the pounding, pounding headache he had experienced for a month was gone!

Twice on the way back he stopped and waited in hotel rooms, but no woman came. On the second night he went to a saloon and found a woman who would come to his room. She said it wasn't usually allowed, so he left first and she went out the back door pleading illness to her madam.

As soon as that one undressed, he killed her. It was a quick, deft thrust with the sharp knife. That was the first time he put the dimes on the woman's eyes after she was dead. His mother always gave him dimes after they played their games. She said it was because he always won the games. This was another way he could pay back the "dirty" money he had accepted.

When the new 20-cent pieces came out, he began using them on the eyes to be sure the lids stayed shut. He didn't like dead eyes staring at him.

At least tonight he didn't have the headache. He stripped off his clothes and lay back on the bed. "Thank you, thank you that tonight I have no headache," he said softly. Then he slept.

Chapter Fourteen

Spur McCoy looked at the list of names that the haberdasher had sent to his hotel room in a sealed envelope. They were the additional names he had promised to deliver of men who had bought the particular handkerchiefs at his store. There were four names, including that of Thurlow Stanwood.

Spur showed the list to Abby Leggett, who scowled. "Stanwood? Isn't he the guy you went to see, the big rancher with the sexy daughter?"

"The same. He's a real power in this town. It'll be easy to check on him for the past two or three weeks. I'll take him and the next one, Triscout, and you work on Ambrose and Kinney."

The merchant had written down who each man was and his residence or occupation and store or business.

"We're skimming the cream off the crop here in Denver," Abby said. "Look at who these people are. One is a big rancher, the next one is the local district judge, the next one a store owner, and the last one a banker."

"We deal only with the finest people."

"The girl, Terri Stanwood. Did she tell you anything new about the latest murder victim?"

"Only that Helen was prim and precise. If she strayed from her year of mourning, it must have been a sudden attack of passion, which Terri said the poor woman might be about due for. Terri felt that knowing Helen as she did, Helen must have enticed our killer in the living room, and by so doing, she fit into his pattern for retribution."

"Let me make a note of that for future reference," Abby said. She twirled her long red hair around so it swept off the back of the chair and let it float down to her back. "Looks like it's time I get busy on my two suspects here. Neither of mine look promising, but we need to check them out."

Spur nodded, and they parted ways at the front of the small cafe where they had been having their morning coffee. Spur checked one of the banks where he had talked to them about the 20-cent pieces. Another man was at the desk, and was friendly. He mentioned the small favor Spur had done Mr. Stanwood saving his money.

"I just happened to be there," Spur said. "Stanwood is the man I need some information about. Not banking information. I'm trying to establish for a fact that Thurlow Stanwood was in town or at his ranch sometime during the previous four weeks. Did he do any banking during those times?"

The banker nodded. "I'm Stacey Jones, and first vice president here. I helped Mr. Stanwood to straighten out one account of his and to open a new savings account about three weeks ago. I can give you the exact date in just a moment. Then a week after that he was back in town to make a deposit of a bank draft he'd received from the cattle buyer in Cheyenne. So I can say for certain that he was in town on those two dates."

Spur stood and smiled. "That's good enough for me. Now, this next man I need to talk about is a banker, but he's supposed to be with the Cattleman and Pioneer Bank. Just where is that?"

"Our main competition. The C and P is down a block and on the other side of the street. Can you tell me what this is all about?"

"No, I'm afraid I can't. I thank you for your help."

Five minutes later Spur sat across from Edwin Triscout, president of the Cattleman and Pioneer Bank.

"Mr. Triscout, I'm working with the United States Government Secret Service and we have a small problem we're trying to track down. I wonder if you could help me."

Spur took out the card on which had been printed his Secret Service identification with a small tintype photo affixed. The card was signed by President Ulysses S. Grant.

"Well, my. I've never seen that signature before on a real document. Of course, I'll be glad to help in anyway that I can."

"Good." Spur took the handkerchief from his jacket pocket and laid it on the counter. "Have you ever seen this before, Mr. Triscout?"

"I'm not sure. Let me check." He reached in his back pocket and took out a handkerchief that was an exact match. "Unless you took that one out of my dresser at home, I've never seen it. But it is the same kind that I buy here in town. I buy them by the dozen you see."

"A handkerchief like this one is an important bit of evidence, and I'm trying to eliminate all of the potential suspects that I can. Were you here in town during the preceding four weeks?"

"Four weeks? No, I made a trip to Cheyenne on business. We have some bank property there which I sold. I also did some work to set up a branch bank in that area. Not a branch exactly but a cooperating bank."

"What were the dates you were out of town?"

"I was gone the entire week, from two weeks ago to one week ago. Since then I've been here in town. I do have some dated documents with my signature on them that should prove the time I was in Cheyenne. Then again, my employees and the vice president here can affirm that I was here the two weeks before that time."

Spur stood. As soon as he'd seen the man, he'd known he was not the killer. He was all banker, small wiry, intense, but with his emotions and everything he thought plain to read on his face and in his body posture and his gestures.

"I think what you've told me will be enough, Mr. Triscout. Thanks for your help."

Abby had no more success with her pair of suspects. William K. Ambrose had not come to work the day after the killing there in town. She went to his home, which was also on the list.

Ambrose was a district judge. His wife answered the door. She frowned at Abby until Abby told her who she was and why she was calling.

"Come in and talk to him," Mrs. Ambrose said. "I made him stay home for three days because of his nasty head cold. He's feeling better and wants to get back to the bench."

The judge sat in a soft chair with his feet up, a towel around his head and face, and a teakettle spouting steam under the towel. He came up for air a moment later and stared in surprise at Abby.

"Goodness!"

His wife explained quickly why Abby was there, and the judge pulled his robe around him closer to cover his long white nightshirt.

"Your Honor, have you been out of town recently?" Abby asked.

Judge Ambrose laughed, which brought on a spate of coughing. When he finished he wiped his eyes, blew his nose, and shook his head.

"Haven't had a day off for six months. This district is overloaded with cases. I keep telling them at the capital but they just ignore me. I haven't ventured out of Denver for almost a year now. Just too busy."

Abby thanked them both and left.

When she called at Kinney Fine Shoes, she was faced with a different problem. The store manager had just fitted a cowboy with a new pair of riding boots. He came over to where Abby was examining a pair of women's high-top button shoes in soft leather.

"May I help you, miss?"

She told him why she was there.

"Oh, my, I'm afraid you can't talk to Mr. Kinney.

He's been out of town now for three weeks and won't be back for another week. He went to Chicago on the train to buy a whole new shipment of shoes for our store. Denver is growing up, so we have to keep up with the latest fashion trends. Say what you will about our cowboy boots, but the fact is, we sell more ladies' fine shoes than any other kind."

"When will Mr. Kinney be back?"

"He's scheduled to be coming to the store in another week. He and his wife went. They go every year to talk to others in the trade, to see the displays of the manufacturers, and to have a small holiday at the same time."

Abby thanked him and went to the hotel. She knocked on Spur's door and he opened it.

They quickly exchanged information and sat on the bed staring at each other.

"Our only clue and it's worthless," Abby wailed.

"Maybe not worthless, but it sure isn't helping us find the killer right now. There must be some reason that handkerchief was in the room. Sooner or later it will fit into the pattern.

"It better be sooner. Our madman killer could take off on the train anytime. There are just too many people here for our description to do any good. We need a stroke of genius or of good luck to get this case moving again."

"Either that or our killer has to hit again and leave us a nice, wide, bloody trail right to his doorstep."

"Yes, and let's hope that the next murder isn't in Cheyenne or Durango or Omaha."

Seven cowboys moved across the Flying S range riding steadily to the east toward Denver. Thurlow

Stanwood led the group, followed closely by his son, Leslie, and his foreman, Dave Bordelon.

"Pa, I told you I didn't want to come on this chase," Leslie said.

His father turned in the saddle and stared hard at his only son. "I told you that it was about time I made a man out of you. Enough of this sniveling and sashaying around. I want you on the range every day now, doing what has to be done. This is one of the goddamned things that has to be done now and then. So pay attention. It'll be your call one of these years."

A rider 100 yards ahead of them got off his mount to study a rocky place. He mounted quickly and angled more to the northeast.

The trail they followed was that of a herd of about 30 cattle, a range mix—some cows, some calves, and a few steers. The rustlers had grabbed whatever they could find late last night and moved them out. The trail had been found at daylight, and now three hours later, the small war party of cattlemen from the Flying S Ranch was gaining on them.

The tracker circled back when the trail was easy to read again. He rode up to his owner.

"Droppings look a lot fresher. The herd is slowing. Can't be more than four or five miles ahead. Not a chance they can keep control of even thirty head at more than a walk, which means about two or three miles an hour. We should be able to make six with no trouble."

"So how soon can we catch them?" the elder Stanwood asked.

"If it all goes according to my figures, we should catch them in less than an hour and a half."

Leslie rode up beside his father and heard the prediction. When the tracker headed back in front of the riders, Leslie watched the grim expression on his parent's face.

"So, Pa, after you catch the rustlers and get our cattle back, what you gonna do, hang them all?"

Thurlow Stanwood turned angry eyes on his only son. He was thinking what his son could have been, how he could be leading this party right now.

"Yes, Leslie. That's exactly what I'm going to do, hang every damned one of them."

About two miles ahead on a small rise, they spotted a dust trail in the distance. It wasn't a big enough herd to raise much dust on the dry mountain valley, but enough.

"Two miles out," one of the riders said. The men loosened the rifles in their boots and checked sixguns as they rode. The pace picked up a little faster now that the culprits were within sight.

They lost the rustlers over another small rise ahead, and when they spotted them again, the cattle were less than a half mile away. Stanwood called the riders to a halt and eyed the land. He put one man on each side.

"Ride hard and get around to the other side of them. I don't want them to see us coming and spook out and the damn rustlers get away." He pointed out where the outriders could pass the small herd behind some creeks that had a line of brush and trees along them.

They rested their horses and gave the outriders a 15-minute start. Then they mounted and charged down the slope toward the slow-moving herd.

One of the drag rustlers on the herd must have seen them coming. A rifle shot jolted the stillness and a hot lead bullet whistled over the heads of the charging Flying S riders. Two of the men pumped out shots in reply at the blue puff of smoke they could spot ahead.

The rustlers must have realized they couldn't keep the animals and get away. Two of them headed due north and two split off and galloped south. The outrider to the north stopped the riders that way with four rifle shots and then turned and rode hard to the east.

"Pick a man and stay with him!" Stanwood shouted. "Shoot the bastard out of the saddle if you have to, but don't let a one of the five of them get away!"

The riders broke into a gallop then, each man heading for the closest rustler he could find. A rustler riding drag had to swing around the herd, and that cost him some time. He was the first one down, taking a rifle shot in the leg and slamming out of his saddle and screeching as he hit the dirt. One Flying S man held him at gunpoint as the chase continued.

Thurlow Stanwood nailed the next one. His rifle round went a little to the side of the target and killed the horse, putting the rider on foot. He quickly raised his hands and stopped running.

Ten minutes later the chase was over.

Two men were designated to round up the 30 head of cattle and start them on the drive back toward the home place.

The rest of them drank from a small creek and

stared at the five rustlers, who were sitting on the ground with their hands clasped on the top of their heads.

"Who the hell is the leader of this damn rustling crew?" the older Stanwood bellowed. Nobody said a word. He repeated the question, kicking the man with the shot-up leg. The man wailed in pain but said nothing.

Stanwood walked around the men, and recognized one who he had seen in town from time to time, but he couldn't remember the man's name. The rest were strangers.

Stanwood looked at the trees and brush along the stream. There were three sturdy oaks within 30 feet of each other.

"Move the bastards over under those three oak trees," Stanwood said. "We might as well get this over with. You rustlers, you know this is the Territory of Colorado, and in this territory rustling cattle is a felony, a capital offense. That means you get hung.

"I and this assembled group of citizens, functioning as a posse and a jury, have witnessed your criminal act, and as judge, I hereby find you guilty of rustling and I sentence you all five to be hung by the neck until dead."

"Pa, that ain't right!" Leslie shouted. "They don't have a lawyer, nobody spoke in their defense. Ain't right."

"Hearing no legal objections, I order the sentence to be carried out at once. Five of you men put your lariats over those oak limbs. Leave enough room for their horses, since we don't have a proper gallows."

Five cowboys rode to the oaks, mashed down

some mountain mahogany brush and some juniper, and threw their ropes over sturdy oak limbs. They tied hangman's knots, but the slender lariat rope didn't make a big enough knot to do a proper neck-break.

"Bring up their horses," Stanwood shouted. The horses were brought up, and one of the cowboys added his own horse to replace the nag that had been killed.

Stanwood took the lariat knot around and showed it to each of the men. Their hands had been tied behind them and their ankles tied together with rawhide.

"This knot won't break your necks, men, but the cinch will cut off your windpipe so you'll strangle to death in two or three minutes. Give you some more time to think about your misspent lives. Anyone want to say who you're working for? Might let you off easier."

"Working for ourselves," one of the men said. "Figured you had enough cattle out here so you wouldn't miss thirty head."

"You figured wrong, dead man," Stanwood said.

Leslie Stanwood came up, and was about to say something to his father when the older man backhanded him hard across the mouth.

"Son, don't you ever contradict me again in front of the men, you hear me? Damn, I thought this would help make a man out of you. You might get your chance yet."

When the ropes were hung, they mounted the rustlers backwards on the five horses, sitting just behind the saddle facing the rump. The nooses were fitted over the men's heads, and then Stanwood himself tied off the long end around the trunks of the oaks and secured all five of them.

He came back from tying the last one and looked at the five rustlers. "A damn sorry collection of the human species," he roared. "Wasted your lives. Probably got wives and kids somewhere. Now what happens to them? Damn shame, but nobody, that is nobody, rustles cattle from the Flying S Ranch. When they find your five bodies hanging here, the rest of the rustlers will get the word damn fast."

He told the five men who had used their ropes to get sticks two feet long. They came out of the brush, and each man stood beside the back of a horse holding a rustler.

Stanwood looked at the five rustlers. "You all five ready to die? You got any last words?"

"You're a bastard, Stanwood," one of them said.

Stanwood snorted. "Probably the last words you'll ever say."

Some of the cowboys were shuffling their feet. Some of them knew how close they had come to a similar fate years back. Stanwood grabbed his son by the shoulder, pushed him forward to the last horse, and took the stick from the cowboy.

"Now, Leslie, when I give the word, I want you to pound the ass end of that horse with this stick. You hear me, boy? You do that and the gent up there hangs. You do this and maybe someday you'll be able to hold your head up like a man."

Leslie took the stick, then dropped it. His father slapped him again and pointed to the stick. Slowly Leslie bent and picked it up and poised it over the horse's rump.

Stanwood walked back a few steps. "Ready, everyone. Allright, do it . . . *now!*"

Four of the men whacked their horses. Leslie tried to but couldn't do it. When the horse beside Leslie's jolted forward, the one Leslie was supposed to hit surged out with the others.

The five men slid off the horses' rumps and hung there for a moment. Then four of them slipped to the ground as the tied-off ropes around the trees snaked up and over the limb, dumping the four rustlers in the dirt. One of them had lost control and wet his pants. A second one voided his bowels.

The fifth one gagged and his eyes rolled as the slender rope, which had been tied off solidly, held. It cut off his air supply. He shook and struggled for a moment. Then his eyes went blank and he was silent. One last furious struggle failed as the lack of oxygen made him pass out. For two minutes his body twitched and his muscles responded with jerky movements. Then his tongue lolled out of his mouth and his unseeing eyes stared directly at the brilliant sun.

Leslie slumped to the ground and vomited. He stayed on his hands and knees as he heaved until nothing more would rise. Three of the cowhands turned and looked away from the dying man. Two of them watched, fascinated by it all and remembering it for a great story they would have to tell.

Stanwood watched the tableau for a moment more, then barked out his orders.

"Untie those four men. Take off their boots and their shirts and kick them in the ass and get them moving."

He walked in front of the four live men. "I should

have hung all five of you. You deserved it. Maybe you'll take this as a sign that you should turn honest and make a living that way. I've got a good memory for faces, and so does my foreman here. If we see any of you again, on this ranch or in town, we'll shoot you down like the dirty rustlers you are. You understand?"

They nodded. One man cried softly. Another's eyes were still wide with the expectation of death. The third man still carried his sneer, but it had little force now. The last man was crossing himself and mumbling some religious incantation.

When given the chance, all four took off, running in their stocking feet toward the east and the railroad.

Stanwood walked over to his son and pushed him gently with his toe.

"Come on, son. Let's find the herd and drive them back to their pasture. Damn, I guess I can't make something out of nothing. That's what you are to me now, boy, nothing. A cipher, a zero. You can stay at the house if you want to, but I'm damned if I'm going to call you my son anymore. Not after what you did today."

The six men mounted up, and led the four horses and carried the men's boots and gunbelts for five miles back toward the ranch before they threw them away. They kept the five sixguns and two rifles the rustlers had used.

On the way back, Stanwood thought about something that had been bothering him for a year or more. What the hell was the use in battling to build up a great ranch if he didn't have a son to pass it along to? Stanwood swore softly. Now for sure he knew that he had no son.

For a moment he brightened thinking about Terri. Then it faded. She couldn't run a ranch, and he wasn't going to take the chance on a son-in-law he hadn't even met yet.

He shook his head sadly. He had no wife, he had no son. Damnit to hell!

Chapter Fifteen

It had been a place for lovers for three or four years. Young people who wanted to hold hands went there to sit in the grass beside Cherry Creek and watch the moonlight on the water. More than one proposal had been made in what became known in Denver as "The Lane."

Lots of first kisses were exchanged below the oaks and the colorful mountain mahoganies along the creek. Many a young man too shy to lead a girl that way had been tugged along by the young woman, who knew what she wanted and would take a small chance along The Lane to find it.

Now six lanterns speckled the darkness of the area, with more coming. Sheriff Warner stared down at the nude body of a young woman. A deputy hurried forward and covered the form with a blan-

ket. The sheriff moved the cloth down from her face
and held the lantern closer.

"Emma Jane Vincent," the sheriff said. He looked
at Spur McCoy, who strode up just then. He had
been notified by a deputy.

"Another one?" Spur asked.

"Looks like it. The doctor was here and said death
was from a stab wound to the heart. That same
thin-bladed sticker used before would be my guess."

"A Chicago ice pick," Spur said.

"True. This was an angry man who killed Emma
Jane. Damn angry. Doc said she was cut up a lot
before she died. Said the wounds all bled buckets,
which meant her heart was still pumping and the
blood flowing. The front of her is not a pretty sight."

"I better look," Spur said. A deputy pulled back
the blanket, and Spur knelt in the bloody grass,
lifted the dead girl's arm, and pushed on her
stiffening shoulder to turn her half over.

"My God!" Spur said. He sucked in a long breath
to steady himself. Her breasts had been removed,
her belly slashed repeatedly, her inner thighs
stabbed and slashed into a solid mass of blood. He
didn't want to think what the killer had done to her
vagina. He let her back down, and the deputy
covered her.

"Sheriff, could you get all of your men out of
here? There might be something dropped or left in
the darkness that we can find, but if we have ten men
tramping down the grass . . ."

Sheriff Warner nodded and spoke quietly to one
of the deputies, and they all moved well back of the
death scene.

"We found her clothes spread over a fifty-foot space from here back toward the end of Fourth Street. It comes almost down to the river. Scattered, but not torn or cut off. Like she took them off herself as she walked or ran this way."

"Who found her?"

"Pair of good kids who were just out walking. The girl was sick and the boy isn't feeling much better. I sent them home."

"What time?" Spur asked.

"Found her about eight-thirty. That's the strange part. There must have been a dozen people through here before that, and nobody reported a thing. All this had to cause some noise. She must have screamed."

Spur looked at the woman's face, bringing up two lanterns. There were red marks across both cheeks, not cuts or bruises, but marks that could have been left by a gag and a tight band around her head. He pointed them out.

"Yeah," the sheriff said, "probably a gag, all right. But still, folks walk through here as a shortcut to Fifth lots of times."

"Who was she?"

"Emma Jane was a waitress at the New Colorado Cafe. Not the best spot to eat, but nice folks. I talked to the owner, who is also the cashier, and she said she didn't see anybody paying special attention to Emma Jane this afternoon. She got off at seven o'clock. No one man stood out as being overly friendly with the waitress."

"Her reputation?"

"Not the best. She had one child without benefit

of matrimony, and it was said that she was more than generous in sharing her womanly favors. It was also said that she often supplemented her income by taking men home to her small house about four blocks to the west. That's only speculation, of course."

Spur looked at the girl again. Her right hand was closed tightly in a death grip. Not unusual. He picked up her left hand and found blood under her short fingernails. Not unusual either, but it could mean that she scratched her attacker. This one might have put up a fight until she was knocked out or cut so badly she gave up. No, this one wouldn't have given up. She must have fought him until she was dead. How long could a body bleed like this, five minutes? He'd ask the doctor.

Two men came carrying a door. The doctor wanted to see the body in his office to examine it in better light.

"I asked him to look her over again," Sheriff Warner said. "He might find something to help us."

Spur waited until the men lifted the body to the door and carried it away. He kept the blanket, and shaped it and put it down to mark the spot where the girl had died.

"Leave that there so we'll know where she was when we come back in the morning. Oh, your men left her clothing where it was thrown, I hope."

"Yes, they understand that much," the sheriff said.

"Sheriff, I want to see the doctor again. Could you have two of your men guard this area until morning? I want to go over it one blade of grass at a time to see if the killer left us any kind of a clue. There must be something here after a fight. I don't think any of the others fought this demented murderer."

Sheriff Warner said he'd detail three men around the area and keep everyone out of it until morning, and Spur left.

The doctor grunted when Spur walked into his small surgical room. He had six lanterns with mirrors on them that threw a bright light. All were aimed at the girl on the long slab of marble.

Both men looked at the girl a moment. They hadn't found her breasts yet, so her chest was a mass of blood.

Spur pointed to her left hand. "Doctor, the blood under her nails. Is there any way to tell if it's hers or that of her attacker?"

"I can't tell. I understand in some of the medical papers now some scientists are studying blood, and they say there are different kinds of human blood. But we're a long way from figuring out just how or why or what they are. From the looks of her hand, it can't be the killer's blood that ran down her hands or her arm. No connection. She might have touched her own wound."

The doctor shook his head. "If I was hunting the man who did this, I'd be watching for a guy with scratches on his face or neck or arms. That's my guess. He might be scratched, and again he might not be."

"Have you opened her right hand yet, Doctor?"

"Nope. Going to have to break her fingers to get them open. Might not mean a thing, but if it would help you . . ."

"Yes, it might be interesting if she is gripping or holding something."

The doctor used an ordinary set of pliers and broke the knuckles and bent back the fingers one by one. When he was through they looked at her palm with surprise. There lay a swatch of hair, as if it had been pulled out of a man's head. The ends of the hair showed larger sections.

"Hair and roots," the doctor said. "Looks like this girl pulled out a fistful of the killer's hair just before she died and he couldn't get it out of her hand."

"Save it, Doctor. Put it in a jar or something and label it. Do you have one of those fancy new microscopes?"

"Indeed I do. We used them at the university. We'll have a look at some of her hair and some of that in her hand. They surely must be different. The hair in her hand is light brown, but her own hair, as you see, is black."

Spur nodded. "Doctor, it looks like at long last we're making some progress."

"How can you call it progress when such a pretty girl gets butchered like this?"

"Doctor, the progress is getting some clues as to who this killer is so we can at last stop him from doing this anymore. I hope he doesn't have the chance to kill again. But we need to know a lot more about him than we do now to find him."

There was nothing more Spur could do there. He went back to the hotel, where he had left Abby, and told her what they had discovered.

"Tomorrow morning at daybreak both of us are going to be out there, and we're going to go over that whole section of the riverbank hoping that there's one more clue there that will help us find the killer."

Abby pouted as she listened. "You should have come and called me. I've seen these bodies before. I might have seen something from the woman's point of view you missed."

"True. That's why I want you there bright-eyed and checking everything tomorrow at daylight."

"We're going to do that?"

"Absolutely. There has to be something more there we can use, especially since it looks like Emma Jane fought him this time. She had time to scratch him perhaps, and to grab some of his hair. We're starting to get some clues to this guy."

Abby stood and walked around the room. "Wouldn't it be great if he dropped his wallet last night in the fight? Inside we could find his name and his address and what he did for a living. Wouldn't that be great!" Her eyes shone and her long red hair swirled around her as she stopped suddenly and turned to him.

"I've got a feeling that we're going to find something valuable there tomorrow." She stepped over to him and put her arms around him and pushed up against him with her full body, and then kissed him teasingly on the lips, twice.

"So, since it's such a big day for us tomorrow, I better sleep in my own room tonight." She kissed him once more and rubbed his crotch gently, then turned and hurried to the door. She grinned at him on the way out. Then she was gone.

Spur laughed softly. She was a handful, in more

ways than one, and he would have her in his bed again before long. In the meantime she was right. He could use a good night's sleep. He looked out the hotel room window at the darkened town. Soon most of the people in Denver would be sleeping. He wondered if the murderer would sleep. The more he thought of it, the more he was sure that the man would sleep peacefully.

He must be mad, must be driven to these fiendish acts by some twisted part of his mind. Perhaps he hated all loose women. Perhaps his wife had deserted him and worked the gambling halls and the cribs and he couldn't stand it. So every so often he had to pretend to kill his wife, and picked the first woman with low morals he could find. Perhaps.

Spur slept without dreaming.

The sun came up the next morning at five-fifteen, and Spur and Abby greeted it as they looked over the murder site. Spur asked the three deputies to hold their positions and warn anyone away from the area until the search was finished.

They walked carefully to the blanket marking the spot where the body had been found. As they did, they passed a woman's blouse, then a chemise, and later a long blue skirt.

When they reached the blanket, Spur picked it up and folded it and put it on the ground. The green grass there was bathed with blood. The blood had dried now to a deep reddish black. Spur started at the end where her head had been, and felt of the bloody grass as he moved on his hands and knees along the length of the death scene.

"What are we hunting?" Abby asked. She had

knelt down and was doing the same just beyond the death spot.

"Anything out of place, like a barn door or a watch fob. Anything that shouldn't be here."

They searched the immediate area for half an hour, working out from the body. Abby sat down in the grass blowing strands of red hair out of her eyes.

"We're not having much luck," she said. "All I've found has been a barrette, a comb, two whiskey bottles, and a man's old shoe."

Spur walked over where she sat and studied the scene again. "Her clothes, what do they tell us?"

"She must have been stripping them off herself. The buttons are undone neatly, not torn open, which means she must have been either teasing or enticing him up to about the point where her chemise is."

"The skirt?" They went over and checked it. The buttons on the side had been ripped open. One was gone, another hanging by a thread, and two of the buttonholes torn open.

"So right here she changed her mind or he got violent," Abby said. "Let's check this area."

They spent an hour moving across and back across the grass. It was more than a foot thick there, sloping down to Cherry Creek, which at times became a raging torrent a hundred feet wide and swept away whole buildings and streets and wagons. Now it had watered the bank well and the grass was luxuriant.

"If the damn grass wasn't so long we might find something," Spur said. "Ouch, damn!"

"What?"

"Put my hand down on something sharp."

"A knife maybe?"

"No, it's right there." A moment later he found it in the grass. Spur bellowed in delight. "Damn, now we've got something. Not a handkerchief. Abby, come look at this!"

She looked in his hand and saw a button, a big button, thick and made of copper with a raised figure of a flying bird on the front. He wiped the dirt off it and it shone with a copper gleam.

"Maybe she pulled this button off his jacket in the struggle, and then dropped it," Abby said.

"This button hasn't been here long. Not like the other things we found. It looks like it came from an expensive man's coat or jacket. I wonder if our haberdasher will recognize it?"

"Worth a try. Now?"

Spur laughed, his spirits brightened. "Just as soon as we get done looking over the rest of this half acre of grass and checking again where the clothes are." He stopped. "Hey, what about her petticoats and bloomers? Where are they?"

A half hour later they still hadn't found her underclothes and they had found nothing new in the grass. They picked up her clothes and took them to the sheriff for evidence, but said nothing about the button.

"First we check it out. It could be nothing. It might come from the coat of some doddering old-timer who always loses his buttons," Spur said. They walked to the clothing merchant and he nodded as they came in. He was measuring the sleeve on a jacket for a man.

When he finished he said good-bye to the man, promising to have the sleeve shortened before six that evening.

"Mr. McCoy, you received my second list on those handkerchiefs, I would guess."

"Yes, and we thank you. Now we have a little different problem for you. Do you sell a lot of jackets to the gentlemen in this town?"

"Not so many jackets. More suits, I would say. However, most of the better-dressed men have one, perhaps two of the sportier jackets for informal wear."

Spur held out the polished button. "Any of the ones you've sold here have buttons like this?"

"Mallard," the haberdasher said.

"I beg your pardon?"

"That's the mallard duck button. Yes, matter of fact, I have had jackets with buttons like that. Copper, you see, and expensive. Each button is cast, not etched, which makes them more dear."

"Would you have any idea—" Abby began.

The haberdasher shook his head. "Not the slightest."

"It's important," Spur said.

"Yes, I know it is. I've seen Emma Jane around town. A tragedy, a damned shame too. When I have time, I'll check my charges for the past year. A jacket like that costs six, maybe as much as eight dollars. I'll have record of the ones I sold . . . somewhere. Might take a day or two."

"We'll come back. Oh, I'll need to keep the button. You know what it looks like, right?"

The clothing merchant nodded, and they went out the front door.

Spur looked at the sun, then at Abby. "Right after we have a late breakfast, we're going to check on the doctors in town. How many are there?"

After breakfast, they split up and each took half the town, and they began talking to the doctors. Someone said there were six medical men in Denver, not counting the coroner, who hadn't said anything about treating a man with scratches.

Spur had no success with the first M.D. he met, but the second one gave him a surprise.

"Yep, sure did treat a man for scratches this morning. They were deep and bad. Said his old tomcat just went wild and clawcd his arms something fierce. Course old Jed probably scared the cat, him and his cane."

Spur thanked the medical man and walked down to the next doctor. He was an older man, had been in Denver since it began on the banks of Cherry Creek. He stared at Spur for a moment.

"You a lawman or something?"

Spur showed him his identification.

"Well, now, President Grant, huh? Impressive. Well, I guess I can tell you I did treat a man for facial scratches this morning, about eight o'clock. Not that bad, but the gent was worried about scars showing."

"What was the man's name?"

"No, sir, Mr. McCoy, I can't tell you that. A doctor can't go blabbing about his patients to anyone. They call it the doctor-patient privilege. Law says I don't have to tell you. Wouldn't, anyway. If a man got shot, that's another thing."

"Doctor, did you hear about Helen Foley?"

"Did. Right sorry to hear that."

"Did you know that Emma Jane Vincent was murdered last night?"

"Fact is I heard it. She's not a patient of mine."

"She was a waitress at a restaurant."

"Oh, yes, certainly."

"She was murdered last night down in The Lane. Butchered actually, cut all to hell. I think the same man killed her who killed Helen. It could be the man you treated this morning with the scratches."

"Dear God! Don't seem possible."

"Can you tell me who got scratched now?"

"Like to, but I still can't. Wish I could."

"I wish you could too, Doctor. You change your mind, you let me hear from you. I'm at the High Country Hotel."

Spur left the doctor's office and spotted Abby down the street. He met her near the courthouse. He told her what he had learned.

"In a trial he'd have to tell," she said.

Spur shook his head. "Not so. The doctor is right. The law says that a doctor can't reveal anything about a patient. The problem, the treatment, the conversations about it all are what is called privileged information. We'll have to watch for men with scratches on their faces. Can't be many."

"The problem is, he'll keep out of sight now until his face heals," Abby said. "He might even move on to a new town."

"If he does we start all over again." Spur kicked at the boardwalk. "Tell you what. You meander up and down the street looking for our man with scratches on his neck or face. I'm going to check in here at the county courthouse to see the history on that Flying S Ranch. I still can't figure out why the army thinks

that Captain Thurlow Stanwood is dead. There has
to be something fishy going on here. I guess I'm
more curious about him than anything else. Meet
you back at the hotel for a late dinner about two
o'clock."

Spur walked into the courthouse. Why in hell did
the army say that Captain Stanwood died back in
1862?

Chapter Sixteen

The Denver county clerk wasn't busy that morning, and he spent the better part of an hour helping Spur find the old records in the big books. They went back to July of 1865, and began going through the pages.

The clerk was a friendly man, with spectacles and a big smile and slightly red cheeks he said were not the result of old Johnny Barley Corn.

"Born that way," he said.

They found the page and the clerk nodded. "Yep, remember that one. Biggest transfer I'd ever done up to that time. I was just a part-time clerk here back then. Colorado had only been a territory for about five years, and it was all new to everyone. But I remember this deal.

"Seems like this colonel had died in the war. Somebody came to claim his ranch. It was the

biggest one anywhere around even then, and worth
a lot of money. The colonel didn't have no wife nor
family here, and the guy who came to claim it was
his brother.

"Yep, here it is right here. The deed of transfer
and the certificate of death of one Colonel Rufus
Harland. The judge awarded the ranch to Josiah
Harland, only living brother of the deceased, and he
was in town for what looks like about two or three
weeks. Then the property was sold to one Thurlow
Stanwood. He still owns it."

The clerk closed the books. "That brings it up to
date. All legal and proper."

"Could I look at that page again?" Spur asked.
The county official opened the book and Spur stared
at the two signatures. The one of Josiah Harland,
and then the one of Thurlow Stanwood. They looked
a lot similar. For a moment he couldn't figure it out.
There were few of the same letters, an *a* an *l* and a *d*.
But the sameness of those letters was not what
caught his attention.

Then he saw it clearly. The writing was done with
a definite slant. He'd seen a lot of people write that
way who were left-handed. All of the letters actually
slanted to the left, rather than to the right. Evidently
Stanwood was left-handed. He thought it a strange
coincidence that Josiah Harland had been left-
handed too.

The army's reported death of Captain Thurlow
Stanwood at the battle of the Chantilly Country
House still bothered Spur. How could the army have
made such a mistake?

What was an even larger mystery was how a
just-discharged army veteran from New York could

wind up in Denver with enough cash money in his pocket to buy out the brother of a dead colonel who just happened to be from Stanton's old army outfit.

There had to be an explanation, and somehow he didn't think that Stanwood was going to be pleased when Spur asked the man about it. If he had a chance. Stanwood hadn't been in town much lately. He must be busy on the ranch.

When Spur got back to the hotel he found a note in his room. Abby had left early and was going to do some shopping. The stores were what she called "interesting" out here. He gave up and went for lunch at a Western barbecue place that had spare ribs that sounded good.

Abby spent an hour in a small women's shop, and found two scarfs that she liked and a new blouse. She paid for them, and saw that it was too late to meet Spur for lunch.

She wandered up the street. She knew most of the business section of Denver by now, and picked a small cafe that said it had the best food in town.

The menu was painted on the wall, and evidently it didn't change much. She picked out a Western sandwich of beef, cheese, and pickles, and found a table. The small cafe was almost filled, and her table had room for four. A woman came in and looked around, then came over and asked Abby if she could share the table. Abby said of course.

They talked for a few minutes as they ate. Then Abby looked up and found a man with the softest brown eyes she had ever seen staring at her. He had a plate of food, and half smiled.

"It's so crowded, would you ladies mind if I shared a small corner of your table?"

"No, not at all," Abby said. He was of medium height and had brown hair and a neat brown suit and a brown-shaded cravat.

He sat down and nodded at them both and began eating. No one said a word. The two women had been exchanging inconsequential remarks about the weather and Denver, but now they stopped even that.

He ate his meal of beans and chili and crackers and some toast, and then was nearly done.

The other woman finished her sandwich and rose to go, nodding at both of them. When the woman left the man across from Abby smiled softly and looked up.

"I don't know why, but I didn't like that woman. Is she a friend of yours?"

"No. I'd never met her before just now. She asked to share the table the way you did."

His smile came easily then and he held out his hand. "Well, in that case I can at least be civil. My name is Leslie Stanwood."

She took his hand automatically. "Oh, well nice to meet you, Mr. Stanwood. I'm Abigail Leggett." His hand was warm and soft, not a workman's hand. They shook and released, and she went back to her sandwich. It was really more lunch than she had wanted. They seemed to serve everything in large and extra large portions out here in the West.

"Been in town long?" Leslie asked.

"No, about a week now, I guess."

"Pleasure or visiting relatives?"

Abby laughed. "You make it sound like visiting relatives wouldn't be pleasurable."

Leslie snorted softly and nodded. "In my case that certainly is true. I happen to live here. At least I have for the past ten years or so."

"I'm really from Chicago, here on some business. I hope it will be over soon and I can go home."

"It's always good to get home again," he said. "I've traveled a little. Home does look the best, no matter where it is."

"Are you part of the Stanwood ranch and mill and mine family?" Abby asked.

"Guilty, but I don't have much to do with them. I do some of the management on the ranch, but just the in-house kind. Afraid I'm no cowboy. I don't even like to ride a horse."

"I'm not much for horses either, since we have lots of buggies and even horse-drawn trolleys now in downtown Chicago."

"Sounds highly civilized. On my next trip I want to go to Chicago."

Abby began to nibble at her sandwich, not in any rush now to finish it. She noticed that Leslie had started eating slower as well. She smiled. She rather liked this young man. He was educated and polite and gracious.

They talked then about the weather, and lingered over second cups of coffee. At last it was time to leave. He reached out and touched her hand.

"I know it's terribly forward of me, but have you had a walking tour of Denver? I'm a lover of history and know most of Denver's past since our town was established back in 1858. That makes Denver more

than seventeen years old now. Not quite as established as Chicago, but we're getting there."

For a moment, Abby hesitated. She should get
back to the hotel and keep trying to find this killer.
Still, Spur had taken a half day off for that barbecue,
and met Terri, who must be Leslie's sister. Why
shouldn't she have a relaxing afternoon?

"Mr. Stanwood, I think it would be delightful to
have a local guide show me the splendors of Denver."

He stood and bowed. "Miss Leggett, I would also
be delighted to tell you about our fine little city, and
even about the mountains if the clouds have blown
away."

They walked out of the cafe and down the street
toward Cherry Creek, and Leslie began his history
lesson.

"This is Cherry Creek, a little stream that flows
into the mighty South Platte River near the Front
Range of the Rocky Mountains. Most of us still
wonder why a town grew up here. Neither the creek
nor the South Platte has enough water to bear a boat
of any size. The South Platte is often said to be the
only river in the world that's a half-mile wide and a
half-inch deep."

Abby laughed and walked beside him. He glanced
down at her from time to time as if surprised to see
her still there.

"You may have noticed our scraggly cottonwood
trees and the chokecherry brush. The chokecherry
has a fruit that will pucker your mouth. The brush
gave us the name of the creek. Our small stream
here in 1864 turned into a raging torrent and swept

away the entire building where the *Rocky Mountain News* was published.

"The publisher, William Byers, didn't let that stop him. A month later he bought the newspaper across the street, the *Commonwealth*, and went right on publishing his own *News*."

They walked and talked, and Abby found this rather shy young man opening up as he talked about Denver. It was easy to see that he loved the town, and knew its history well.

They went up one side of the main street and down the other.

"Oh, did I tell you that Denver didn't become the name for this town until 1860? Before that on one side of Cherry Creek the town was Denver City, and on the other side it was called Auraria. At last the editor of the *News* convinced the locals to unite for the greater glory and we became Denver."

They stopped in a small shop for a doughnut and cold lemonade. Abby saw a clock in the shop and she raised her brows. It had been nearly two hours since they had left the cafe.

"My goodness, look at the time. I've enjoyed your guided tour and the refreshments, but really, I must get back to the hotel. There are several things I simply must get done yet today."

"Could I be of any help?" Leslie asked, his smile growing more ingratiating every minute.

"Thanks for asking, Mr. Stanwood, but this is part of my work and it's something I have to do. I thank you again for the walk and the history lesson."

"At least let me escort you back to your hotel. Which one is it?"

She told him, and a few minutes later she shook

his hand at the steps to the High Country Hotel. He held on to her hand.

"Miss Leggett. I've enjoyed this afternoon. Could I have the pleasure of taking you to dinner sometime, perhaps tonight? We do have some rather good restaurants here in Denver."

She hesitated again, not sure why. "I do have a lot of work to do. Why don't you leave a note in my box at the hotel, perhaps tomorrow?"

He smiled. "That I'll consider a firm engagement." He dazzled her with another smile, then let go of her hand, turned, and walked smartly away.

Abby lifted her brows. Well, the young man was kind and intelligent and gracious, but he was a Stanwood, and she knew that there could be some question about the father. But the sins of the father did not set upon the son.

Did she twist that around? Abby smiled as she hurried up the steps to Spur's room. It had been the most pleasant afternoon she had experienced yet in Denver. Who knows, he might even try to kiss her the next time.

She knocked on Spur's door, and he called for her to come in.

Spur welcomed her and showed her his notes about the Stanwood situation in Denver.

"How could a soldier just out of uniform and two thousand miles from home in New York have fifteen thousand dollars with which to buy the Harland cattle ranch?"

"Fifteen thousand?"

"That was the figure entered in the transaction and bill of sale and on the grant deed. Where did he get that kind of cash money? That's as much as an average workingman earns in over thirty-four years!"

"It is a mystery." She went to the window and looked out. "Guess who just gave me a guided tour of Denver?"

"President Grant?"

"No, silly. Leslie Stanwood." She explained how they met, and told him about the walk.

"Sounds uninterestingly platonic," he said.

She smiled. "It would be my guess that Mr. Stanwood had some other thoughts, but it wouldn't be ladylike for me to mention them."

"You better not. I still don't trust his father. Something is wrong here somewhere. But back to the case. I've heard nothing up the rail line about our killer working up that way. He could, of course, go up on the train, kill someone, and be back here the next day."

"So we still have the hair, the button, and the handkerchief. Which isn't much."

"And a description," Spur said. "It's a lot more than we've had in the past." He rubbed his neck and looked out the window as the light began to fade.

"Damnit, somewhere out there is our killer. We should have enough to find him, but nothing seems to be going together. Maybe when Mr. Johnson tells us who he sold those mallard-button sport coats to, we'll have some new names to work with."

"Maybe."

"Yes, and maybe not. We will go see Johnson tomorrow and help him sort through his sales slips and charge tickets if we have to."

"Agreed." Spur watched her a minute. "Want to play some poker?"

"You do mean cards?" she asked, grinning.

"Yes and no."

Abby sat down on the bed. "Let's make it no cards. I have this strange little itch I need you to scratch for me."

Spur chuckled and sat down on the bed beside her. Soon he scratched her itch exactly the way she liked.

Chapter Seventeen

Dave Bordelon sat in the far end of the bunkhouse nursing a bottle of whiskey. He had worked the level down nearly a third of the way before he called over his best friend on the crew. As foreman he had to keep apart from most of the men.

Bordelon stared at Yancy through half-open eyes. "You know how I loved that horse," Bordelon whispered. "Ain't a thing I ain't done in seven years without Scout. Best damn horse any man ever had. Them sons of bitches of sheep-gutters sliced his throat wide open!"

"Yeah, Dave, I know. Damn shame. We found you another good horse, though. Not as good as Scout, but a damn fine chestnut stallion."

"Not good enough. Sure, I got a horse, but I ain't got no damn sheep-gutter's blood. I need some of their blood, damnit. You go with me?"

Yancy was in the middle of rolling a cigarette. He spilled half of the tobacco at the request, and had to add more. When he finished he looked up.

"Go with you where, Dave?"

"Go get us some of that damn sheep-gutter's blood!"

"Don't rightly think so, Dave. Remember, the boss said we wasn't to worry about some two-bit sheep-herder. He can't hurt us if we just don't rile this guy. He's the kind who hits back, and there ain't many like him. Remember, we lost the barn and your stallion that one night when they scattered our remuda."

"Horseshit, Yancy. He killed my Scout and he's gonna pay with blood. Him or his kin, don't matter none to me."

"Better count me out, Dave. I been off my feed a little lately. The damn rheumatiz from all those nights sleeping on the cold ground is kicking up too."

"Yeah, another damn yellow-belly. Hell, I don't need no help." Dave surged to his feet, grabbed a rifle from near his bunk, and buckled on his sixgun belt. He walked to the door, maintaining a better balance now.

"Gonna check the herd," he said to no one in particular, and slammed out the bunkhouse door.

It was full dark outside. Dave walked quickly to the corral and brought out his new mount, a chestnut of exceptionally deep red color with four perfect white stockings.

He saddled the mount automatically. He moved quickly now, not acting drunk at all, and soon stepped into leather and rode.

Bordelon knew it was at least 20 miles, so he took his time, pacing the horse. He could do 40 miles and be back in the bunkhouse before anyone woke up. It had been just after dark when he left, he figured about seven o'clock. He had at least 11 hours before sunup. Plenty of time.

By eleven o'clock that night he could smell the sheep. He had followed the route he'd used before when they had surprised the young kid with the sheep and put down the dog and scattered the damn wool growers. The main place should be around close.

It took him another hour to find the cabin. There were flocks of sheep in pens made of brush and poles. The horses, they must have horses. He found them just outside the area where the sheep had bedded down. He dismounted and took the rifle and began moving up on the two animals.

Bordelon was halfway there when he heard a growl and then another one. He froze in place and watched. Two damn sheepdogs were creeping up on him. No way he could get to the horses now. He couldn't even see them anymore. One of the dogs barked and raced toward him.

He brought the butt of the rifle around just in time to deflect the white teeth away from his thigh. The dog rolled over twice, and then whined and turned back to the attack. Bordelon didn't like dogs, especially smart ones like sheepdogs. He ran back toward his horse.

The dogs trailed him for a while, as if they were herding him, then they turned and went back to the flock.

Bordelon lay on the grass next to his horse for half an hour trying to figure it.

Not a chance he could get close enough to slit the damn horses' throats. That's what he'd dreamed of doing. Return blood for blood!

But now that was not possible. He checked the Big Dipper. It was getting on toward two o'clock. Not a chance he could be back to the ranch now by daylight. Bordelon fingered the rifle. He could pump about a dozen rounds through the damn window in the small log cabin the squatters had built.

He shook his head. That would just scare them and not hurt anybody. He wanted blood.

Again he watched where he had seen the horses, but they were now out of sight. He would wait. Hell, he could wait until daylight and then hit the horses and ride away. They wouldn't see him, never know who did it. Yeah!

With the first streaks of dawn, he lay in his concealed spot about 300 yards from the cabin. Smoke came out the chimney first, then one of the boys came out and walked to the outhouse. Before Bordelon could decide whether he wanted that son's blood, he saw the horses moving toward the house. They were evidently on long picket lines.

Bordelon grinned, sighted in on the back horse, and concentrated on the animal's head. He squeezed the round off, and through the haze of blue smoke from his muzzle saw the horse jolt backwards and fall. He shifted his sights to the next horse, and fired once but missed. He worked the lever and pumped a new round into the chamber, and fired again with more accuracy. This time the round found the mark, and the second horse went down with a .52-caliber rifle round in its head.

For a moment Bordelon lay there gloating. Damn! He'd paid back the bastards. His Scout was worth any six horses, so they owed him four more. But he wouldn't wait around. He slid backwards to the reverse slope of the hill and ran for his chestnut.

Two hours later he was well away from the sheep herd. He checked at one of the ranch's shacks well out on range where riders stayed sometimes during roundups. Nobody was there. At least the sheep-herders hadn't been using it. He found some tinned food, a can of beans, and some kind of canned meat, and heated it over the small stove.

Then he rode for the home place. He'd tell the men that he'd been making a long-range survey. He knew that the boss would be in town today.

Alfonso Ortega had heard the first shot when he was stoking the fire in the fireplace. He dropped to the floor.

"Down! Everyone on the floor!" he shouted. He crawled to a firing slot he had made in the front wall and looked out at the far ridge in front of the house. It was 300 yards away. As he watched it, he saw a new puff of blue smoke, and a heartbeat later the round whined into the area and he heard one of the horses scream a terrible sound.

That was followed by another shot and then nothing. The smoke haze faded and mixed and was gone. Ortega pushed open the door and made a hard dash toward the sheep. He stopped halfway there when he saw both the horses down in the dirt.

One wasn't moving. The second was making small keening sounds and pawing the dirt with her front feet. Then a moment later, even that movement stopped.

Ortega ran to them and saw that both were dead. Slowly he shook his head. So it was a war. He had answered their attack with one of his own and now it was an exchange of death, one after the other. So far it had not touched his family. If Stanwood's men hurt any of his family members he would burn down the whole damn Flying S Ranch and kill everyone there!

Jose ran up with tears streaming down his face. "The cattlemen!" he said. "Do we have to move again, Father?"

"No, we are through moving. This is our land, we are going to fight to hold it. It might mean we have to camp out for a time, but we are not moving."

Ortega looked at his other two sons, who had walked up slowly, tears in their eyes as well.

"The ones who did this will pay for their crimes," Ortega said. "Now have your cheese and bread and get the sheep out to the usual pastures. We won't have a lot to worry about until tomorrow."

Ortega went back into the cabin, drank his strong coffee, and ate the meager fare for breakfast. His wife watched him from dark eyes. She had cried too, not for the horses, but with worry about what he might do now. She knew him too well.

He kissed her lightly as he finished his coffee.

"The breakfast was good. You're a good woman. Take care of the boys until I get back. I must go to the north and east a ways."

She blinked back the tears. "Be careful," she said. "We have no riding horse. How will you go?"

"Wife, I am a shepherd. I can run thirty miles a day every day of the year. I'll use my own two feet as God intended. Perhaps we were getting too rich and contented owning horses we could ride."

Then he left quickly by the door, taking his sixgun and his sturdy knife, which was so sharp it could cut a whisker in half.

Ortega used every bit of cover he could find as he trotted and walked to the north and a little east. He knew where the best cattle range was. He had ridden all over this entire part of the country before selecting his homestead.

By noon he was within ten miles of the Flying S Ranch and he had not seen a cowboy. He paused beside a stream and washed his arms and his face, then drank and ate some cheese from his pockets.

There were plenty of cattle here, but he wanted to be close enough to the home place that the results of his work would be found quickly by the Flying S riders.

He pushed another five miles along a creek that threw up a good growth of brush and small trees on its banks. He found what he wanted a half mile later. It was a small gathering of a dozen brood cows, each heavy with calf. Alfonso Ortega took out the knife and tested it.

A minute later he walked up beside a big brown and white cow and in one deft stroke, slashed the knife across her throat. She bawled a moment, then dropped to her knees, blood gushing to the ground. She tried one more bellow, then blood spewed out of her mouth and she fell to her side, dead in a minute.

Using his skill with his knife and his understanding of animals, Ortega worked from the back of the herd toward the front, killing six of the brood cows before he nodded to himself, turned, and jogged toward the south and his homestead.

He had heard much of this Stanwood when he was in town looking for a ranch. He did not tell anyone it would be a sheep ranch. The people in Denver who knew Stanwood said they had known for sure that he rousted settlers off land he claimed to be his. But they said he could claim it only by use, not by ownership.

Ortega had selected his homestead well away from the rancher, just to avoid the confrontation that he now faced. If the big rancher came at him with 20 riders, each with a pistol and a rifle, he and his whole family would be slaughtered.

There had to be a better way to convince Stanwood that there was plenty of room in this wide-open land for both of them. Their animals need never see each other, let alone feed on the same grass. Usually his sheep were in the rugged sections of the mountain where cattle would not venture.

But the big rancher knew all of this. No doubt his men had told him, when they'd found the sheep, that they were well away from any pasture that the Flying S Ranch even considered controlling. Why then the conflict?

Ortega figured it out as he walked. It was most likely the man who owned the big stallion that had

died. He was keeping the battle alive. He was
thirsting for more and more revenge, more and
more blood. It must have been that man who shot
the horses this morning. Who else would shoot
horses when there were people there to kill? Yes, it
must be the foreman of the Flying S. He was the
man who had to be convinced—or killed.

A dozen plans surged into Ortega's mind as he
jogged across the green valley and up the slender
ridges and down the other side. He could run all day
this way. It seemed to stimulate his brain, to make
him think and plan and evaluate things with a
deftness and certainty that he often didn't have.

Most of the plans were not practical. He could not
ride up to the Flying S and have a reasonable
discussion with the owner. He could not buy a rifle
for each of his boys and launch a first attack on the
entire crew of the Flying S. They must have lookouts
and guards by now, 24 hours a day.

What could he do? He knew no one in Denver to
appeal to. He had seen the newspaper there, but he
had no idea what the editor thought about sheepmen, or if he would dare to attack the biggest
rancher in the entire Colorado Territory.

As he trudged along, the miles started telling. It
had been a long time since he'd walked 20 miles.
Today he would go more like 35 before he got home.

Nobody was going to help him. It was the same as
it always had been. The sheepmen had to go it alone.
The rich ranchers could even band together to get
their way. The ideal solution had come to mind
several times as he walked. The more tired he
became, the more realistic it seemed.

Then he had a drink at a creek and rested a moment.

"No, by God!" he thundered for the whole world to hear. "I won't kill Thurlow Stanwood unless he kills one of my family first!"

With that settled in his own mind, Alfonso Ortega continued his long walk back to his small cabin and his sheep ranch.

Chapter Eighteen

That morning Spur and Abby walked into the Johnson Haberdashery as soon as it opened. Johnson himself hurried up, his eyes glowing. "You got my note. Good. I have three names for you. It took me hours of digging through my old records but I found them. Two of them were charged on a regular tab. The third paid cash. Here they are." He handed Spur a piece of paper.

Spur held it so Abby could read it as well. "Thurlow Stanwood, Judge Ambrose, and Quenton Ingles."

Spur looked up and frowned. "Two of these men are the same ones who bought handkerchiefs here."

"Absolutely. That's because those two are two of my best customers. They buy almost all of their wardrobe from me. Fact is, I didn't even tell them they both have similar jackets. At least all four that I got in were of different styles and colors, so there isn't that problem. A local merchant in a town this size has to be careful with things like that.

"Now, In Chicago it wouldn't make any difference, but here in Denver, well, we don't want two prominent citizens showing up at some official function wearing the same jacket."

"Yes, we understand, Mr. Johnson. You said you had four of the jackets, but sold only three?"

Johnson went to a rack and brought out the fourth jacket. "Figured that you'd want to see it. Fine material, solid attractive buttons, the famous mallards. I was hoping you might be interested in this one, but it's about two sizes too small for you, Mr. McCoy."

"Yes, nice jacket," Spur said. He opened the front of the jacket and looked at it a moment. Lined and deluxe. He let the flap down and thanked the store owner.

Outside, Spur turned to Abby. "So we have two men on our list who we already checked. Both were in town during the out-of-town killings. So that narrows it down a little, wouldn't you say."

"I get a feeling we might have some good luck on this case after all," Abby said.

"Not good luck, Miss Leggett. Good detective work. If we hadn't found the button, the killer probably would have made it away free and safe."

The merchant had written the address of the third man on the bottom of the note. Also a line that said he was a teller at one of the banks.

"I guess we check the banks. Which one is closest?" Abby asked.

Five minutes later they talked with the manager at the closest bank.

"Quenton, yes, one of our good employees. He's been home the last three days with a bad cold and fever. If you have any questions for him, I'm sure he's feeling well enough to talk to you now. His wife stopped by and said he was planning on coming to work tomorrow."

They thanked the manager, and soon found the small white house with a picket fence and lots of flowers around the yard. A lot of work and care had gone into the place.

A knock on the door brought a quick response. A small woman with striking brown hair and brown eyes opened the door and smiled at them.

"Yes?"

Abby took the lead. "Mrs. Ingles, my name is Abby Leggett and this is Spur McCoy. We're here to see Mr. Ingles. His bank manager said he was feeling well enough to have company now."

"Oh, my, yes. Goodness, come right in. Quenton wanted to go back to work, but I persuaded him to rest another day. He doesn't have the strongest constitution, you know, so I tend to mother him a little."

She smiled and led them into the parlor where a thin, frail young man sat on a sofa, surrounded with pillows and covered with a comforter. He turned. His eyes were deep set and his hair jet black. He smiled and held out his hand. When he spoke, his voice was so low they couldn't understand him.

"Quenton, you'll have to speak up for the folks to hear," his wife said gently.

"Yes, I forget. Good morning. I'm Quenton Ingles."

Spur introduced himself and then Abby. "Mr. Ingles, we're just checking some references. I wonder if you'd mind answering a few questions for us."

"Not at all."

"Were you in town continually during the past six weeks?"

"The past six weeks? Yes, of course." He looked at his wife. "Yes, that was two months ago we went up to Cheyenne for the weekend, but I had to be back to work on Monday. Outside of that, we've been here, both of us.

"My manager at the bank can confirm that easily enough. I had a perfect work record up to this dratted cold."

"In that case the alibi you gave us should hold up well," Abby said. "That's all we need to trouble you with. We thank you for seeing us, and we hope you're feeling better and back at work soon."

Outside, they stopped at the street and frowned at each other.

"Not a chance Quenton could be our man. Wrong size, wrong coloring, wrong color hair," Spur said.

"Besides, he doesn't look like he'd have the strength, let alone the explosive personality to be a killer," Abby said.

"So, we're right back where we started from," Spur growled. "We have two good clues, and both point directly at two men. Those two men happen to be the most prominent and influential in town and we can't prove a thing against either of them. Especially since they were not out of town to start the string of killings."

"Enough to make a preacher swear," Abby said. They walked down the street toward Main.

"There has to be a logical, reasonable connection between the clues we have and our suspects," Spur said. "We've just got to keep digging until we find it."

"The only trouble, we don't have any new ground to dig in," Abby said. "We've got nothing to go on."

"Not true. We have our four clues; the linen handkerchief, the hair from the victim's grasp, the mallard button, and the fact that the killer has scratches on his face."

"That and a nickel will get you a cup of coffee," Abby scoffed. "But it won't catch a killer."

"Let's work over the clues again. The handkerchief. It could have been left there at any time by anyone, but since the lady was a widow who had not been socially active, it's a fair assumption that the handkerchief is a valid clue. We just have to figure out who dropped it.

"Number two, the brown hair. If we can find some suspect, there is a chance, a fairly weak chance, that the doctor's microscope could match the hair from the victim's hand with that of the killer. I don't know if a court would allow such evidence, but the doctor said he'd heard of it happening."

"Number three is the button," Abby chimed in. "But so far we have three suspects, all of whom were in town and all eliminated as good suspects."

They walked toward the hotel.

"Unless there's something about the button and the handkerchief that we're missing. Something about the ownership. Could they have been stolen?"

Spur answered his own question. "Who would steal a jacket or a handkerchief? Of course the jacket could have had the handkerchief in the pocket . . ."

"Right, pretty weak logic," Abby countered. "What about the scratches? Isn't there some way we can force the doctor to tell who that scratched patient was that he treated the morning after the killing?"

"Not a chance. He can tell us who the scratched man *wasn't*. That might help, but not now. The description we have of the killer is good, but still too general. We need an eyewitness who lives."

"Don't look at me. I'm not about to try to seduce every man I meet just to hope we find the right man."

"I didn't think you'd go for that one, but it was worth a try. Hell, I couldn't do that part." They both laughed.

Spur told Abby to wait while he ran in and checked his box in the hotel. He did and came back with a telegram. He scowled and handed it to her to read.

"TO SPUR MCCOY. DENVER. HIGH COUNTRY HOTEL. NEED PROGRESS REPORT ON CURRENT PROGRAM. BOSS GETTING UNHAPPY. WIRE ALL DEVELOPMENTS AT ONCE. HALLECK SENDING. WASHINGTON DC."

"Great. What happens now?" the red-haired girl asked.

"I wire the developments, our clues and description. That might keep them from lynching me for another couple of days. We better get down to the telegraph and do it now."

* * *

Christopher Perry led the way through the thick Rocky Mountain woodland. Giant ponderosa pine and Douglas fir lifted as much as 150 feet straight into the heavens. Beside Perry walked Thurlow Stanwood wearing heavy woods boots, rough pants, and a red checkered cotton plaid shirt. He had a Winchester rifle in his hands, hoping for a shot at a white tailed deer.

"Why the hell is this so far off the drag trail?" Stanwood snapped.

"Just want to be sure you understand the problems getting the sticks out of this ravine," Perry said. "Sure, the logs are good, but it's a hell of a job sometimes to get them to the mill. You asked why it cost so much per log. I'm showing you."

Stanwood stopped in a small cleared space. "Perry, you always did have a quick mouth. Now let's get to the spot so I can look it over and get back to the horses."

"Right this way," Perry said. He was halfway across the open space when he started limping. "Damn, twisted my ankle back there. I should get out here more often myself. The spot I want you to see is just past that next bunch of brush. About thirty yards and you'll be able to see it all. I better wait for you here. Damn ankle is starting to swell inside my boot."

Stanwood looked at him and shook his head. "How in hell you ever get through one day without killing yourself is beyond me, Perry. Christ, how do you keep this logging-lumbering operation in the black? Hell, how far, another thirty yards? I guess I can do that alone. Remember, I walked over all of these hills before we bought the timber rights." He turned and snorted, then walked ahead. Perry waited until Stanwood was into the brush, then slid backwards six feet to a four-foot-thick Douglas fir stump three feet high and leaned against it.

He could hear a crosscut saw working ahead. That was where the fallen trees were "bucked" into 20-to-25-foot lengths so they could be dragged to the mill.

Perry heard the man above yell, and then there was a sound of something crashing and careening downhill.

Thurlow Stanwood had heard the bucksaw—he'd heard and seen them for years—but when the man yelled, he looked up. A 30-foot length of a three-foot-thick log rolled down the steep slope toward him. It hit a stump and bounced into the air, came down, and shattered half a dozen foot-thick pines and steamrolled toward Stanwood.

For a moment Stanwood was too startled and surprised to move. Then he picked the best way to run in a fraction of a second and leaped that way. The log smashed through another tree, uprooted a two-foot-thick stump, and bore down on him. It was less than 20 feet up the hill now, and there was no chance he could outrun it. He couldn't move fast enough to escape the mammoth log that crashed through and flattened everything in its path.

It was like the war all over again. Punish the enemy if you could, but make sure you stayed alive yourself. His glance covered the area between him and the log in one sweep. Nothing. He tried again, and found an upthrust of granite two feet high.

He ran forward three steps, then dove beside the upthrust and put his hands and arms over his head, as he crashed to the ground right beside the heavy granite ledge.

Then the time was gone. The monster log smashed another pine and thundered down on him. The green Douglas fir log hit the ground hard right in front of the upthrust of granite and rolled forward.

If it had come down hard on the rock it would have pulverized it, but since most of its downward thrust had been absorbed by the ground behind the rock, it jolted over the top, crushing only a foot of the rock off as it lifted slightly again and became airborne, then destroyed a line of brush 25 feet below, and at last came to rest on the upslope of the far side of the small ravine.

Stanwood lay where he was, not sure if he was dead or alive. Then he coughed from the rock dust around him. He was covered with six inches of pulverized granite. He sat up and brushed the rock off himself and looked around. The path of the log looked like a disaster area. He'd seen a tornado do something like this once, only not this bad.

"Stanwood!" somebody shouted.

He looked up and saw Perry in the fringe of the brush on the trail they had been on.

"Goddamn, Stanwood, are you all right?"

Slowly Stanwood lifted to his feet. He flexed his arms and legs and back. Then he wiped more of the rock dust off his face and blew his nose on a big red handkerchief.

"I'll live," Stanwood said. "Which is more than that damn bucker will who cut this damn log loose if I catch him."

"That must be the logger I saw running like his

shirttail was on fire. I'll never be able to find out who worked in here now. Not a chance. These guys lie for each other. He must not have seen you coming."

"I was in plain sight for at least two minutes." Stanwood shook his head, slapped more of the rock off his pants and shirt. "Now where the hell were we going?"

They walked another ten minutes to a much larger ravine where they were logging as well. Perry explained how it worked best to roll the logs down to the bottom of the ravine, then hook up the choker chains on them with a pair of oxen and drag them out.

"This all takes time. Now if we had a spur rail line in here, we could get the logs out in two hours instead of two days."

Stanwood listened and nodded. Then they walked back to the horses.

"Your ankle seems to have recovered," Stanwood said with a touch of anger.

"Just a turn, not a sprain. Doc said sometimes it's best to walk something like that out rather than coddling it. Looks like it worked this time."

Perry rode along behind Stanwood as they moved through the woods toward the mill. He touched the derringer in his jacket pocket. A two-shot .45. He could do it now and no one would ever be able to prove a thing. They could set up a log smash. He gripped the small gun and drew it carefully out of his jacket pocket.

Slowly Perry rode forward until he was beside but a little behind Stanwood. He couldn't miss from four feet. Two rounds in the back would do it! He lifted the weapon, then closed his eyes and let his hand fall to his side.

With a sudden anger he pushed the weapon back in his pocket. He couldn't kill this man in cold blood. His chance had passed. Now it would take another plan, another day. He didn't have that much time left.

An hour later back at the mill office, they went over the books and production figures. Stanwood hadn't seen the new heavier wagons they used now to haul lumber to their lumberyard in town and to the siding where they loaded it for shipment to the east.

Thurlow Stanwood left in his buggy a half hour later. Perry watched him go and swore softly. He'd had his chance. That damn ledge of rock had saved Stanwood from being squashed flat. It was one of those little details that you couldn't foresee that always spoiled a good plan.

Now he would work out another accident. This next one simply could not fail. There was too much at stake. He figured the whole operation would soon be worth over a million dollars! Just as soon as he got that spur line railroad built so he could move logs and lumber faster.

Perry walked slowly back to the mill office working on a new surprise for Thurlow Stanwood, a fatal surprise.

Chapter Nineteen

After they sent the telegram to Washington, D.C., Spur and Abby went to the sheriff's office, but there were no new developments. They had not been able to find anyone who had seen the killer go in or go out of Helen Foley's house, or who had been with the waitress.

Sheriff Warner shook his head in regret and frustration. "I just don't see how we'll ever catch this guy. He seems to be so slick and careful. He doesn't leave any tracks. This last one fought him and we've got some evidence, but damned if I know where it can lead us."

Spur said some polite things and they left. Abby said she wanted to be in her room the rest of the afternoon.

"Big social event tonight or something?" Spur asked.

"Matter of fact, I have an engagement. I'm being taken out to dinner at the best eating place in all of Denver."

"Roundup Cafe. We've been there."

"No, silly. I don't know where it is, but Leslie Stanwood is escorting me."

"Stanwood?"

"The very same. I told you we met yesterday and he took me on a walking tour of town. He's quite nice, in spite of what you told me about him. He was a total gentleman."

"Them's the kind to watch out for. All good manners right up to the point of their sneak attack."

Abby laughed. "Now you're sounding jealous."

"Not a bit. I have no claim and no call on you. This is one hell of a lucky gent."

She watched him from bright eyes, and smiled. "Kind sir, that's a wonderful thing for you to say. I appreciate it. I like compliments as long as they aren't intended as a softening-up process."

"Hey, you're soft enough already." Spur touched her shoulder. "You run along and have fun. Oh, be sure to ask in plenty of time for bathwater. It isn't always ready. I'm going to chat with some of the merchants around town. I might pick up something about that Helen Foley killing. Somebody between that store where they met and her place might have seen them and can give us the name of the man."

She touched his shoulder and hurried up the street toward the hotel.

In her room, Abby looked at her best dress, the light green and black one that was her favorite. It was the only dress-up dress she had brought. It would need a good ironing. The room clerk said that

he would send a boy upstairs to her room with two
hot sadirons and a small ironing board.

By six she was ready and sitting in the lobby
waiting for Leslie Stanwood. He was two minutes
early and seemed nervous. He bowed in front of her
and smiled and held out his hand. She let him help
her up and they exchanged quiet greetings.

"All ready for a fine dinner?" he asked.

"I've been starving myself all day waiting for it,"
Abby said with a little laugh. "Not really. Where are
we going to eat?"

"Oh, I thought I mentioned that. The only really
fine place to eat in town is at the Stanwood town
house. My father has the ranch, but he also keeps a
house in town for when he comes to town and for
the rest of the family. I stay there quite often, and we
have a fine cook. Does coming to my family town
house distress you?"

"Will it be a big group?"

"No, just the two of us."

"Well, this all is a surprise. I'm sure my maiden
aunt in Kansas City would tell me to slap you in the
face and march back to my room. But she's a little
old-fashioned." Abby looked at Leslie a moment,
then nodded. "Of course your cook will be there,
correct?"

"Yes, and the maid and a gardener. Oh, my sister
could be there. I'm never certain when she might
pop in to town to buy a new dress or something. I
assure you that you will be as safe as in a church."

"In that case, let's go."

He had a carriage and driver waiting at the front
steps. They sat in back and the rig rolled down the
street, turned twice, and came to a large house at

the edge of Denver right beside Cherry Creek. It was a three-story wooden house with gables and pointed domes and two wings.

"Father built it for Mother when she wanted to come to town to live. But she soon tired of it."

He led her up the front steps and into the entryway. It was elegantly furnished. Then they went into the parlor. The furnishings were all from Chicago or the East Coast, she was sure. It was plush, and expensively decorated with heavy drapes across the windows and a chandelier with at least 40 candles on it, each with glistening cut glass around it to spread the light.

"It's beautiful!" Abby said.

"Actually, I helped in the decoration. I have a feeling for good furniture and what goes together. Mother did a lot of it as well." He went to a cabinet and opened it. The doors revealed an array of liquor and wine bottles.

"Would you like a sherry before dinner? We have one that's very light and not too sweet."

Wine! She lifted her brows for a moment, then nodded. She had sampled wine before, but had never learned to like it. Someone said you had to acquire a taste for wine the way you did pickles, mushrooms, and olives.

"Yes, please, just a small one."

Even though it was summer, the big house had a touch of a chill to it, and a small fire burned in a four-foot-wide fireplace. He seated her in an upholstered chair facing the fire, and brought the sherry in small glasses with long thin stems and flared bottoms. The stemware was expensive, and for a moment she was afraid she might drop it.

"Tell me what you do, Leslie. Where did you go to school?"

"School, yes. Not the best memories. I went here in Denver for a while, then father brought a tutor to the ranch where he said Terri and I could learn twice as fast as in the school. We did. I tried to go away to a prep school, but I didn't like it."

"What do you do now for the company?"

"Mostly bookkeeping and some management. I'm not a cowboy, if that's what you're asking. Sure, I know how to ride, but I do that only when I must. I prefer town to the ranch, and Father doesn't like that at all."

The maid came and curtsied. "Mr. Stanwood, the dinner is ready to serve."

"Fine, Linda. We'll be right in." He turned to Abby. "Now, isn't this a lot better than some noisy old restaurant? Here we won't have to kowtow to anyone, and besides, we could never get the dinner I've arranged for us tonight."

He helped her up, and they went through two rooms to the formal dining room. The table was eight feet long and the table settings were at the opposite ends of it. For a moment Abby wanted to giggle, but she didn't. She saw that Leslie had a fine linen suit on and that he was dressed up for the occasion. It was going to be a formal dinner just for the two of them.

The room was stunning. Reflecting mirrors seemed to be positioned on half the walls. Lamps lit the room as brightly as daytime. The table was set with sterling silver and fine china, and there was a small ceramic coffeepot at both settings. The table was polished mahogany, and the chairs matched with soft cushions built into each on the bottom and back.

He led her to one end of the table and seated her, then went to the far end and sat down.

"I rather enjoy eating in the grand style now and then," Leslie said. "Of course, I like picnics and barbecues as well, but this is fine dining."

He rang a small bell, and the same girl in her black and white uniform brought in soup dishes and a tureen of soup. She held the bowl for Abby to help herself.

Leslie smiled. "Abby, this is a special vegetable soup with some delicate spices in it that I brought back from the East. It's a French style of soup that I think you'll enjoy."

She waited until he had been served, then sampled the soup. It was delicious.

"Well, what do you think?" Leslie asked.

"That's the best-tasting soup I've ever had. What goes into it?"

He waved his hand. "Too many things to count. Just enjoy it."

She did.

The soup was followed by a green salad with a creamy topping, then salted bread sticks and delicately flavored mashed potatoes with butter. Before she had barely started on the potatoes, the maid brought in a roast fowl of some kind, the whole bird, and placed it on a platter in front of Abby.

Leslie smiled. "For you, miss, the very finest of the house, a roasted pheasant with special sauces and an herbal basting and stuffing that I think you'll like."

As he spoke the woman placed a second platter in front of Leslie with a whole bird on it.

"I sent our driver out into the countryside this morning to bring back these birds. He shot them with a rifle, so we don't have to worry about a lot of buckshot in the meat."

Abby looked up in near panic. She had no idea how to start eating such a feast.

Leslie smiled at her and laughed softly. "Don't worry, Abby. Eat it any way you wish. Tear off a drumstick, slice down the breast meat, cut off a thigh. It's yours to devour any way that you wish."

He tore off one of the drumsticks and began eating it by holding it in his fingers.

"I think this is what is known as finger food," he said.

It was almost an hour later before they finished their dinner. There were two more courses after the pheasant, then a light dessert of pudding and an after-dinner mint.

He led her to the third-story balcony that faced west.

"Father had this built so he could come up here and look out over his cattle ranch, and so he could watch the sunsets. We get some tremendous sunsets when there's about a half cloud cover in the spring and fall."

They watched the sun go down, and he caught her hand as he led her back to the parlor.

"Now, Abby, wasn't that a lot better than being in some stuffy old cafe downtown?"

"A thousand times better. I'm afraid I didn't do justice to that pheasant. Everything was so good. I'm amazed that you don't weigh three hundred pounds if you have this kind of food to eat every day."

"Oh, no, I don't eat like this every day. This was a special occasion. I seldom find a woman in Denver who truly attracts me, who is bright and beautiful, but not pompous and nasty. I like you, Abby Leggett, so I arranged this little dinner."

"This is quite the nicest compliment I've ever had, Leslie Stanwood. Thank you. I'm impressed."

He moved and sat beside her on the sofa, which faced the sunset. Gently he picked up her hand and kissed it. His glance came up slowly to lock on hers.

"Miss Leggett, if your father were here, I would go to him and ask if I could come courting. I believe in the old ways, that a time of formal courting is an absolute necessity for young people. But since your father or family isn't here, could I ask you if I may come courting?"

Abby was surprised by his suggestion. She showed it on her face and eased back from him.

"Well, Mr. Stanwood, this is quite a surprise to me. I thought we were just having a friendly dinner."

Suddenly he hovered closer to her. His face was smiling, yet it wasn't as convincing as it had been.

"Miss Leggett, may I kiss you?"

She frowned, eased back again, and shook her head. "No, I should say not, Mr. Stanwood. That would not be proper at all. No chaperon, no courting, no kissing, certainly not."

His face broke into a delighted smile. "Good, that was a test. I wanted to see how you would react. Instead, let me assure you that I am now prepared to ask you again about courting, but at another time."

"I think you better take me back to the hotel right now, Mr. Stanwood. It would be most proper."

He stood, his face smiling. "Yes, exactly what I hoped that you would say. You may be surprised how hard it is to find a really moral woman these days. I thank you for being so patient and kind and letting me bring you here to dinner. It's been a total delight for me. Now, this way to the front door and the carriage will be waiting."

It was.

Abby smiled softly as they went out the door and into the rig. It had been a delightful evening. Such a dinner, and a man who was more worried about her honor than she was. That was certainly a change. He helped her into the carriage, and instructed the driver where to go. Then he sat beside her on the far side of the seat as the rig rolled downtown.

Abby let him help her up the steps and into the hotel lobby. Then he bowed, smiled, and said he would contact her the next day.

Leslie Stanwood hurried out the door and into the carriage, and five minutes later was in his pair of rooms on the third floor. He tore off his formal suit and threw it on the bed, and paced up and down in front of the window that faced the balcony and the west.

He stared out the window for a moment, then dove on the bed and flailed it with both hands. He screeched out his rage and his anger as his mind traveled back. Most of it had happened in this very room.

She had been there. She had been there with him.
No! He would not re-live another moment of it . . .
not another second. But then all too suddenly she
was there with him and he was 12 again and she let
him pet her breasts, and then she touched him
"down there," and at first he was frightened, so
frightened.

But she coaxed him and told him it was all right.
"It can't hurt a thing, Darling Boy. Mother will be
good to you. Has Mother ever hurt you? Of course
not. Just like last time, you touch Mother and
Mother will touch you. That's fair. Isn't that fair?"

His 12-year-old mind reeled. But dutifully he
nodded and let her touch him. He let her put his
hands on her body in places he had never seen, and
then she . . . then she told him what else to do.

One time he ran away. He screamed at her and
ran out into the hall and down the stairs. She had to
dress before she came after him. He wore only his
shirt, no underpants nor britches. The maid had
caught him and herded him back toward his room
by the time his mother came down the hall.

She took charge of him, gently scolding him until
they were back in the room. That was the first time
she hit him. He was only 12. She slapped him on the
head so hard his whole head ached for days, and for
a while he saw two of everything he looked at.

It was fun at first, but then it got scary when he
started running into things he didn't think were
there and going around things that weren't there at
all.

But for a long time that afternoon he just kept his
eyes closed as his mother undressed him and played
with him. She kept telling him to make it hard for

her, to make it hard. He didn't understand what she meant. This wasn't like the apple tree, not at all.

She finally made him use his finger, and by then he was so confused and mixed up and ashamed that he'd do anything she told him to.

Afterwards she gave him the 20 cents as usual, and then she gave him a silver dollar.

Leslie Stanwood sat up on the bed and wiped the tears from his eyes. All those times, all those years.

Then, just last year, she had left. She hadn't bothered him for almost a year before that. Then that night she slipped into his room and found him sleeping, and before he awoke she had him aroused and so worked up he couldn't make her stop and he couldn't stop himself. He was 21 years old, a grown man. She was a wanton, demanding more and more, and he at last pushed her away and ran into a spare room down the hall and locked the door.

The next morning he heard his mother and father having a terrible fight. His father threatened to send his mother back East to a hospital, and she laughed at him and told him he was just crazy because he couldn't make his work anymore. His father hit her then, knocking her down, and she screamed at him and rushed out of the house and drove into town by herself.

That was the last time Leslie ever saw her. But he had been ready. After he got back to his room that night, he found the long knife—the Chicago ice pick, the men called it. It was over 12 inches long and slender, and so sharp it would cut through flesh and small bones.

He had made up his mind he had to kill his mother. A monster like her could not go on living and hurting other people, other small boys perhaps. Yes, he had to kill her.

Leslie had planned it that night. He would ask her to come to his room, and then when she was worked up, he'd use the long knife on her and cut out all of her evil, slash away her vile and terrible sins.

But she didn't come back, and then his uncle shot himself. So he had to find a substitute for his mother. Someone else like her, wanton and evil and easy, who would flip up her skirt and lay on her back just for the fun of it.

Loose women! He must kill them all!

He took the Chicago ice pick from the special hiding place behind the books in his room and honed it. Yes, it was sharp. Yes, he would use it again.

For a moment he thought about Abby Leggett. She had seemed almost on the verge of kissing him tonight. Then he'd asked her to kiss and she'd pulled back. One more afternoon and she would be like all the rest. She would want him and use her body to confuse and get him excited. Then she would try to make him do it with her and he would kill her. It was simple. Abby Leggett would turn out like all the rest of them. A slut, a whore, a wanton—and she would have to die. Like all the rest of them.

If he kept looking, someday he would find his mother and he would kill her. Then the deaths could stop. Then he would be purified and clean. But not until then.

Not until he at last killed his slut of a mother.

Chapter Twenty

Alfonso Ortega waited for a response from the Stanwood Flying S Ranch. He knew there would be one. He wasn't sure what it would be. It would come through Thurlow Stanwood, he was sure of that. He had moved most of his sheep away from the big cattle ranch. The closest flock was now at least six miles away from the ridiculous borders that the ranch claimed.

He had been watchful and would continue to be so. Ortega looked around their rough log cabin. It probably would be burned down before this fight was over. He was through running away. This time he would battle with them to his last breath if necessary.

He'd thought Thurlow Stanwood might be different, but he was just another cattleman.

Ortega had worked hard for everything he had.

The cabin was rough and unfinished inside. His wife cooked over an open fireplace with swing-out iron hooks and one rack. They slept on bunks built into the wall, with ropes tied around the poles to form the bottom of the bunks for the springs. Pine boughs and dry grass formed the mattresses. Well-worn blankets and sheepskins kept them warm.

Ortega had two pair of pants. The boys had one each, and his wife patched and stitched on each of them nearly every night so the boys could wear them the next day.

They lived on the meagerest fare. Lots of mutton from sheep that didn't survive. They dried the mutton in the sun to preserve what they could. His wife baked a kind of unleavened bread from a supply of flour that they treasured.

Once in a while he could get to town and bring back a few vegetables and coffee, sugar, and salt. But the trips were few, and months went by between them. They did have goat's milk from three old goats they kept. That produced a kind of soft goat's milk cheese.

Ortega sighed and cleaned his sixgun. He wondered if it was all worth it. Was he only being stupid trying to fight someone so powerful? Stanwood could send ten, 15, even 20 armed men after him if he wanted to. When things really got desperate he knew he would have to move his family. He already had picked out a spot, straight into the mountains about six or seven miles. They would go up slopes the flatland riders would never even try.

The sheep would have to move as well, and it would soon be time to shear them and then figure out the best way to get the wool to market. That was going to be a full-time job itself. He'd have to build wagons to haul the wool to the railroad, then consign it to some market in Chicago or perhaps farther south. Charleston? He would work on that problem.

The next morning he sent his oldest boy, Jose, to the flock nearest to the ranch, and then studied the sky. It could rain before the day was out. The grass and weeds were dry in spots. A good rain would give better grazing for the sheep, and they wouldn't have to move them up to the higher meadows quite so early this year.

It was nearly noon when Jose came running back to the cabin. He was exhausted, his face was black with soot, and there was a burn mark on his cheek and one hand and arm. He waved Ortega away and drank a cup of water before he could talk.

"Fire!" he croaked. "Fire, in the valley, killed most of the flock!"

He slumped on the bunk, and his father grabbed his revolver and raced out of the cabin. It took him nearly an hour to trot and run to the small valley where they grazed the flock of some 200 sheep. He could see the smoke and smell the burned flesh well before he got there. A light rain fell as he struggled up the last hill.

When Ortega came over the final rise and looked down, he fell to his knees. The whole valley was a blackened funeral pyre. He could see the carcasses of more than 100 of his sheep in the blackened ruin. The sharp sides of the valley and the rain had stopped the fire, but not before it had killed at least half of the flock.

The two sheepdogs worked a quarter of a mile

away rounding up the panicked sheep, bringing them into a flock again. They worked slowly, calmly, without any human instructions other than what they had been given two hours before when Jose left.

Ortega stayed on his knees as he sobbed. Tears flowed down his cheeks, and he took off his dark hat and pounded it on the ground. A hundred sheep slaughtered! He had worked for two years to buy that many new sheep. Now they were gone. He knew who did it and he knew why. Slowly he stood and walked into the pyre itself and through to the far side.

A light wind blew in his face. The fire had started on the far side and blown its killing breath toward the sheep. They'd run, and some had made it. Half had not.

He came to the edge of the fire line and he walked along it, dull brown dried-out grass on one side, blackened ash on the other side of the ragged line. It had started here somewhere. How had it started?

Ortega walked the burn line for an hour. Then at the far end of it he turned and walked it again. On the third trip he found what he hunted: the wax end of a package of waxed sulphur matches. They were often carried by cowboys because they were water-proof. The matches had been used up and the useless end thrown away.

Somebody had ridden along and dropped lit matches in the dry grass, or perhaps had walked and used matches every few feet. The matches themselves must have burned up without a trace.

Now he checked the land behind the place where the fire started. The horse tracks were plain to see, shod horses—Flying S horses, he knew. He found at least three different sets of prints. It took three of them to kill 100 defenseless sheep? His anger grew and grew until it was white hot.

He walked toward the dogs, signaled them to form the sheep into a long line, and then told them to begin moving the sheep back toward the home cabin. There was a small valley where he could hold them for a day or two. By then his plans would be complete.

It was nearly dark when he got the sheep into a safer spot near the other flocks. He left the dogs around them and went into the cabin. His wife had dinner ready, a mutton stew with some of their precious potatoes and carrots.

"How many?" Jose asked.

"Half," he said, his face set, grim. His wife gripped the spoon she stirred with and caught her breath.

"A hundred—dead?" Jose asked.

"Yes. This is the last night we'll spend in this cabin, at least for a while. Tomorrow we move into the mountains, ten miles from here. We'll herd the flocks into the same general area, but keep them scattered for the next few days."

Jose had recovered, except for the burns on his right hand and across his face. The burns had been cleaned and bathed with oil. He watched his father slowly grip his right hand into a tight fist, then relax it.

"What are you going to do now, Papa?"

"I'm going to move my family and my flock where they can be safe."

"After that, Papa?"

"We will see. But it will be me who does it, not you, Jose. You think of yourself as a man, and that's good. But this is something that I must do alone."

"And if there are more of them than you expect and you never come back to us? What then, Papa?"

"Then my worries will be over, and yours will be just beginning. The flocks will be yours and you will take care of your mother and brothers as I have always done."

"Yes, Papa."

It took them all day to get the household goods loaded on the cart and moved into the mountains. They pulled the cart with the one mule they had left. They drove the mule as high as they could go in a beautiful meadow with spring flowers still blooming. Then they carried everything high into a patch of heavy brush near a small chattering stream. There they cleared a spot and put up a tent they sometimes used on long trips with the sheep.

They made an outside fire pit and put an iron plate over it for a stove.

The next day they drove the sheep into pastures two miles from the tent, but so far off the track that no one would think to look for them up there.

That night Ortega slept fitfully, disturbed by dreams that chided him for thinking he could challenge a big cattle rancher and survive.

By morning's first light, he'd awakened and left the pallet. He had a quick breakfast of coffee and bread before he rode the old mule back to the cabin on his homestead. He made it look lived in again, then found two green, strong saplings and tested them. Yes, they should do. He found a long straight branch and sharpened the end of it. Then he bent the saplings back and used the cabin door as a trigger. After two tries he had the spear and the saplings set just right. He eased out the window and then closed it. There would be a deadly surprise for the first man to rush through the front door.

That done, he adjusted the gunbelt on his hips, checked the sixgun to make sure it was loaded, and then with his knife firmly thrust into his right boot, he headed for the Flying S rangelands. The mule was old, and slow, but steady. She could walk three miles to the hour all day and never get tired.

He rested when he saw the first Flying S brands. Then he moved again just before dusk. As he went, he slit the throats of a dozen cows and calves. They would die quickly. He should take a calf back to his camp for the change of diet, but he was not killing the animals for food. How many sheep did it take to equal the value of one cow? He didn't know.

He saw only one cowboy, and he was driving half a dozen animals toward the main ranch. Ortega slowed and let him move ahead. There was no rush now. The hurry would be moving the other direction.

It was well after dark when he saw the first lights of the Flying S ranch buildings some two miles away. The yellow light of the kerosene lamps cut square holes in the sudden darkness. As he came closer, he became more cautious. Surely Stanwood would put out sentries and lookouts. Surely he would expect that there would be some kind of a counterattack even from a lowly sheepman.

When he was 500 yards from the buildings, Ortega left the mule in some brush along the creek and walked slowly toward the barn. When he was 100 yards away he found a small ravine that had been choked with dry weeds and grass. He took out his plug of sulphur matches and quickly started the pile burning.

Then he ran away from it and got as close to the barn as he could before he heard any response.

A man yelled from near the well. Another shouted from the porch that they had a fire! A moment later a dozen hands stormed out to the ravine with shovels and wet gunnysacks ready to put out the blaze.

Ortega hurried the other way. He lit the big barn on fire first, then ran to the bunkhouse. A few men were coming back from the diversion fire in the gully and saw the barn burning. They ran there, and gave Ortega plenty of time to set the bunkhouse on fire.

Then, as lights glowed in several windows in the big ranch house, Ortega pulled his sixgun and fired 20 rounds at the place, smashing every lighted window he could find.

Half a dozen rounds snarled back at him, and he realized they were rifle bullets. He dodged one way, then the other, and ran into the deep darkness.

He had to walk in a large circle to get back to his mule. Once he was cut off by two men riding slowly carrying revolvers and rifles as they patrolled the remaining buildings. Stanwood had finally gotten smart.

There was still a bright splash of light from the barn as it burned hotly and the roof fell in. Then one side went in to feed the fire and the other two fell outward.

Ortega nodded grimly as he saw the last wall of

the big barn go down. Then he hurried toward his mule and waited to be sure no one was near. He stepped into the saddle and rode to the southeast watching for cattle.

On the way home, he butchered 20 more cows, calves, and steers. He would leave a trail of blood heading back toward his ranch, hoping that someone would follow it. He was counting on them following it.

Well before the night was over, he came to the cabin on his homestead. He rode on, leaving the mule a half mile into the woods. Then he came back and checked the cabin. It was as he wished it to be. A shirt and undershirt flapping on a clothesline. Smoke coming from the chimney.

He climbed in the window and banked the fireplace so it would burn the hour until daylight and then at least until noon. He was sure there would be visitors before that time.

Ortega found a concealed spot 50 yards into the brush in back of the cabin with a good view of the whole area, and settled down to wait.

They came an hour before noon. He counted six as they edged out of some trees a hundred yards from the cabin. The smoke still came from the chimney and the wind blew the shirt on the line. A peaceful mountain cabin.

A moment later six rifles fired half a dozen times each into the cabin. The heavy log walls took up most of the lead. The window on the left side shattered, and he could hear things breaking inside. When no one came out or returned fire, the six stopped shooting.

One man rushed forward from one spot of cover

to the next, and soon charged into the open, a sawed-off shotgun in his hands. He raced for the cabin door and kicked it open.

At once the shotgun went off, but it was aimed at the sky. The man who slammed open the door staggered backward, an inch-thick spear sticking out of his chest. He dropped the shotgun and grabbed the spear, but it was too deep to pull out. He screamed, then bellowed in fear and rage.

A few seconds later he dropped to his knees, then bent over on his back and jolted onto the ground. He didn't move again. The men in the brush fired at the cabin again. Then the shooting stopped and some-one raced up to the cabin on the windowless side, crept around, and peered in through the shot-out window.

"Nobody here!" the cowboy shouted.

The other men ran forward. One of them looked at the man on the ground.

"Bordelon is dead," one of the men called. "Damn spear went right through a lung."

"Guess the sheep man pulled out," another voice said.

"Hell, looks that way. We better get Bordelon on his horse and take him back to the ranch. Old Man Stanwood is gonna shit his pants when he hears about this."

Alfonso Ortega watched the men pull the spear out of the dead man and tie him facedown over his saddle. They looked at the cabin, shrugged, and rode away, northwest toward the Flying S Ranch.

When he was sure they were gone, Ortega went down and looked at the cabin. It wasn't hurt much. A new window, some minor repairs inside, and it would be home again. But not right away. He and his family could live in the tent for all summer or more if they had to.

He wondered what Stanwood was going to do. Would this end it? Had the rancher suffered enough? The riders from the Flying S had come looking for blood, and they'd found it, only it was one of their own who'd died. That might just be enough for Stanwood and his Flying S Ranch.

Ortega walked back to where he had tied his mule, and began the long ride back to his summer place. He had a feeling that he might just have seen the last of the great sheep war in Colorado.

Nobody had won. Stanwood hadn't gained a thing. Both of them had lost a lot of livestock. Nobody won in a war, especially a range war. He kicked the mule in the side. He was getting hungry. Some bread and cheese and a glass of goat's milk sure would taste good about now.

Chapter Twenty-One

Spur and Abby had wasted another half a day talking to people along the route that Helen Foley, the murdered woman, had taken the day she met the stranger and took him home with her. Or was he a stranger? It didn't matter. No one in the area had seen the pair or remembered either one of them. Spur and Abby even knew what Helen was wearing that afternoon, but it didn't help. They had a late breakfast for lunch, and that was when Deputy Sheriff Sanders found them.

"Sheriff says he's not sure what it is, but we got a screamer in one of the fancy houses and a guy who won't come out and says he has a long knife and he's about ready to use it. We can go in fast and hard, but figured you might want to talk to the man."

Spur came to his feet and pushed back the chair in one smooth motion.

"Talk to you later, Abby," he said, and he and the deputy hurried out of the cafe and jogged down the street toward the Happy Harem bordello. It wasn't the best one in town, but it had 16 choices, more than most. The lobby was full when the two came through the front door, and the sheriff pointed up the stairs.

Four ladies in bathrobes in various states of closure leaned on the stairs and against the banister waiting. It was still business as usual, even though one of their members was about to become skewered on a 12-inch knife.

Sheriff Warner led the way.

"The girl's name is Florence. She screams a lot. Nobody seems to know this guy, but he's yelling and he's got a knife and he's wedged the door shut. We figure we can break it down, but if we do, he said he'd slit Florence's throat. Then she screamed again."

The hall was clear of customers and girls, but there were three armed deputies waiting there. Spur motioned for them to come to him.

"Sheriff, why don't you take your men downstairs and go on about your business. This is a talker, so let me talk to him. No chance we can use force or we lose the girl. It probably isn't the man I want, but I'll find out soon enough. Maybe he'll tell me what he's so pissed about."

The sheriff looked at Spur and shrugged. "Hell, seems like a good plan. One whore more or less don't matter much, but then we'd have to hang the son of a bitch. Yeah, McCoy, you go ahead and try to talk him out." Sheriff Warner waved at his three men, and they all went down the stairs grabbing at the whores as they went past them and getting humped at and some flashes of bare breasts in return.

Spur sat down with his back to the door of Room 12 and knocked twice. "Florence, my name is McCoy. I'm not with the sheriff. I just sent him and his men downstairs. I'm not even a cop. Why don't we talk about this. Who is your gentleman friend in there?"

"He's no bloody gentleman, I can tell you that."

"Shut up, bitch! This Florence ain't no fucking lady, so we're even."

"Sir, what's your name?"

"Wally."

"Hello, Wally. My name's Spur McCoy like I said. What seems to be the problem?"

"Hell, I ain't got no problem," Wally said.

"Must be some difference since you've barricaded the door. Wouldn't Florence do what you wanted?"

"Oh, hell, yes, she done it fine, and so did I. She just got all high and mighty and swore I wasn't any good at it."

"No good in bed? Florence, you told Wally that? You told a paying customer he didn't fuck good?"

"Hell, he pissed me off, saying I wasn't the best-looking woman he'd ever bedded."

"Not a good thing to say, Wally. Not very smart even if you *are* the paying customer."

"Hell, she's a fucking whore. I can say anything I want to. Why do I have to be nice to her? I'm paying her, not the other way around."

"You had a few shots of whiskey before you came up here, Wally?"

"Yeah, one or two. Hell, Florence is so ugly I can't stand to see her naked without some whiskey in me."

"How many drinks?"

"Well, eight, the truth be known. And I have trouble getting it up when I'm smashed, but I done it."

"You did not, you arsehole. I already told you that. Limp as a dishrag. I told you, dumbbell. You didn't even get it inside me."

"I done it, damned if I didn't."

"What you kids need is a referee. Tell you what. You open the door and I'll come in and watch and be the judge if he can get it up or not."

"Yeah, sounds good to me," Florence said.

"Not a chance," Wally roared. "Not letting you see me with my pants off. You outside there, you Spur guy. No, sir."

"Well then, Wally, what would you suggest?"

Spur settled down to a long conversation. He'd done this before.

It took almost an hour, and at the end of that time, Spur had convinced Wally that he was so tired that he slumped against the bed and let his head lay on the pillow and the knife slid from his hand. Florence picked up the knife, tiptoed to the door, opened it, and was in the hall in a flash.

She was still naked.

Spur grinned at Florence. "The man in there lied," Spur said. "You're the prettiest thing I've ever seen."

Florence brightened. She stood straighter. "Well, aren't you the nice bloke, though. You get a free one whenever you stop by. Wally is snoring already. I figure he'll sleep it off and put on his pants and go home."

Florence turned and walked down the hall as unconcerned as if she'd just been to the general store for five pounds of flour and three bars of lye soap.

Spur looked in the door out of curiosity. Wally was short, fat, and bald. Not a chance he could be the Chicago ice pick killer.

When he walked out of the bordello, Spur saw Abby's long red hair half a block down as she walked toward him. When she spotted him she hurried. "You all right?"

"Fine."

"How is the killer?"

"Sleeping, and the gal is unharmed. What are you so excited about?"

Our haberdashery friend, Mr. Johnson, called me in off the boardwalk. He said he remembered that several of the men who bought the handkerchiefs said they bought some for their sons as well. They were talking about grown sons. The ones he remembered were Mr. Kinney, the store owner, and a man named Wilson, who is a saloon owner."

"We already have talked to Mr. Kinney," Spur said. "Let's see where his grown son was during that fatal five weeks."

Kinney was pleasant about the talk with the detectives, but he was a little smug about giving them the facts about his son. "My son Charles has some of the handkerchiefs. The fact is, he moved to Chicago six months ago, and the handkerchiefs were part of a new wardrobe I bought him before he left."

They thanked Kinney and moved on to the next man, Wilson.

"He's the owner of the Wilson Sporting House," Abby said. "I've been asking people. He runs the saloon and has six girls upstairs. Mostly drinking and gambling, though. They do have some big games there. Biggest in town, I'm told."

It wasn't the kind of saloon where ladies were welcome, so Abby paced the boardwalk outside. Spur talked to the apron, and he took a message to the owner, who soon came out.

"Yes, McCoy, I've heard about you. Gunned down that robber and saved Stanwood a pile of cash. So, why do you want to talk to me?"

"I'm trying to run down an alibi a man has. He says he was with your son here in town about three weeks ago. Is that right?"

"Hell, I don't keep track of that boy. He's a gambler and is on the road a lot. He has to find new pigeons to pluck, you know. He's sitting right over there. Why don't you ask him your questions."

Spur looked where the owner pointed. The man fit the description of the killer almost exactly. Soft brown hair, not too tall, on the thin side, clean shaven, and at the moment he had a big smile as he swept in a poker pot. The only problem was he didn't have any scratches on his face.

Irv Wilson looked up as Spur rattled a chair at the table.

"Room for one more?" Spur asked.

"As long as you have money in your hand," Wilson said.

Spur sat down and stacked five double eagles in front of him. "Mr. Wilson, your father tells me you travel a lot. I work for a lawyer, and he has a client who says he talked to you and played poker with you here in town three weeks ago. Is his alibi good?"

"Three weeks ago? Hell, no. I was on the road then. I was hitting Chicago and Kansas City and a bunch of little towns about then. Fact is, I was gone for four or five weeks and just came back about a week ago. You playing or not?"

Spur sat in for three hands of poker. If the man were telling the truth he was the best candidate so far to be the killer. He was in the right place during the killings—he could have any kind of motive. Then he was back in town in time for the murders here. Spur watched Wilson carefully.

Irv Wilson knew his cards. He won all three pots. One because he had good cards and evaluated the other hands correctly. The other two times he cheated, dealing himself aces from the bottom both times.

He said he was out of town and then back in town at the right times. He was definitely a suspect. He also had access to the handkerchief in question. Spur wondered if he had a sport coat with mallard buttons on it.

Spur pushed back his chair and stood. Irv Wilson was a man to watch. Any man who could cheat that well at poker couldn't be trusted in the rest of his life as well, including how he answered questions.

After Spur pulled out of the game he went outside. Abby caught his arm and they walked up the street, her soft green eyes blazing now.

"Well, well? What do you think? Does he have a son?"

He told her about the possible suspect. "Irv Wilson is a gambler, and a good one. Why would he jeopardize all of that with these killings? He's too smooth and self-confident.

"But that doesn't mean we won't watch him. I'm going back in and find another game and watch Irv for a while. See what he does beside playing poker."

"Just what am I supposed to do?"

"Go find some clues or solve the case while I'm drinking and gambling and pinching the whores on the bottom. Have dinner and a nice hot bath and get a good night's sleep. While you're at it, get some shut-eye for me as well. Before tonight's over I might need it.

"I'm going to shadow this young man until he tucks himself into bed somewhere, whether it's his or not."

Abby flounced off, and Spur went back in and bought some chips and played at an inexpensive game. He had two beers and watched as Irv won almost every pot in his game. There was a quick turnover of players at Irv's table. The young man should let the suckers win more to build up the pots. He'd learn if he didn't get shot by a derringer sometime from under the table.

Irv played right through the supper hour, and then about ten o'clock he got up and left.

Spur followed him to the fanciest whorehouse in town, where Irv invested a whole hour before he came out. By now he was more than half drunk, but he managed to get back to a neat house that must be owned by his parents, two blocks off Main Street.

Irv Wilson went inside and locked the door behind him, and soon a lamp glowed in a second-floor window. The young man was going to get some sleep without the services of a night maid.

By midnight the light had been blown out and the suspect was evidently settled in for the night. Spur decided it was time for him to try the bed route as well.

Back in the High Country Hotel, he knocked on Abby's door, but she was either asleep or not there. He opened his own door two keyholes away, and his room was empty.

Spur shrugged, locked the door, and turned his key halfway around to prevent the use of a skeleton key. He stripped off his clothes and fell on the bed and promptly went to sleep.

Chapter Twenty-Two

Spur and Abby had breakfast at the hotel, then went to talk to the haberdasher again. Mr. Johnson smiled at them, finished with a customer, and walked up nodding.

"Did my last bit of information help you?" he asked.

"Some, Mr. Johnson," Spur said. "Now we're wondering if any of the other men who bought the handkerchiefs have grown sons at home. It's just a chance, but we need to check it out."

Johnson thought for a moment. "Well, yes, matter of fact some do. Triscout the banker has a son who must be eighteen or nineteen now. He could be a possibility. Then, of course, you know about Leslie Stanwood, and there was one more I thought of yesterday after I sent the note. Who was that?

"Oh, yes, Lenny Quade. Bill Quade's son is twenty-two as I recall. He's a clerk in a store or a bank or something. Those three more would have access to their father's fancy handkerchiefs."

"Good, Mr. Johnson," Abby said, her green eyes flashing. "This will help. Now if you can give us the addresses of Quade or his son, we'll get back to work."

Outside, they paused on the boardwalk. The Denver sun was shining down on them warmly. The fresh clear air had just blown in high-country clear from the Rocky Mountains to the west and blown away all of the wood smoke from town.

"We have to do this again?" Abby asked, a touch of weariness creeping into her voice.

"Nobody said being a detective was glamorous and exciting, did they?" Spur asked. "If they did, they were lying. You take the banker and ask him about his son being in town the vital weeks. Use the checking-on-an-alibi excuse."

"And you'll find this Quade guy. We really don't need to check on Leslie Stanwood. Didn't we rule him out as a suspect once before?"

"Afraid we did. Anyway, I wouldn't want to interfere with your social life."

She looked up quickly. "It wouldn't be an interference. It's just an outing. He's really not my type. Too thin, and he looks like he worries a lot. But he's sweet and attentive and a girl likes to go out to a fancy dinner now and then. I was treated like a queen the other night. It reminded me of some times in Chicago. It was wonderful."

"Right now we don't need wonderful, we need a

killer. Meet you at the Right Way Cafe for lunch—as they're calling our noon meal back in Washington."

Spur found Lenny Quade in a saddle shop where he was an apprentice to the saddle maker. He did the preliminary cutting of the leather and some of the tooling, and learned the trade as he watched and helped.

Spur stopped talking to Quade and took a deep breath. "Do you ever get jaded to the smell of leather? Damn, but I love that smell. Is it the tanning fluids they use or the leather itself? One of the best smells I ever get."

Quade looked up. "Know what you mean, Mr. McCoy. That's why I came to work here. I love the smell too. But to answer your question, I haven't been out of town for over two years. That time I went with my folks to Cheyenne on the train as a little outing. Went up one day and back the next."

"Yeah, I guessed as much. Well, it's been interesting talking to you, Mr. Quade. Good luck in your saddle making."

Spur met Abby at the cafe a half hour later, and neither of them was smiling.

"You too?" she asked.

"Dead end. Not a thing. The best suspect we have is still Irv Wilson. I'd be a lot more enthusiastic about him if I saw some scratches on his neck."

As they ate lunch, Spur shook his head. "More I think on it, the more it seems that Wilson couldn't be our man. He spent an hour at a bordello last night, and I don't think he was playing piano. If our man had been in a whorehouse, we'd have a dead whore this morning. My guess is that by this time he's in such a pattern that he couldn't stop even if he wanted to."

Abby watched him from wide green eyes. She pushed red hair back from her face and stared at Spur. "Then you think we can count out Irv Wilson as a suspect? He sure seems to qualify on all the other counts."

"Except the scratches," Spur said.

"I've been thinking about the scratches," Abby said with a frown on her round face. "Why did we assume they had to be on the killer's face? I mean, if he's in the heat of passion, he must have at least his shirt off. He could be scratched on his back or his shoulders or his chest."

"Right," Spur said. "Now that you mention it, I remember being scratched sometimes on the back."

Abby laughed. "That doesn't embarrass me at all because I know those scratches were from passion, not from fear of being murdered." She paused. "Maybe we should do some research along those lines."

"Passion?"

"We might be missing something," she said.

Spur moved his legs to ease a growing pressure in his crotch. "Young lady, are you finished with your lunch? I think it's about time we go over our notes and our strategy—in my hotel room."

Abby laughed softly and nodded. "Ready when you are, Mr. McCoy."

Five minutes later they slipped into Spur's room without anyone in the hall noticing them, and Spur locked the door and put a wooden chair under the knob.

Abby turned around once in front of him, then reached up to be kissed. The kiss came soft and gentle, then stronger, and didn't end until he had pushed his tongue past her lips and into her warm, eager mouth.

When their lips parted, Abby sighed. "Now that is more like it. This is the part of being a detective that I like the best. A conference with another detective."

Spur went over and sat on the bed. "Hey, red, why don't you seduce me this time. Just pretend that I'm a sixteen-year-old virgin and you're going to show me the wonders of making wild, passionate love."

"You're joking. I wouldn't know how."

"Of course you know how. You've been seduced. Apply the same techniques and get me all excited."

"You're hot and hard already. I felt you."

"So pretend. What would you do first?"

"What the hell, let's try it. First, what would I do first? I'd kiss you about six times and push you down on the bed."

"Don't tell me, woman, do it."

She laughed and stepped to the bed and sat beside him, then leaned over and kissed his cheek, then moved around and kissed his lips and parted them. As soon as her tongue entered his mouth she pushed him gently back on the bed and lay on top of him. She held the kiss a long time, moving on his chest so her legs spread and she covered him.

When at last she came up for air, he grinned. "Damn, you're good at this. Maybe you're really the killer and you like girls, and want them all naked and—"

She stopped his tirade with another kiss. Then she

found his hand and lifted it to her breast. He let it lay against her pulsating mound.

She broke off the kiss. "Spur, you're supposed to caress my breast, to rub it, to play with it." She sat up, straddling him, her bottom on his hips but not crushing his penis. Quickly she unbuttoned the top of her dress and lifted her chemise. She pulled out one breast for him to see, and then took his hand and pressed it against her warm flesh.

Then slowly she lay back down and kissed him again. His hand massaged her breast and she whimpered. "Yes, yes, for a sixteen-year-old, you're doing very well. Just try to control yourself!"

She ground her hips against his growing erection and giggled. "I like this, it's fun for a change. I get to set the pace and the movement. Of course if you were a real sixteen-year-old you would have popped your first load right there in your pants as soon as you touched my tittie."

"So concentrate on the second, third, through seventh loads," Spur said, grinning. She closed his mouth with a kiss and began humping her hips slowly at his. His hand moved around one breast and drove into cloth until he found her other one, which he promptly brought up to heat with his caressing.

"Oh, yes, dear Lord! But that is fine. Why is sex so good? Just to keep the babies coming, I guess. Thank God it hasn't happened to me yet. I may be sterile. Oh! Yes! Play with them, play with my titties!"

She moaned low and with feeling. Then she broke off the kiss and sat up. Slowly she pushed her arms and shoulders out of the top of the dress. She made sure he watched. Then she lifted off her chemise gradually, revealing just a bit of her breasts at a time as it rose until they were bare and she threw away the chemise.

She bent and rubbed her breasts on his face. Then when he opened his mouth, she lowered one heavy and full breast gently into place.

"I'm in heaven!" she said as he sucked on it and chewed gently on the sturdy engorged nipple. "Oh, God! That is so fine. Right now when I'm all sexed up and hot and all mushy-feeling, I can't figure out why people can possibly want to do anything besides making love. It's so glorious!"

She bent and unbuttoned his shirt, pushed it back, and toyed with the reddish brown hair on his chest. She brought her head forward and let her red hair rain down on him, covering his face and then his chest. She laughed as he blew strands aside so he could see her.

"What are you going to do now?" he asked.

"Undress you!"

She moved and sat beside him, lifted him up, and took off his shirt, then pulled at his belt and undid it. She had trouble with the buttons on his fly, but he made her do them. She stopped and caressed the long lump under his pants. Abby looked up and grinned, then licked her lips in anticipation and got the last buttons open.

She pulled off his boots, then his pants, and giggled at the way his short underwear tented out, hiding what could only be his full erection.

"Let's see what you have under there, you naughty boy. Are you thinking impure thoughts right now? I bet you are." She pulled at the back of his underwear and he lifted his hips, and she tugged the cloth down until it cleared his erection and she stopped.

"My God, so beautiful!" A tear came to her eye. "What a marvelous organ, so adaptable, so ingenious, and so hard and pulsating and purple on the top!" She bent and kissed him, then again, and pulled half of his long shaft into her mouth for a moment.

"So good!" She stood and worked on the dress. A minute later it lay at her feet, and she slid out of two petticoats and her bloomers and watched him staring at her.

"Oh, dear boy, you've never seen a woman all naked before. Forgive me. First my breasts. You've met them." She knelt on the bed and pushed her chest up to his face. He kissed them and she pushed him down.

"Now meet the rest of me." He lay on the bed and she knelt over him, her crotch coming down to his face. He kissed the soft red hair, parted it and found her very center, and kissed her soft, moist and pink nether lips.

"Oh, God!" She screeched in wonder and fell beside him, her whole body jolting and vibrating as a climax soared through her. She generated spasm after spasm, her body shaking and trembling and then slamming back and forth, her face a mask of intense concentration and delight.

When it was over she curled against him and his arm came around her shoulders and she shivered again.

"So fast, so quick, and you didn't even touch me! Amazing. This is one day I'll remember the rest of my life. It simply can't get any better than this. Not even with you plunged as far into me as you can go. Nothing can top this."

"At least we can try." He lifted her back on top of him and chewed at her swinging breasts. He let go of one nipple after biting it gently. "Hey, pretty woman, you know one of your tits is chocolate and the other one is strawberry?"

"Yeah, and I've got a sweet little plum pudding down here between my legs I want you to eat some more of."

He rolled her over on the bed and hovered over her. His mouth planted kisses down across her breasts and over her flat little tummy to her crimson crotch swatch.

"Oh, dear Lord!" she wailed. "Yes! Yes! Yes! Eat me up down there!"

He dove through the tangle of her steamy red hair into her very heartland, pushed the dripping lips apart, and kissed them deeply.

Her shriek of delight pierced through half a dozen rooms of the hotel. Her hips jolted upward at him, and he held to her nether lips as she surged again, and then once more before dropping down to the bed and parting her slender, shapely legs. Her knees lifted and her hips came up again.

"Do me, McCoy! Push that spur of yours deep inside my little cunnie and fill me up. Oh, God, fill me up until I run over. Do it right now!"

He brushed his hands up her satiny white thighs almost to her muff, then reversed them. She moaned in anticipation. He drew one hand hard up her thigh directly to her dripping vagina lips, crossed them, and went down the other side.

She bleated in a sense of loss.

The next time his hands came up her thighs he paused at her nether lips, and then pushed one finger deep inside her as far as it would go.

She yelped in surprise, then stared at him and shook her head.

"No substitutes, big cock. I want your prick rammed into me as far as it can, push it right up to my ribs if you can. Come on, right now. *Fuck me hard!*"

The pressure had been building in Spur as well. His tool throbbed with anticipation. His scrotum was pulled up tight, drawing his testicles high into his crotch.

Gently he went between her thighs and lowered. Her hands came around his buttocks urging him forward.

For a moment he probed, then bathed the head of his penis in her juices, and a second later her hands found his shaft and she guided it to the promised entrance.

He felt the opening and plunged forward.

She screamed in wonder and joy and pure animal sexual fulfillment. Her scream descended into a wail of awe and delight as he stroked gently, then harder, and stopped.

Her eyes snapped open and she watched him. "Right now, great lover, right now as hard and fast as you can go. Later we'll have time to be soft and gentle. Fuck me hard, McCoy, right now!"

He drove forward now, and her legs lifted around him changing the angle, plunging him in deeper. They shifted again, and he surged ahead again as her legs came around his sides and locked over his back.

Now he rocked forward and back like some mad pile driver on the slant, pushing her higher on the bed with each stroke until her head was against the metal frame of the bed. She grinned and kept up her wailing and moaning, punching him back each time he came forward until they hit bottom and their pelvic bones grated before he pulled back for another stroke.

"Yes, darling, yes! Poke me for all you've got. I've missed you these last few days. Do me now so good I won't want you again for at least fifteen minutes. Hell, I don't plan on getting any sleep tonight at all."

Just then she rattled into another climax, her body twisting and trembling, vibrating and jolting as one series of spasms after another rocketed through her slender frame. Tears gushed out of her eyes as she shrieked a dozen times as the climax peaked, and then she dissolved onto the bed and her legs dropped down, her whole form loose and pliable and spent.

He stopped pumping.

"No, no! Don't you dare stop. I want to feel that hot cum spurt into me and warm me and make me feel like a real woman. Keep going, damn you!"

She grinned as she said it, and slowly she lifted her legs over his back and squeezed him in her grip as he poked into her again and the gentle smile on her face broadened into pure ecstasy.

"You're slow today, McCoy. You been jacking off when I wasn't looking?"

"Not a chance," he said. "That's only a special

demonstration for virgins about the third time around."

His voice tightened at the end of the sentence, and his face creased into a frown and then wonder as his hips pumped harder and he lifted her, then pounded her deep into the mattress as he jolted into her vagina as deep as he could go seven times. Then once more, holding it as long as he could before he bellowed out a roar of dominance and achievement and fell spent and half dead on top of her.

She wrapped her arms and legs around him, locking him in place, a beautiful smile on her pretty face, which glowed now as she held her man.

It was ten minutes before either of them moved. Then he pushed upward and she unwrapped her arms and legs, and he rolled away from her, still breathing hard to recapture spent oxygen.

"Oh, damn!" he said softly. "That was great. How do you get me so worked up so fast?"

"Special talent," she said, grinning. "It also helps that you're one hell of a big sexy stud horse who simply loves to fuck."

They both laughed.

"This is just the start, you know," Spur said. "Once is never nearly enough for me. I'm thinking four times. That sound about right to you?"

She shook her head where she lay beside him. "Spur McCoy, I'm surprised you think I'm that kind of a girl. I couldn't possibly do this again. I mean, it wouldn't be ladylike. That is, not unless you can promise me at least six times."

He pinched her bottom and she grinned. "Hey, do that again, or do you need a little more rest between times?"

"A little more rest. You damn women can climax a million times in a row, I swear."

"Jealous?"

"Absolutely."

"Why didn't we bring anything to eat up here? Fucking always makes me hungry."

He jumped off the bed. "I'll run down to the general store and get something."

"You do that and I'll pay for the food."

Spur dropped back on the bed laughing. "Not a chance. We can always take a break for supper."

They did, between number three and number four.

Chapter Twenty-Three

Christopher Perry sat in his house at the mill site in the edge of the woods and stared into a small fire in the fireplace. He often built a blaze when he wanted to think.

Now he needed to. He had worked out a new trap for Thurlow Stanwood. This one had to work. The man must be brought down, and Christopher Perry must take his place as owner, ruler, boss of Flying S Enterprises.

He had it worked out to the last detail. The first Wednesday night of the month Stanwood went into Denver to his lodge meeting. He never missed. He always went by himself, driving that small black buggy. There was only one dangerous place on the whole trail between the ranch and Denver, where the buggy road went down a steep bank to ford a feeder stream into Cherry Creek.

The drop was over 75 feet. He couldn't count on the horse to panic at that special spot, but he certainly could help out a little. It was well out of town, far enough away so no one would be around late in the afternoon. The meeting began at eight, and Stanwood always drove in for dinner at his town house. The routine never failed.

That Wednesday night Christopher Perry lay in some boulders less than 20 yards from the side of the trail at precisely the right spot across from the dropoff into the canyon. First Stanwood, then the horse. It wouldn't be hard.

Yes, there would be a bullet hole, but Stanwood was going to suffer many scrapes, gouges, and broken bones in the fall. If the one bullet hole in Stanwood's chest still showed, Perry would use a rock or a branch of a tree to mess up the wound so badly that no one could tell it had been a bullet.

The horse might be harder, but it would be dead as well before it went over the side. One shot to the head would do the trick. The horse would be in such a position that when it fell, it would pull the buggy with it over the side and down 75 feet into the canyon below.

Simple, easy, quick.

Perry began to sweat as he waited. Soon the sun was down, but the heat from the rocks still came at him. He wiped his brow, then his forehead, and at last pushed his handkerchief back over his dark hair. Maybe a half hour more to wait.

He kept thinking of all the things he would do with the company. He had gone to Cheyenne, where a lawyer had drawn up a full partnership between him and Thurlow Stanwood, with the survivor to inherit all of the company except for ten thousand dollars for any surviving children. Easy. Fair.

It would get the two kids off his neck and gone to the East and he would have his empire!

Stanwood wouldn't alter his habits at this late date. He would come.

By the time Stanwood was ten minutes late, Perry stood and looked down the trail. The black horse and buggy were less than 200 yards away and drawing up quickly. He dropped behind the rock and checked the rifle. It was loaded, it was ready.

He sighted in on the spot he wanted and waited. He had shot a rifle a lot lately, just for the practice. Now he knew he had to hit his mark or all would be lost. Stanwood never drove to town without his sixgun along. He was good with the iron.

Now Perry could hear the rig coming. The jangling of the harness, the creak of the wood in the buggy, and the beat of the horse's hooves on the hard ground. Sweat ran down his forehead and touched his right eye. He slashed it away. The rig was damn close now. Any second it would appear.

Again he dreamed of everything he would do. Women, travel, buy anything he wanted!

The black horse surged into sight around the boulder. Then the rig straightened and slowed as it came to the dangerous section. Perry had counted on Stanwood to drive it cautiously the way he always did.

Perry sighted in with the rifle, aimed again, tracked the target, and fired. Just as he pulled the trigger the buggy jolted over a rock in the trail and Stanwood pivoted forward.

Too late the rifle bullet fired and jolted through

the air, cutting a delicate line of blood across
Thurlow Stanwood's back. He looked toward the
sound of the round, ducked down and drew his
revolver, and slapped the horse with the reins, then
pulled her around in a tight turn and drove straight
at the rock where Perry crouched.

Furiously Perry worked the lever to drive another
round into the chamber so he could fire. It took him
two tries, and by then Stanwood was almost on top
of him. Perry lifted the rifle to fire, but a .45 round
from the revolver came first, slicing through Perry's
right hand and driving with nearly full force into his
chest.

Thurlow jerked the horse's head around again
and turned the rig back toward town, crouching
over in the buggy until he couldn't be seen and
slapping the reins on the black's rump as the rig
charged down the trail faster than was safe.

Perry tried to lift his right hand. The rifle was still
there. Enough time left, he just had to concentrate.
He got the rifle into position and fired three times.
Working the lever with his right hand was torture,
but he got the fourth cartridge into the chamber
and fired it. But by then the black buggy was up the
far side of the ravine and around a cluster of
boulders.

Stanwood had escaped.

Perry considered his wound. His hand could be
wrapped up with a kerchief. But what about his
chest? He looked down and saw no blood. Gently he
undid his shirt and looked at his chest and saw the
small purplish black hole. The .45 had gone in there.
But it hadn't come out.

Why wasn't he dead? He moved and felt the pain.

It hurt a lot, but he could breathe, so it hadn't hit a lung. His heart still beat, so it hadn't hit his heart.

A doctor. He needed a medical man. Could he stand? Could he ride? It took him nearly five minutes to lift up from the rocks and stand. The horse? Where the hell did he leave his horse? For a moment panic hit him, but he beat it down. Just like a bad run of luck at a poker game. A man had to settle down and play the odds, take it as it came.

Now, first he needed his horse. Yes, down about 30 yards in that clump of brush. He left the rifle where it was, then changed his mind and used it as a cane with the muzzle in the dirt as he worked slowly down the side of the road to the brush.

The bay was there, but how could he mount? He tried to lift his left foot into the stirrup, but couldn't get it that high and nearly fell. For a moment a wave of nausea and light-headedness hit him and he almost passed out. Not quite. He blinked, and then led the horse to a tree that had fallen years ago. Perry crawled up on it, holding the reins to the bay.

Once there, he threw his leg over the bay. She looked back at him, wondering why he had mounted in such an unusual way. He settled in the saddle and knew he had to go to town. He went the long way. It was no more than three miles away now. He came in from the south instead of the west and rode directly to the doctor's office.

A stranger helped him down from the saddle and into the doctor's office. He had his story all set. The loggers were fooling around with their revolvers and one went off by accident and the bullet clipped his hand, then went into his chest.

The doctor harumphed at the yarn and began to work. "By rights you should be dead, Perry. A half inch either way and that slug would have killed you dead. You're one lucky damn sawmill man."

"About time I got some good luck. Hey, Doc. Isn't there some kind of a detective in town? Guy named McCoy?"

"There is. Working on finding a guy who hates whores and loose women. This guy kills whores, fancy ladies, and unfaithful women."

"That's the detective guy. I need to talk to him."

"Staying at the High Country Hotel. You can see him just as soon as I figure out where that slug is that went in your chest. Course after that I dig it out, you're not going to want to do anything for a day or two."

"Gonna hurt much, Doc?"

"Perry, it won't hurt at all. I've got this new stuff called ether. You won't feel a thing." He put a cloth over Perry's mouth and nose.

"Now, just breathe normal, Perry. Don't fight it. Breathe regular and you'll be all well before you know it."

Perry fought it for a moment, then the fight went out of him and he took long, even breaths and soon slumped on the table, unconscious.

The doctor grunted. Now all he had to do was try to find the slug. If it went through Perry's hand first it had to have slowed down. Maybe it didn't go in very deep. The doctor took a thin metal wire probe and pushed it into the wound, going deeper and deeper until he felt it scrape on metal.

Over an inch into flesh. How did it miss all the

vital organs? the doctor asked himself. He took out a
thin, small knife and began to open the wound so he
could get the slug out. It wasn't his favorite job, but
it had to be done.

Ether, great stuff. He'd only had it for six months
or so, but from now on he'd never be without it.

Spur McCoy had been talking with the sheriff
when Thurlow Stanwood stormed into the office.
He was red-faced and furious.

"In plain daylight somebody tries to gun me
down, Sheriff. What kind of a county are you
running here, anyway? I demand that you go out
there and capture that madman."

"Mr. Stanwood, settle down. Take it easy. I don't
have the slightest idea what you're talking about.
Start at the beginning and maybe I and my men can
help you."

Stanwood told them about the attack, how he'd
turned toward the gunman and fired—hitting him,
he thought—unable to see who the man was. Then
he'd turned and raced for town.

"So you didn't see who it was, and you think your
life was saved by a bump the buggy hit in the road
just as the bushwhacker fired."

"Yes, yes, that's what I said. Now send a man out
there and see what you can find before it gets dark."

"Did you see a horse?" Spur asked.

"No, but there's lots of brush around there. A
horse could be hidden anywhere."

"So the man might be half a county away by now,"
Sheriff Warner said. He held up his hand. "Easy, Mr.
Stanwood. I've already sent a man out there to
check. In the meantime you go to your lodge

meeting and we'll look around the bars and see what we can hear."

Stanwood stood there for a moment, rubbed his back where the bullet had barely grazed him, and nodded. "Just be damn sure you find the bastard. Next time I might not be so lucky. I don't want to duck and hide from every shadow for the rest of my life."

Spur walked with the sheriff as they checked the saloons.

"This sort of attack happen often?" Spur asked.

"Not on Thurlow Stanwood. We get a shooting from time to time. I've got a rule that any bullet wound must be reported to my office by the doctors. We have six doctors now."

"Why don't we check on them instead of waiting?" Spur asked.

They came to Doctor Partlow's office ten minutes after he had dug the slug out of Christopher Perry. Perry was still groggy from the ether, and had thrown up once already.

Perry looked up at Spur and the sheriff and he wilted. "All right, I took a shot at him, I didn't kill him. He shot me and I want to charge him with attempted murder."

Sheriff Warner chuckled. "Self-defense for Stanwood. You couldn't win your case, Perry. I won't even let it get started. Why did you try to kill Stanwood?"

Perry drank some milk that the doctor's wife brought to calm his stomach, then took a deep breath and told them about the swindle so many years ago.

"My name wasn't on any of the papers. I didn't

break any laws. I was just moral support. But Stanwood, now there's a man who should be in jail."

"What happened at that battle in the Civil War?" Spur asked.

"What battle?" Perry asked.

"The Chantilly Country House fight. That's where the War Department says that Captain Thurlow Stanwood died back in 1862. Did this Colonel Harland die and Stanwood change identifications with him?"

"Yes," Perry said. "His face was shot off, and Stanwood knew about his ranch out here and his lack of relatives. Stanwood switched wallets and rank and then deserted the next day. Being officially dead, he was free to head for Denver. I met him on the way, and he knew he needed help.

"He pretended to be the dead colonel's brother, took control of the ranch and bank account, and then a week later sold it to a new man in town, Thurlow Stanwood."

Spur nodded. "Sheriff, if you don't want to file charges against Stanwood, I damn well will, federal charges of impersonating a U.S. Army officer, of fraud and larceny on a U.S. land grant."

"No need, Mr. McCoy. From what I've heard we have plenty of evidence to charge Stanwood with fraud, conspiracy, misrepresentation, theft, and half a dozen more felonies. He'll spend the rest of his life in a prison somewhere."

"We better arrest him right now," Spur said. "News like this can travel faster than a telegram."

They went to the lodge hall and asked for Thurlow Stanwood to come out.

"We need you to sign a complaint down at the office," Sheriff Warner said.

"You catch him? You find out who shot at me?"

"We certainly did. We'll explain it all down at the jail."

Once inside the jail, Sheriff Warner told Stanwood he was under arrest for grand larceny, theft, and a dozen other felonies in connection with the unlawful takeover of the old Rufus Harland cattle ranch.

"You're crazy," Stanwood bellowed. "I bought that ranch from Harland's brother, Josiah. It's all legal and notarized down at the county clerk's office."

"You're left-handed, aren't you, Stanwood?" Spur asked the rancher.

"Yes, what does that have to do with it?"

"When the experts compare your left-handed writing with that of Josiah Harland down at the county registrar's office, they're going to find the writing is almost identical. The fact is they were both written by you. I also understand the real Josiah Harland died in New York State a month before his brother was killed at the Chantilly Country House battle. That will be easy to verify with the county clerk of his home in New York State."

Stanwood stared at them a minute. "Lies, all lies. Who was it who shot at me? Don't bother, it had to be that damned Christopher Perry. He's the only one who knew all of this. Did I kill the little bastard?"

"Nearly did, but he's alive and well and he'll testify against you. You should have thought of that, Stanwood, before you humiliated him and took away half of the business. Oh, I still want you to sign that complaint against him for attempted murder. That charge will stand, and you can testify against him. It should be an interesting court docket when the circuit court convenes next month."

Stanwood stood there a moment seething. Then he turned and walked back to the cell a deputy held open for him. "You can charge Perry with part of this Harland ranch deal too, you know. He swore before a judge that I was Josiah Harland. He was an equal partner for a time, and he was in on the conspiracy. I'll be glad to testify about his part in it. He deserves just as much time as I get."

Stanwood frowned. "The ranch, the mine, the lumber business. Who will get it? There are no more Harlands that I know of."

"There must be some relatives in New York somewhere," Spur said. "You know how well those New York towns keep records. I'll wire my office in Washington and have a man sent up to the little town they came from and sooner or later, we'll find some kin."

"My children. They'll have nothing," Stanwood said.

"So what," the sheriff shot back. "They're young. Let them make their own way. Most of us had to do that. Now get in that cell and be quiet for a change."

Spur walked out of the jail smiling. He'd have a little bit of good news to tell Abby after all.

Chapter Twenty-Four

The next morning Spur talked to Sheriff Warner to make sure the Stanwood matter was taken care of.

"Yes, all tied up, McCoy," the sheriff said. "I got a temporary restraining order from Judge Ambrose preventing anyone from selling any goods or property from Flying S Enterprises. The court appointed a custodian of the outfit until the legal heirs can be found or the court makes a permanent ruling."

"What if there really are no heirs to the Harland estate?" Spur asked.

"From what the judge says, the son and daughter could then be named the legal owners of the property and businesses. Lord knows that Stanwood built it up from a fifteen-thousand-dollar scratch outfit of a ranch. He deserves a lot of credit, even if he did steal it in the first place. All this could take months to settle by the courts."

"The court will make a search for heirs in New York?"

"That's what Judge Ambrose said."

"Good. That wraps up one of my small worries here in your city. Now if I can get the other one settled, I'll be satisfied. Any developments on our maniac killer?"

"Nothing new."

Spur growled at the sheriff and walked out to the street. A few minutes later, Spur met Abby in her room. She let him in and was dressing. He watched with appreciation.

"You enjoy watching a lady dress, don't you, McCoy?"

"True. Of course I'm just as interested in watching her undress." He told her about his talk with the sheriff, and she shook her head.

"I know he stole the ranch in the first place, but it doesn't seem right that he should lose everything. Ten years of hard work and all gone for nothing."

"That's the law, Abby. If you establish a fortune on a foundation of stolen money, the whole damn thing gets taken away from you. Tough, but true."

Abby hesitated a moment, then swung her long loose hair around as she looked at him. "I guess it has to be." She finished dressing and grabbed his arm. "Take me out for breakfast, I'm so hungry I could eat Montana."

"Don't forget the mustard. Montana is too dry without mustard."

She hit him with a pillow.

"Of course I can't eat much. You see, a gentleman friend is coming courting at eleven o'clock. We're going on a buggy tour of Denver."

"Watch him if he has a blanket along. This the same young whippersnapper as before?"

"Yes. Jealous?"

"Of course not. He's a soft-handed town man. Not your type. Besides, he's a Stanwood and his father is in jail."

"Leslie is just sensitive and you don't understand him," she said, but with little enthusiasm.

"You don't even believe that yourself. But you have fun. Oh, and take that derringer in your reticule. You might need it—in case there are any rattlesnakes in the grass or anything."

She grinned. "Talk about softics. You, Spur McCoy, are concerned about me. I think that's sweet." She moved over and kissed his cheek. He grinned. The front of her dress was open. She turned to him, her full breasts showing grandly through the thin chemise.

"Could you button me up? It will be a big change for you but I bet you can do it."

He bent and kissed each breast through the soft cloth, then buttoned her bodice all the way to her neck and inspected her.

"Yes, I think that will do. Nothing showing to make Leslie go crazy and attack you."

"He isn't the type. If anything happened I'm sure I'd have to seduce him, like I did you the other night."

"One of the top events on my social calendar."

"See, you try so hard to be tough, but you're just an old softy." She twirled around. "Do I pass inspection?"

"Grandly." He kissed her lips with a feather touch and let her go. "You be good. I still don't trust that poor excuse for a man as far as I can kick him."

"Relax, Spur. I'll be as safe as I was in my crib beside my mother in Kansas City."

They went to the lobby and Spur bought a copy of the *Rocky Mountain News* and read the local gossip. The paper was a day old, so it had nothing about Stanwood. Spur was sure it would be the lead story soon and for weeks to come.

Spur watched as Leslie Stanwood came in the front door of the hotel, looked around the lobby, spotted Abby, and went over to her. Spur didn't like it, and he wasn't sure why, but there was nothing he could do about it. Not yet at least. Maybe he could dig up something.

By noon the fancy-lady houses were open, and Spur spent an hour talking to seven madams, but every one of them swore that they didn't know Leslie Stanwood. They were almost certain that he had never frequented their houses.

"Hey, some men do and some men don't," one of the madams said. "Some men prefer to get it from the straight women who only wish they were whores."

He had a beer and thought about it. Then he put Stanwood out of his mind, both Stanwoods, and concentrated on the case again. He went over the clues one more time. The handkerchief. It could have been dropped by a father and it could have been borrowed or used by a son. That left it wide open. The button. Same damn thing. The hair. Now there they had a real clue that could be tied down to one man. But how did you get hair samples from every suspect and put them under the microscope?

Scratches. Yes, Abby was right. The scratches could be anywhere on the killer's body. He was probably naked when he seduced the woman, or she seduced him. Spur would probably have to face the fact that there were no face scratches. Not much help unless they caught somebody quickly. He'd have to ask Doctor Partlow how fast scratches would take to heal on a man.

The description. It fit too many men in this town. He ordered another beer. It was a damn dead-end case unless he could turn up something damn fast. But what?

Abby sensed the new, driving, building pulse of Denver as they drove leisurely down the streets. She saw where Cherry Creek had become a raging torrent one spring and washed into town with a vengeance, carrying away whole buildings and streets and wagons. The ruined area had been quickly rebuilt.

"And here we have the nicest, most expensive houses in Denver," Leslie continued. "A banker owns that three-story white-painted mansion, and a gold miner who struck it rich and saved his money has the place next to the banker. Some people say the man's gold in his neighbor's bank has made them both rich. Now both of them concentrate on raising fine horses and giving riding demonstrations."

The tour continued. They stopped an hour later at a small restaurant for a special meal. It had been arranged beforehand, and two waiters hovered over them like they were royalty. They had a fine soup and then delicate sandwiches of six different kinds, followed by the new chipped and flavored ice that was all the rage back East.

He watched her critically. "Abby, how do you like the new ice dessert? Everyone back East is eating it. That is, where they have ice that's fit to eat."

"I like it. It's quite unusual. At first it made my teeth hurt, but now it doesn't. Yes, I like it, really good, and the crushed strawberries in it are wonderful."

He smiled at her pleasure. She was so uncomplicated, so direct. Leslie liked that in a woman. Of course he had to give her the test, but that could come later. In case she failed it, the little interlude with her would be over. He sighed, then watched her again as she took the last bite of the iced strawberry dessert. She was like a lovely child, but a woman too.

"So, are we ready to continue our grand tour?"

"Ready, Leslie. Where are we going?"

"Up along the river. I want you to see where Cherry Creek wanders to the south. Then we'll tour the famous Denver saloon district, but only from the carriage."

They went out to the buggy, and since Leslie was driving, they had complete freedom about where to go and when to stop. Twice they turned in at small shops that Abby saw. At one place she liked an attractive printed silk scarf and Leslie bought it for her. She wrapped it around her neck, and they continued.

"I'm enjoying this guided tour even more than the walking tour," she said. They had stopped the buggy three or four miles south of Denver along Cherry

Creek near a small falls, and walked down to the river.

"For a long time this was my favorite spot in the whole world," Leslie said. "When I got feeling low, I'd come here and throw rocks in the water and sometimes dangle my feet in it."

"I bet it's cold, coming down from the mountains."

"Terribly cold, but refreshing on a hot summer day."

"Like today. Let's go wading in the stream!" She looked up at him with such an innocent face, and with such a little-girl smile, that he nodded.

"Fine, but it's your fault if we're late for supper tonight at the house."

They waded for a half hour, and threw rocks to see how many times they could make them skip along the surface of the water. Leslie got seven skips.

"You've done that before," Abby said, frowning at him in mock anger.

"Once or twice. Your rock made three skips. The secret is to get the flattest rock you can find and then throw it so it hits flat. See, like this."

He skipped another rock, but Abby gave up. She waded out of the water and sat in the grass to let her feet dry. Two places on the bottom of her long skirt had gotten wet in the stream, but she didn't care.

"It will dry quickly," she said. "My feet are almost dry, so I can put my stockings on and my shoes. You'll have to turn the other way. I'm sure you'll do it if you're a real gentleman."

He laughed and turned, his expression showing

that he was pleased with her demand and her modesty.

"Oh, I see you now and again with that detective, that Spur McCoy. Do you work with him?"

"He's an old family friend and I'm along on a lark—oh, quite proper and all. We each have our own hotel room, and he won't let me go with him when there's any danger."

"Then are you a detective too?"

She sensed something strange about this young man and lied again. She wasn't sure why she didn't tell him the truth, but something warned her. She had made excuses about being with McCoy twice before in this town. The people seemed to frown on it, and there was more of that feeling now, so she lied again.

"Not really. I like to pretend I'm a detective, but Mr. McCoy assures me it's no job for a woman. I think he's right."

"What is McCoy doing in town?"

"I'm not too sure. Something about a bank robber from back East who came here and took a new identity. Oh, my! I shouldn't have told you even that. It's all a big secret. I'll have to ask you to promise not to say anything that I just told you. Don't breathe it to a single person."

He laughed, and she thought the tightness around his eyes relaxed a little.

"Well, now, I can be as close-mouthed as anyone," he said. "In fact, I've forgotten it already so I won't be able to tell a soul. Are your shoes on quite firmly? It's time we start back."

They drove slowly through the sun and the shade of early afternoon.

"Leslie, thanks for taking me on this tour. I'm growing to love Denver. It's so high and bright and the air is so pure. Then there are the nights! Oh, my, the night sky is so beautiful. The stars are a mile closer than anywhere I've ever been before."

"That's why we call this the mile-high city. Someday Denver is going to be the hub of the whole western United States. We're right in the middle of things here."

"What will you be doing by then? You said you don't like being a cowboy."

"I imagine that I'll be working with the lumber mill and the timber. I'll probably manage the logging-lumbering operation. That's more my style of work. I could be comfortable working there in the office or setting up new lumberyards around the country."

He shrugged and slapped the reins on the black, who moved out smartly.

Leslie looked over at her. She had picked some daisies and small sunflowers and some other wildflowers along the stream, and held them now with some young shoots of fern. He thought she made a perfect living picture. He smiled at her for a moment, then turned serious.

"But who knows what any of us will be doing in ten years, or even one year from now. Usually I have a hard time thinking out what I want to do even a week ahead."

He drove slowly, and as the town showed ahead, they could see the pall of wood smoke from the thousands of fires. The smoke clung to the settlement like a shroud.

"I guess a little wood smoke won't hurt us," Abby

said. "It's certainly better than eating raw food and going cold." He laughed as they drove back into Denver and through to the other side and the Stanwood town house.

Abby suddenly remembered what had happened to Leslie's father last night. She hadn't even mentioned it. That was unthinking of her.

"Oh, about your father. I'm sure it will work out all right. I mean about his being arrested."

Leslie looked straight ahead for a moment and he shivered. Then he relaxed and looked at her.

"Thank you. I had a talk with Judge Ambrose this morning. Terri and I are to be given use of the town house until the matter is settled. We'll have adequate funds to maintain the house and the staff, but we can't draw on the company funds. It's going to be a trial and a struggle, but we'll come out fine in the long run, I'm sure.

"But we'll have to be frugal. This may be the last fine dinner I can give, so let's go in and enjoy it."

The dinner was as good as the one before. This time they served sizzling steak with six vegetables, three kinds of rolls with jam and jelly, and a delicious soup and a salad, a cream pudding dessert, and delicately flavored coffee.

"If I ate this way very long, none of my clothes would fit me," Abby said. "Everything was so good I just couldn't stop eating."

It was almost six when they finished dessert, and they took their final glasses of wine out to a large veranda built on the west side of the first floor. They lounged on benches and waited for the sunset.

"Leslie, if the courts take everything away from your father, what will you do?"

"When that happens it looks like I'll have to settle down and find employment and earn my own living. I haven't had to do that yet. I could work when I wanted to. But soon I'll have to work, at least to earn enough money to live at some second-rate boarding-house.

"This place will be gobbled up by the courts and any heirs that they find in New York. The judge was quite frank with me about it. He said he had known Rufus Harland, and knew for a fact that the man had no children or wife. But he said there's a real chance that the original ranch, and all of the development of it and the other two businesses, will be forfeited because of the original fraud. Father could even face some time in prison."

"But that's not fair. The original ranch was only worth about fifteen thousand dollars, I heard. Now all three of the businesses are worth what?"

"Well over a million dollars, I'm told," Leslie said, and she saw the tightness come back around his mouth.

"Oh, my! That's really not fair. Your father did it all. He took fifteen thousand and turned it into a million dollars. The heirs should be praising him, not throwing him in jail."

Leslie smiled faintly. "You're a romantic, Abby Leggett. I'm a realist. If the court takes it all away, I can accept that. If my father has to go to prison, I can understand that. Even if I'm penniless and have to go to work to stay alive, that too I will get used to. I'm a realist, a practical man. I'll do whatever it takes to survive."

An hour later they watched the sun rim the mountains.

"I should be getting back," Abby said.

"You know the soft twilight makes you remarkably beautiful tonight," Leslie said. He bent and kissed her cheek and then came away.

"Oh, my. Leslie, you shouldn't have done that."

"I know. We've only just met. But I can tell that the two of us have a lot in common. Such a lot."

He reached for her, and Abby didn't pull away. His arms went around her and they stood facing each other. His face was a handsome mocking presence there only inches away.

Abby wanted to kiss his lips, just to see how it was different from kissing Spur. She wanted to throw her arms around him and kiss him a dozen times. A hot flame ignited deep inside her, and for a moment she let it burn and flare up and start her blood boiling. It felt so damn good!

Then with a terrible logic, she ground down the flame and made it sputter and die. Then she caught her longing with a firm hand and shattered it against reality.

Gently she took his hands off her waist and backed away.

"No, Leslie. We don't even have a chaperon. You've said nothing about a formal courting. I can't let you touch me that way. Will you please take me home now?"

The sudden spark that had come in his eyes faded as she stepped away. He took a deep breath, then stood as tall as he could and clicked his heels together.

"Yes, Miss Leggett, I'll have our driver come around. He'll be quite pleased to see you safely to the High Country Hotel."

She hesitated. "Leslie, I had a wonderful time today. It's just that there's a man back home who I really like a lot. It wouldn't be right, or fair to him. . . ." She looked away. "Thank you again, Mr. Stanwood. I had a wonderful time, and the dinner was delicious. I hope to see you again sometime."

He nodded, took her hand, and led her out to the carriage, which had been waiting at the front porch for an hour.

"Good night, Miss Leggett. May all of your dreams be pleasant ones."

She got in the carriage and waved at him. Then she took a deep breath and let it out slowly. She didn't know why, but there was something strange about Leslie Stanwood. It was nothing that he did or said. Perhaps it was only the way he looked at her sometimes. Abby shrugged. It was early. Maybe she could play some cards with Spur. Maybe learn more about poker. Maybe.

Chapter Twenty-Five

He picked her up in the worst saloon in town, the Last Roundup. It had only four whores working there and no madam. They played it almost any way they wanted to, and when he offered her forty dollars for all night, Maud told him to go out to the alley and she'd be right with him.

He touched the derringer in his pocket as he stood in the alley behind the Last Roundup Saloon. Nobody came out, not even to go to the privy. No one moved in the alley. Three minutes flat after he stepped into the alley, Maud came through the door wearing a street dress, a hat that pulled down over her face, and no gaudy makeup. She carried a package, but he didn't pay any attention to it.

"Figured you didn't want to advertise none," she said. "Yeah, I seen you around town. You're Leslie

Stanwood. Too bad about your old man, but long as you got cash, we can do business."

An hour before, he had rented a room in the Colorado Hotel, the worst hostelry in Denver, under the name of Andrew Blade. He thought the name was a good touch. They went down the alley, across the street, and into the next alley, and then were half a block from the side door of the Colorado Hotel.

"Just walk down the street like we belong here, and no son of a bitch is gonna notice us," Maud said. "Hey, cheer up, we're gonna have ourselves one hell of a night. Can you come eight times? I always try for eight with my all-nighters. Want you to think you're getting your fucking money's worth. Get it? Your fucking money's worth?"

Leslie didn't laugh at her joke, just propelled her down the street, in the side door, and along the hallway to the second door, Room Four.

"Yeah, nice and easy to get in and out," Maud said as he opened the door, which he had left unlocked, and they slipped in without a soul seeing them.

Maud lit the lamp. She'd been in this hotel before. She checked and made sure the shade was down. The window was on the side of the establishment that had a four-foot space between it and the pair of stores next door.

"Hell of a good view," Maud said, and giggled. She took the package out from her arm and unwrapped it. It contained a pint of whiskey and two bar glasses and a square of cheese.

"Hell, something extra. Most men start getting hungry and thirsty about the third time. You want a snort right now?"

He shook his head.

"Damn, I do." Maud opened the cork and tilted the pint of amber liquid, then lowered it, smacked her lips, and drove the cork back in the bottle with her fist.

"Yeah, now, you want the first one fast or slow? How about a little game. I'm this young maiden, see, and you grab me from behind and rape me. Oh, I'll struggle a little, but you can rip my bloomers off and everything and then take me from the back. I like to get poked from the backside. What do you think?"

Leslie shook his head. "No, no nothing like that. Just strip off your clothes and lets have a look at you."

She shrugged, and pulled open a few buttons and dropped the old print dress to the floor. She wore nothing else but a pair of soiled bloomers of dirty pink.

Leslie stared at her coldly, making no move to touch her.

"Maud, how did you get into this line of work?" he asked.

"Mostly my old man. He introduced me to the male cock when I was twelve. Then at fourteen I was as big as the other girls and he was selling my body in a little town down in Texas. The madams in town got mad at him and run us both out of the place. He kept at me twice a week in the next town, and he got a job, so he was stuck but I wasn't. I stole forty dollars from his wallet one night when he was drunk and caught the stage west as far as my money would take me.

"Then I been working the whore saloons ever since." She shrugged. "Hey, ain't all that bad. Most men are downright reasonable." She reached for his jacket. "Let's get your clothes off and get the first one going here. Then you'll relax just a hell of a lot."

Leslie growled and hit her with his fist so hard he knocked her across the room. She sprawled on the bed unconscious and with a broken jaw. He rubbed his hand and made some strange noises in his throat. Then he put a gag around her mouth and tied her hands behind her.

Not a good whore. She didn't even have big tits. He tied her ankles then, one to each side of the cheap iron bedstead. He untied her wrists and put them over her head and fastened them to the top of the bedstead with leather thongs he'd brought with him. She was spread-eagled on her back.

The headache came with a rush. He moaned and swayed and dropped to his knees trying to fight it off. It wouldn't go away. He got to his feet to push his head as far from his heart as he could, but still he could count every beat in the pulse as it sledgehammered in his brain.

Leslie moaned, and grabbed the bottle of whiskey and took a long pull on it, but it only burned his throat. He didn't think there was enough left there to get him drunk. Sometimes that worked. Sometimes that killed the headache.

Two minutes later the whiskey bottle was empty, and he threw it on the floor where it shattered. Somebody, evidently in the next room, pounded on the wall and said something he couldn't understand.

Yes, he had to be quiet. No more noise.

The fluttering black wings swept into the room and chased him, driving him into one corner, where he cowered against the wall. In a swift move he bent and pulled the long thin knife from his boot sheath and slashed at the black, ugly wings, driving them back. He cut them and they bled black blood, but he drove them farther and farther until they vanished, dissolving right through the wall into the hallway.

Leslie shook his head and looked at the girl on the bed. Whore! Jezebel! Fallen Woman! He bent over her and saw now that she was conscious. Her eyes moved back and forth as she tried to figure out what had happened. She turned her head and saw the way her hands were tied, and nodded. She said something, but he couldn't understand her through the gag.

Then her jaw must have hurt her because she cried.

"You're a filthy whore," he said softly to her. As he said it he sliced a line of blood across one breast. Her body stiffened and she screamed, but only a gurgle came through the gag. He had learned well how to make an effective gag.

"You're a filthy whore who preys on men!" he whispered to her, and slashed her upper arm, bringing a stream of blood that flowed down and at last dripped off her lower arm to the old blanket on the bed.

"Slut, Jezebel, wanton, whore!" Each time he spat out one of the words he cut her again, not deep, but so the wound would bleed enough to cause her great pain.

Before he could think up more words he heard his mother calling him and he slumped to the floor. He would hide here and she couldn't find him. Then he wouldn't have to play the game with her again.

Sure it felt good for a minute or two, but then he screamed at himself because he knew it was wrong. He was 18 already, and still his mother played games with him. She made him do the most terrible things. She told him a good woman had three holes and a man had to know how to use all three of them. Then she made him do all three, and he was usually sick after she left the room.

She always hummed and told him how big and strong he was, and what a fine pecker he had, and how he was going to make some woman a damn fine fucking husband some day.

"The slut!" he whispered to himself. "The damn slut!"

Then he was gone in a memory whirl that started when he was only ten and his mother was giving him a bath and washing him everywhere. He figured he was too old for her to be giving him a bath. But she insisted. His mother always insisted.

He shook his head. What time was it? How long had he been remembering? He saw by his pocket watch that it was only nine-thirty. Good.

He got to his feet and watched the girl Maud. The whore Maud. She had done her last man, only she didn't know it. He slashed her ten times in a row and watched her faint from the pain. Then he stopped and waited until she revived. He took water from the pitcher and wet her face so she'd come back to consciousness again.

When she did he smiled at her.

"Maud, Maud. You've been a bad girl, and now you're going to pay for all of that sinning and for being a slut and a whore. You're going to pay with pain. A thousand cuts. Have you heard of the Chi-

nese form of torture? Probably not. They take a
prisoner and cut him a thousand times, and make
him bleed. You're bleeding now just fine, Maud, not
too fast, but enough to make it hurt so bad."

She passed out again.

He couldn't help but spin back in time once more.
He had planned so carefully how he would kill his
mother. She might as well have killed *him*. She had
ruined him for any other woman. She had stifled his
natural instincts. She had kept him from working
on the range so he'd come to think such work was
unmanly, not worthy of his time.

He had planned to kill her slowly, make her suffer
the way he did. Then he would bury her body so no
one would ever know. She would simply have vanished.

As it turned out she did vanish, but not the way he
wanted her to. She was alive, still alive, and he was
hoping to find her. His next trip he would go to San
Francisco. The railroad was through now. He could
ride all the way. Yes, he would go to San Francisco.
She might be out there.

He stood and looked down at Maud. She was
awake again, her eyes frantic now, her mouth working but no sounds coming through. Her breasts
would be next, not large, but big enough. He lifted
the knife and knew just what to do.

When Leslie stopped using the knife it had been
over two hours. Her breath came in ragged gasps
now. Very little blood came from new cuts. There
wasn't much left. He stood over her. He was blood-
splattered now, his clothes ruined. He would burn
them the way he had before.

He checked his watch. Almost midnight. She had

lasted longer than any of the others. It was time. He took the knife and thrust it between her ribs into her heart. She gave a gasp and then died.

It took him a half hour to cut off the gag and the short pieces of leather that had held her arms and legs. Leave nothing behind. He had learned his lesson well. He still didn't know how he had dropped that handkerchief. But he had.

He checked the room again. Nothing remained that could be tied to him. He slid the knife back in his boot and unlocked the hotel room door. A quick look showed no one in the hallway. The outside door was only 15 feet away.

He slid outside, closed the door, and was six feet from the door when someone barged through the side entrance and slammed into him. It was a man and a woman. She screamed and looked up, and the man caught her and mumbled an apology, and then they both vanished down the hallway and into a room.

Leslie was too stunned to move for a moment. Then he rushed out the side door and ran down the street to the alley. No one else had seen him, only the woman and the man. Had she seen his face? Was she sober enough to remember it?

A hundred questions drilled at him as he walked quickly through the alleys and then took the last street to the Stanwood town house. He slipped in the basement door and stripped off his clothes. Quickly he put them in the furnace, poured kerosene over them, and set them on fire. He stood there in his short underwear and undershirt watching the fire burn. All of his clothes would be gone by morning. Nothing left. They usually didn't have a fire in the furnace this time of year. The big wood burning box was half full of ashes. He'd remind the caretaker to move the ashes tomorrow.

He was in his room when he heard a knock on the door. When he opened it, he found Terri there in a bathrobe. Her eyes glanced at his underwear and she grinned.

"I've been waiting for you to come home. You said you'd talk to the judge. What did he say?"

Leslie took a deep breath and waved his sister into the room. They sat on the edge of the bed, and he told her the bad news about the house and the fortune that probably wouldn't be theirs.

When he finished, she stood and walked around the room.

"Damn. Just when I thought I could get some money and go to Chicago." She shrugged. "I guess that's out now. We'll have to wait and see what the court decides. That could take a year."

She paced up and down, but watched her brother. "Leslie, what's the matter?"

"I don't know what you mean."

"I remember when you used to be naughty. You'd break one of mother's favorite dishes or something and you'd come running to my room to hide. You always wanted me to hold you tight and protect you. Did you break more of mother's dishes again?"

"Not exactly."

"I knew that Mother was . . . was not being good to you. That sometimes she was with you and you both had your clothes off. She made advances to you, didn't she?"

"I didn't think you knew."

"You came to me afterwards, lots of times. I

figured it out. But now, you must have broken another dish."

"In a way I did. Would you hold me?"

She put her arms around him and held him tightly. Then she began to sing a song she hadn't thought of for years. Five minutes later he stretched out on his bed and dropped off to sleep. Terry smiled and put a sheet over him and blew out the light. In some ways her big brother was still a little boy.

Chapter Twenty-Six

Spur and Sheriff Warner were on their second cup of coffee in his office the next morning when the call came in. The owner of the Colorado Hotel ran into the outer room screeching and in shock.

"Damn, somebody got murdered—butchered is a better word! Come quick!" He stopped and shook his head and tears squeezed out of his eyes. "Hell, ain't no damn rush. She's so dead nothing gonna help her."

Spur, the sheriff, and two deputies ran to Room Four at the Colorado Hotel and pushed open the door.

"My God!" Sheriff Warner said.

Spur caught the sheriff's arm and pulled him out of the room.

"Sheriff, please don't touch anything. This has to be our whore killer. Who's the girl?"

The sheriff motioned for one of his men to step into the room and take a look.

"Yeah, Sheriff, that's her all right. Maud, one of the whores down at the Last Roundup Saloon. She's been in trouble before."

"This is the last time she ever gets in trouble," Spur said. He began examining the body without touching it. Both breasts had been cut out, and there probably were a hundred knife slashes on the body. The blankets were soaked with blood. Three flies feasted on some of the blood that hadn't dried yet. He brushed them away.

Spur found the broken whiskey bottle in the corner, then saw the two glasses and cheese on the top of the dresser.

"Looks like they made a party of it," Sheriff Warner said.

Spur kept checking the rest of the room. He looked on the floor, under the bed, in all the dresser drawers. The pitcher of water had been partly used but not the bowl. Odd.

He found bloody marks on the door handle.

One of the deputies came in and reported that there was a bloody mark on the wall outside down from the door. Spur checked it out, and went to talk to the owner at the front desk.

"I want to know everyone who registered on the first floor for last night," he said.

"Six people," the owner said quickly. "I usually ain't full. Two of them were single men looking for jobs in the mines. One was a cowboy heading for Cheyenne. One was a drummer pushing household brushes, and the other two were Mr. and Mrs. John Smith."

Spur snorted. "You know the Smiths?"

"Fact is I do know John, but he wasn't supposed to be here. Mrs. Smith wasn't the real Mrs. Smith."

"And John Smith isn't his name. Who is he and who was she? This is a murder case and damned important."

"Damnit, you know I can't tell you all that. I got to be discreet when things go on that shouldn't. No skin off my shins. You sure I got to tell you?"

"Unless you want to get thrown in jail for a few days to think it over. What's it going to be?"

"Gent's name is Bob Vuylsteke. He's the jeweler here in town. His lady friend is one of his clerks in the store he runs along with the jewelry business."

"I want the names of the other tenants for last night. Any of them still here?"

Two were, and he talked to them. They hadn't seen anything unusual. One of them, who stayed in Room Six right beside Four, said he heard some loud noises about nine or nine-thirty, but he pounded on the wall and it quieted down.

The two miners had taken off early that morning to get in on a hiring out at one of the gold mines.

The undertaker was in the room when Spur got back. He shrugged.

"Might as well take her away," Spur said. "I've seen enough here." He stood outside in the hall and slammed his palm against the wall. Sheriff Warner came out and scowled.

"I don't like this maniac running loose in my town," Warner said. "He's so damn clever. Nobody saw him go in, probably nobody saw him come out."

"The saloon," Spur said. "He must have picked her up there. When does that one open?"

"Hell, it's open all night and all day. It's the worst hole in town."

"Where else would you go to pick up a victim?" Spur ran out of the hotel and down Main Street to the Last Roundup Saloon. There was only one customer. He was sitting at a table, leaning over with his head on his arms, and snoring. A half-filled glass of stale-looking beer was at his elbow. The barkeep looked up from a magazine. "Yeah?"

"You on last night?"

"Nope, not until six this morning."

"When do the girls get up?"

"You want one or two?"

"Just some talk. Lawman business. Go roust them all out. Tell them they have five minutes to get dressed and down here. They don't have to be all fancy."

The barkeep shrugged. "Hell, they gonna bitch and scream."

"Doesn't matter. Get them down here."

It took ten minutes before all three sat at a table in back and glared at Spur. He walked up and nodded. They were in various types of dress, from a loosely wrapped robe to a street-dress outfit.

"Ladies, my name is Spur McCoy and I have the task of telling you that Maud was killed last night."

One of the girls gasped, another shrugged. The third's face went white and she gripped the edge of the table.

"I told her not to go," the white-faced one said.

"What's your name?"

"Ursula."

"You told Maud not to leave with a man last night?"

"Yeah. Told her. I saw her talking with him. A Fancy Dan. Clean white shirt, necktie, fancy vest and jacket, pants that had been pressed with creases. Told her not to go with him."

"Did you know who the man was?"

"Not sure."

"We're pretty sure that was the man who killed Maud last night. Ursula, think hard. Who was the man she left with?"

"He's never been in here before. I used to see him sometimes on the streets. I remember him three or four years ago. He must have been eighteen or nineteen. Handsome young man. Saw him with his father sometimes. I just can't remember who either of them were."

"You think about it, Ursula. If you get a name, you run . . . I said run . . . right down to the sheriff's office and tell anyone there who you think the man was. You understand?"

"Yes, I'll try. I really will. I liked Maud. She was a real friend to me."

"I'll be back to see you this noon, Ursula. You do some powerful thinking between then and now. It might help if you remember what the young man's father did, what kind of work."

Spur turned and walked out of the saloon. It wasn't ten o'clock yet. He went to the only jewelry store in town, Vulysteke Jewelers. He walked in, checked the store layout, and found that the jewelry business was on one side, with a watch and clock repair section, and a giftware and fancy dishware and china store on the other side.

He went to the watch repair section and found a thin man with dark hair bent over a naked pocket watch movement on his bench. The man wore a magnifier in his eye, and only looked up when Spur cleared his throat.

"Bob Vuylsteke?"

"Right, what can I do for you?"

"You can help me identify a cold-blooded, crazy man who has killed eleven women that we know of and will kill a lot more unless you help me stop him."

The man chuckled. "Afraid you have me mixed up with somebody else. I'm a jeweler, not an international jewel thief."

"You're Bob Vuylsteke and you were in Room Two last night at the Colorado Hotel."

"How in hell . . ." He stopped. "Just who are you, mister?"

"Name is Spur McCoy and I'm a United States Secret Service agent working for the President. I need to have a long, private talk with you."

"Hell, last time I ever go to that damn hotel. Nobody's damn business—"

"I'm not trying to expose your indiscretions, Mr. Vuylsteke. Now where can we talk?"

They went to his small office in the back of the store, and Spur told the man exactly what had happened in the room next to his last night. Vuylsteke shivered, and before the story was over he was gasping.

"My God! That must have been the same man we bumped into when we came in. We had been gambling, and just got back to the room about midnight somewhere. My God!"

He stood and went to a closet and pulled out a jacket. There were deep reddish-black stains on the sleeve. He held it up and frowned. "Mr. McCoy, is this blood? It sure looks like it. I must have got this blood off that man we bumped into."

Spur examined it and sniffed. "It's blood, all right. This man you bumped against. What did he look like? How tall was he? How big? Did you see his face?"

Vuylsteke held up his hands. "I don't know. I was drunk. I don't remember even seeing his face. But Mar . . ." He stopped. "The lady I was with said she saw him plainly." He hung up the coat and went back behind his desk.

"The trouble is, I'm a happily married man. Last night was just a fling, a wild, stupid night out. It was something I shouldn't have done. If it gets out that I . . . I mean, the woman will be ruined and my wife will probably leave me and take the kids, and my business here will be ruined as well. The public needs to trust a jeweler, the way they do a banker. Don't make me tell you."

"I can, you know. I can swear out a felony warrant on you and put you in jail until you tell me what you did that night, who you were with, and everything that happened. Of course, that would all be open to the public and the newspaper reporters."

"No, no, don't do that." He stood and paced the floor of the small office. "Could . . . could you be delicate? The woman works here, and we both had too much to drink. She's as ashamed of it as I am. But if you could do it quietly . . ."

"We should be able to arrange that. I'll be sitting alone in the coffee shop across the street. You have her come in and sit at my table and we'll talk quietly. Remember, this man has killed eleven women already. If he thinks this lady can identify him, he'll surely make her his next victim. Will you send the lady over?"

"Yes, but be gentle and dignified with her. I don't want her hurt by this."

Spur left the office and walked out of the store. Across the street, he ordered two cups of coffee and two doughnuts and waited. He had taken only one bite from his doughnut when a woman came in the front door, looked around, saw him, and walked straight to his table.

"Mr. McCoy?"

He nodded, and she slumped in the chair. "I don't know what happened last night. I've never done anything like this before, and . . ."

Spur held up his hand. "Did you see the man who got blood on Mr. Vuylsteke's jacket?"

"Yes, plainly. Brown hair, a youngish face, twenty-four, maybe twenty-five. Slender, as I recall, and no scars or moles on his face. Quite a handsome young man. He wore a jacket, shirt, and tie. When he bumped us he left a long streak of blood on my dress. I noticed it as soon as I got home, and I washed it out with cold water before it set."

"Did you know who the young man was?"

"No. I've seen him around town before. But I just can't be sure of a name. Let me think about it for some time. I might get a name associated with some other event and be able to put the name to him."

"We don't have much time. You heard about the woman who was murdered in the room next to yours last night?"

She looked down. "Yes, I heard. I cried for her."

"You may have to do more crying if you don't

come up with the name. You see, he must have seen you as well, and if he thinks that you can identify him, he very well could make you his next victim."

She gasped and pulled back.

"I've warned Mr. Vuylsteke. I hope you don't live alone."

"No, with my older mother."

"I'll have the sheriff put a guard in your house when you're there."

"All night?"

"That's when this man does his killing. You come up with his name as soon as you can so we can capture him."

Spur took another sip of his coffee and went out the door. The woman stared at him, her coffee and doughnut untouched on the table. A moment later she stood and hurried out of the cafe and across to the jewelry store.

Spur watched her go. She was his best hope yet, she and the softhearted whore at the Last Roundup Saloon. If either of them came up with a name he'd have a chance.

Spur hadn't seen Abby this morning since breakfast. She said she was going to do some shopping and then just waste the rest of the day.

He checked with the undertaker.

"Find anything unusual besides the slashes and the butchering job he did?"

"A couple of things," the round-faced undertaker said. "Her face and hair were not touched. Not a scratch, which seems unusual balanced against the state of the rest of her body. Then the other unusual finding was that her vagina had not been violated in any way.

"There was no sexual penetration or any insertion of any other blunt or sharp instrument. No sexual torture other than her breast removal."

"What does that mean?" Spur asked.

"Damned if I know. Just figured it was strange."

"How did she die?"

"First I thought it was loss of blood, but there was one deft stroke with a long thin knife between her ribs and right into her heart. That was the final thrust that killed her."

"But only after she had bled a great deal and suffered. Oh, she evidently didn't make any noise in the hotel. Why?"

"Marks around the sides of her mouth and cheeks," the body man said. "She had been gagged tightly so she couldn't make more than a groan.

"And there were bruises and scrapes and torn skin on her ankles and wrists, as if she had been tied up. Spread-eagled on the bed most likely."

"Nice guy, this killer. Thanks. I appreciate your help." Spur left the death room and wandered up the street. It was close enough to noon. He went to the Last Roundup Saloon. Ursula was busy. He waited for half an hour and she came down, lines of sweat still on her forehead. She dabbed at the sweat, and when she saw Spur she started to back away.

He caught her wrist and they sat down at a table.

"I don't want to talk to you, Mr. McCoy."

"Why not, Ursula? How can I hurt you? I'm hunting a killer, not trying to hurt you."

"You can hurt me terribly. There are powerful men in this town and if they don't like you, you don't get any business or you simply vanish in the night and most everyone thinks you took the stage, but what really happened is the girl is dead and buried deep. I've seen it happen."

"What are you talking about?"

"Girls who work here who aren't here anymore. A man in town wasn't nice to some of the girls."

"How can that hurt you, Ursula?"

"I could be killed next."

Spur stood and walked around the table. "Ursula, I don't understand. Why would you be next?"

"Because I think I know who the man was who took Maud out to the alley last night."

Spur sat down and held her hand. "You tell me and I guarantee that no one will hurt you. You can live at the sheriff's office for the next few days until I catch this madman."

"Oh, no, I'm not worried about the madman. It's his father I'm afraid of."

Spur squinted and turned his head away, then looked back. "You're worried about his father? Who are we talking about here? Who do you think that you saw leaving with Maud last night?"

"If I tell you, will you protect me, not let anybody hurt me?"

"Absolutely. I guarantee we'll protect you. Who was the man who left with Maud? Who do you think the man was who killed her?"

Chapter Twenty-Seven

Ursula looked at Spur and shivered. "You must protect me. His father is an extremely powerful man."

"Yes, yes, yes! We'll protect you. You can stay beside me twenty-four hours a day. Now give me a name."

"I think the man I saw leave with Maud could have been . . . Leslie Stanwood."

"Stanwood? The son, Leslie?" Spur scowled. "Some of our evidence could point toward him. Are you definitely sure that it was Leslie Stanwood?"

"No, not positive. I've seen him only a few times, but he was dressed the same way, like a swell. I saw the side of his face and the features were the same. If I had to guess, I'd say it was Leslie Stanwood."

"Would you swear to that in court?"

"I don't know. I'd have to say that I thought it was Leslie Stanwood, but I couldn't be sure."

"Great. That doesn't help me one whole lot. As far as being afraid of Thurlow Stanwood, you can forget that. He's in jail on a fraud and grand larceny charge and he won't be getting out. So don't be frightened." Spur stood and walked around the saloon. The girl stayed where she was, seated at a back table.

He came back and stared down at her. "You can't be positive, but you *think* that the man was Stanwood."

"Yes, Mr. McCoy. I can't be sure."

"At least that's a pointing. We have some other evidence and it can also point to Leslie. Maybe that's enough. Certainly not enough to convict him— but maybe enough to scare him and make him run."

He thanked Ursula. "If I find out anything else I'll let you know. If you think of anything that makes you more positive, you get in touch with me at the High Country Hotel."

Spur was halfway back to the sheriff's office when he remembered the woman at the jewelry store. She'd had some time to stew and think about it as well. He changed directions, and walked up the street to the store and entered.

Vulysteke saw him coming and hurried up. "Martha wants to talk to you. I think she remembered something."

"Any idea what it is?"

"She wouldn't tell me. She's frightened. Hell, so am I. If he thinks we recognized him, he'd have to kill both of us, I guess."

Martha came around a counter and saw Spur. She put down some papers and walked quickly toward him. He motioned her into the office where he had talked with her boss. Spur closed the door, and she looked first at Vuylsteke, then at Spur.

"I think I remember where I saw the two men, especially the younger one. It was one of the celebrations they have now and then here in Denver. This one was the Yahoo Roundup, a mock gathering of the herd, only they gathered people and it was a big charity event.

"Anyway, I was there and that's when I saw both of them. The younger man was with a man I remember well now. He was Thurlow Stanwood. So that makes the young man with him his son, Leslie Stanwood. That's the man I saw briefly in the hallway, I'm positive. The man with blood on his clothes and a surprised look on his face was Leslie Stanwood."

"Will you identify him in court if it comes to that?"

"Absolutely. There's nothing to fear from his father now that he's in jail too."

Spur grinned. "That makes two votes for Leslie. I think it's about time I had a talk with that young man. Oh, I don't want either of you to say a word about this. It's my hope that we won't have to go to court with this case. Make it easier all the way around." He shook hands with both of them and hurried out of the office and the store.

It took Spur five minutes to walk to the Stanwood town house. It looked the same. There was no maid to answer the front door. Terri did it herself. She smiled when she saw Spur.

"Well now, what a nice surprise after so much bad news. Come in, come in and let's talk."

He stepped inside, and Terri moved close to him and kissed him hard on the lips. She grinned and edged back.

"Hey, I've been wanting to do that again ever since you left here. Did you come to give your condolences or to get kissy and take off all of our clothes?"

"That's damn tempting, I admit." He reached down and picked her up and kissed her thoroughly, then eased her back to the floor.

"Well, now, we could continue doing that here in the hall or we can go directly to my bedroom."

He took her hand and steered her into the parlor. "First we have to talk."

She snuggled up to him and pulled one of his hands over so it covered her breast. He could feel the heat of her through the light dress.

"You talk. I'll feel your hard body."

"Terri, how well do you know your brother?"

"Better than anyone else in the world, including my father. Leslie is not a happy person."

"Does he travel much? Was he out of town, say, about six weeks ago for a period of almost a month?"

"How did you know?" She looked at him and frowned. "This isn't just some boyish prank that Leslie is in trouble for this time, is it?"

He shook his head. Terri sighed. She pushed one hand inside his shirt past an opened button. "Matter of fact, Leslie did go to Kansas City about six weeks ago. He went on the train, then down from somewhere by stage to Kansas City. They might even have a train down there by now.

"Then he came back here from Kansas City by stage through a lot of little towns."

"He got back about two weeks ago, just before I came into town and saved your father that money near the bank, right?"

"Yes. I remember because Father told Leslie that he had to be back in time for the Saturday barbecue out at our ranch. He made it. So did you."

Spur stroked her breast almost without thinking about it. She purred softly and kissed his neck.

Terri, have you ever seen one of these?" He reached in his pocket and took out a 20-cent piece. She turned it over in her hand and shrugged.

"I think so. That's a twenty-cent piece. Most of the people don't use them because they are almost the same size as a quarter. I always get them mixed up myself. I heard someone say they won't last long."

"Does Leslie ever use them?"

"Sure, that's where I saw them. He says he loves to use them because the merchants hate them, but they have to accept them. Leslie is a little strange that way."

"Leslie is what, about twenty-two now?"

"No, he's a little over twenty-three."

"He isn't married. Has he ever been married?"

"No, not Leslie."

"What's his relationship with women? I mean does he like them, go out on social engagements, go courting, that sort of thing?"

"Sometimes. Why are you asking this? Don't you think it's time you tell me exactly how bad the trouble is that Leslie is involved in?"

"Not yet. No, really. I can't. You're saying that Leslie likes women, but he doesn't like women."

"Yes, that's right. Oh, damn. I shouldn't be telling you this. Leslie was always our mother's favorite. She fawned over him, she made things for him, bought him presents. Then when he was twelve or thirteen it changed, and he seemed to resent the special treatment.

"I found out why one day when I heard noises in Leslie's bedroom and I turned the knob slowly and opened the door without making a sound. Leslie was about fourteen then and he and Mother . . . I mean, they were both naked on his bed and she was teaching him . . . she was showing him how to have sex. They didn't see me. Then they did it. I couldn't stop watching. I'd never seen anything like that in my life.

"The next day I made Leslie do to me what he did to Mother. I told him if he didn't I'd tell Father. That was the first time I had sex. He said Mother made him do it, that she'd been playing with him and using him since he was twelve."

"So he hated his mother."

"Not at first, but I guess it kept on right up to the time Mother left home. You know about that."

Spur nodded.

"Toward the end I saw them again. I tried to sneak up on them after a while, just to watch. Crazy, right? But then toward the end Mother had to threaten him and force him. Yes, toward the end I'm sure he hated Mother."

"Did he ever try to hurt her, to kill her?"

"No, of course not."

Terri's eyes widened, she gasped. "You mean

those three women in town who were . . . who were murdered? You think it might have been Leslie?"

"There's a chance. We have a witness who said it could have been Leslie she saw with one of the dead women. We have some clues. Maybe you can help prove it *wasn't* Leslie."

"My God! Leslie. I think he built up enough anger over the years that he probably was thinking about killing Mother. He hated her so terribly. Oh, you said I might be able to help Leslie. How can I help?"

"Is Leslie here?"

"No, he left before noon. Took the carriage. I don't know where he was going."

"Are most of his clothes here?"

"Yes, he lives in town now. I live both places."

"Could we see if he has a dress jacket with a button missing?"

Five minutes later they found the jacket in his closet. All three of the mallard buttons were in place. Spur took the jacket to the window and looked at it more closely. Inside where the spare button had been sewn, there were only a series of small holes, needle holes where it had been fastened.

He looked at the sewing and the thread on the three buttons. Two of them were the same. The middle one was sewn on in the same manner, but with a slightly darker thread.

"One of the victims had a button like these in her closed hand when we found her," Spur said.

Terri blinked back tears. "Damn, Leslie. You could have talked to me about it!"

"I'll have to take this jacket as evidence."

She nodded.

"Now, what about a trash barrel or a burn barrel? How do you dispose of your household trash?"

"Some of it we bury, some we burn in a barrel outside. Then there's the furnace, but it isn't used in the summer."

They looked at all of them, and in the furnace he found the half-burned flap of a jacket pocket. He fished it out of the ashes and dusted it off.

"That's from one of Leslie's jackets," Terri said. "One of his favorites."

Spur saw heavy dark bloodstains on it, but he didn't mention it.

"Any idea where Leslie went today?" Spur asked, his voice tight, showing urgency.

"He didn't say. I'll ask the cook. The court said we could keep on one servant." They went to the kitchen, where the cook was starting to get supper ready. Terri talked with the sturdy, well-fed cook for a moment in low tones. When she came back she frowned.

"Cook says he left about eleven o'clock, but first he asked her to make a special picnic lunch. He said he was going to surprise a special pretty girl and take her for a picnic out along the river."

"Did he say who?"

"She asked him, but he said it was no one that cook knew."

"Abby," Spur said softly. "The woman I work with has been out to dinner with Leslie twice now. She thinks that's he shy and harmless."

"He wouldn't hurt her, would he?"

"The pattern with his other crimes seems to be that Leslie kills women who are whores or who are generous with their womanly charms, loose women and those he can seduce."

"Where would he go?" Terri wondered. "He loved the river. He had several favorite places. Let's hitch up the light rig and I'll show you where he often went when he was feeling happy or when he was furious with Mother. He could be at any of five or six places."

Spur checked the time on his watch. It was a little after one P.M. "Yes, Terri, yes, let's get that rig hitched up. Abby might be in desperate danger right now."

Alfonso Ortega rode into town on his mule pulling a small cart he used to haul supplies back to the ranch. He had left his family in the hidden tent well away from his homestead and cabin. The sheep were well hidden. For two days he had watched to the northwest, but he had seen no riders coming his way. He couldn't understand it. Surely Stanwood would make a murderous assault on his place.

Ortega tied up outside the general store he liked and went in with his order. It was a spartan list of supplies. Flour, sugar, salt, a dozen apples, a bag of local cherries, and some peaches that had come in on the train. He bought three new pair of pants for the boys, and needles and thread and a pair of shearing clippers the merchant had ordered for him from Chicago.

When the bill was totaled up, Jed Longly looked at the sheep man. "Comes to twenty-two dollars and forty-three cents. I threw in an extra pound of cherries."

Ortega frowned. He reached in his pocket and took out the last cash money he had, a gold double eagle.

"Looks like we'll have to take back the pants, Mr. Longly. I'm a little short." Ortega handed the merchant the gold coin.

"Close enough for now. I'll put the two and forty on your tab."

"Don't take credit or charity, Mr. Longly."

"Hell, this ain't either one. Half the folks in Denver owe me a few dollars. Almost all of them pay. Know you will. You got wool to ship, right? Bank will loan you cash for the shipping cost. Then in two or three weeks a letter will come in on the train with a bank draft. It's called credit, Mr. Ortega. Getting to be the going thing.

"Now you take these goods and say howdy to the missus for me."

Ortega stood there a moment, tears almost brimming out of his eyes. He took two big breaths and nodded. "Guess I can do it this once. Going to make a go of that homestead of mine, in spite of the Flying S Ranch. Stanwood is pressuring me some."

"Stanwood? Oh, hell, guess you ain't heard. He won't bother you no more." The merchant outlined the trouble the rancher was in. "Word around town is that he's going to lose the whole thing, ranch, mine, and lumber mill. Stole the damn ranch ten years ago. Ever hear of such a thing?"

"Is this really happening?" Ortega asked.

"Right as rain, Mr. Ortega. If Stanwood was bothering you about your sheep, you don't have to worry a whit about him no more. He's as good as in the territorial prison right now."

Alfonso Ortega smiled. "Mr. Longly, that is good news. I wonder if I might impose on you for two more small items. I'd be ever so thankful for some real tobacco for my pipe. I've been out now for about six months. Then I'd like a dress for my wife. She ain't had one in three years or so."

A half hour later, Alfonso Ortega loaded his cart and turned the mule back toward his homestead. First he'd get his family back in the cabin. Then he'd start the shearing. Jose could help this year. He'd need to build racks to put the wool in to haul it to town. For that he'd need a bigger wagon and a team of draft horses. He'd talk to the bank next week about borrowing money against his wool. With the market up this year he figured his long wool would bring in more than a thousand dollars cash money.

Ortega whistled as he walked beside the rig and drove the mule back toward his cabin.

Spur McCoy and Terri Stanwood had driven north along Cherry Creek for three miles and found two of the places that Leslie had told his sister about, but he was not at either of them.

They turned and Spur drove faster back to town. "So we try to the south. The river gets smaller there and there are some nice places off the road. We'll check out each one of them as they come."

It took them a half hour to come to the first one. No one was there or had been there. Spur got out of the rig and looked at the trail that followed the river. There were half a dozen prints of horses, and he spotted the wide tracks of a wagon or a carriage.

Terri looked at them as well. She frowned. "I'm no good at this sort of thing. But it could be. This is the most logical way that he would have come. Leslie is a creature of habit. He likes to do things that work, and go places where he feels secure and where he's been before."

Spur thought of the Chicago ice pick and frowned. That certainly was something that worked that Leslie had used repeatedly. The farther they drove the more certain Spur was that Leslie Stanwood was the killer.

Now his job was to find him and Abby. He was sure that Abby was with him. Leslie had taken her to dinner twice in two days, and Abby probably had been at the hotel most of the morning where Leslie could find her. He was a smooth and courteous man. He'd persuade her to go on a picnic.

Spur slapped the reins down on the back of the sorrel pulling the buggy, and Terri held on to his arm as the rig raced forward faster and bounced over the rutted dirt trail.

He had to find her and find her soon. Damn, why couldn't he see this coming?

Chapter Twenty-Eight

Leslie Stanwood walked into the High Country hotel a little after noon and went up to Abby Leggett's second-floor room. He knocked, and held a bunch of violets in his hand as she opened the door.

"Pretty flowers for a beautiful lady," he said, offering the violets.

Abby had been brushing out her long red hair, and she still held the brush in one hand. She tossed the groomer on the bed and took the flowers, a wonderful smile wreathing her face.

"How thoughtful! What a nice thing to do. Let me put them in some water so they'll last." She left the door open and found a glass, poured water in it from the pitcher, and arranged the violets.

"There, now they'll last for days."

"Miss Leggett. It's a beautiful summer day. I have a picnic lunch and the carriage. How would you like to come on a picnic down by the river? We can even go wading in the water again if you like."

"A picnic? Goodness, it's been years since I've been on a real one. Would there be sandwiches and ants and just everything?"

Leslie smiled. He liked this uncomplicated girl with the waist-length red hair. "Of course, lots of ants. I'll find them myself."

"Yes, an outing sounds like fun. But I'll have to change." She motioned him out the open door. "You wait for me in the lobby. About ten minutes. Will the lunch spoil?"

"Ten minutes will be fine. I'll read the newspaper. Remember, we'll have a blanket on the grass and everything." He smiled as he pulled the door closed and headed for the lobby.

It was nearly an hour later when they spread a red plaid blanket under some tall oak trees on lush grass beside Cherry Creek. The stream made a small curve in front of them, and there were rapids on the far side where the water chattered and splashed over the rocks.

Leslie brought a wicker basket from the carriage and put it in the middle of the blanket.

"Let me look inside!" Abby pleaded. He nodded, and she began to take out covered dishes and carefully wrapped packages. She found roast beef sandwiches, ham sandwiches, and cheese and bacon sandwiches.

"You invited the whole regiment along from the fort?" she asked.

"Wanted to have something that you liked. No chances this way. I'm partial to the cheese and bacon. I could probably live on them three times a day and be happy."

There was potato salad, pickles, and five large slices of three different kinds of pie—cherry, apple, and rhubarb.

"So much food, I'll get fat by the time we drive back to town."

"Not true. You run off everything you eat. You're what my father calls a hard feeder, an animal that just won't get fat. You feed it all it can eat and it doesn't gain a pound. Hard feeders. You're lucky."

"Well, I decided that I won't get fat, so I'm being careful. Are you ready to eat?" She gave him a napkin and set out the sandwiches and salad.

He took from the basket a heavy crock pitcher that had been wrapped with warm insulating towels.

"Hot coffee," he said. "Don't let it be said that Leslie Stanwood forgot a thing on this picnic."

They ate, and threw acorns into the stream, and talked about places they wanted to visit. Abby had two sandwiches and a mound of the potato salad and then a piece of cherry pie.

"I can't believe how much I eat when I'm with you, Leslie. I think you're a secret agent of some evil food supplier who has as his goal getting me fat."

They both laughed. When the lunch was over, they moved the blanket into the sun to warm up, and he touched her long red hair.

"It must take a lot of work to keep your hair so beautiful," he said.

"No, I just wash it twice a week and spend three hours a day combing and brushing it. No trouble at all."

"You're a strange girl, Abby. I know almost nothing about you. You were born in Kansas City. What about your family?"

"Hard-working parents. Not much else to tell. Oh, I'm sorry about your father. It's going to be hard on you and your sister, I'd guess."

"Hard enough. I think he'll come out of it without any prison time. He's going to claim a deathbed statement by the colonel in which the man gave the ranch to Father, but he had no legal proof. So it wouldn't be fraud or theft at all, just a little manipulation to establish what the deceased wanted all along."

"Do you think that will work?"

"He's got the best lawyer in town, so it certainly might. We'll have to wait and see."

"Let's go get our feet wet!" Abby said, changing the subject to something more pleasant. "You turn around while I take off my hose, and no peeking!"

He chuckled, and turned and threw acorns into the water. When he looked back at her, she was squealing at the chill water as she waded into it up to her ankles, holding her skirts around her knees.

He pulled off his boots and socks and rolled up his pants legs.

They splashed, and built a little dam of rocks at a shallow place, and once Abby almost sat down in the water. He caught her and held her up, his arms tightly round her, her breasts pressing against his chest. Their faces were close together. She pushed away from him and caught her balance.

"Oh, dear, that would have been a disaster. Thanks, Leslie, for rescuing me."

"Just part of my job as protector of the weak and terribly beautiful," he said.

"There you go again with that line of talk. I swear, Leslie, I don't know what I'm going to do with you." She waded out of the water then and fell on the blanket in the sun.

"Oh, that sun feels so good, so warm!" Abby said.

Leslie sat down beside her, and took a towel from the basket and dried off her feet. "I knew we'd need this to take care of our wet feet."

They sat there a minute without talking. Then she watched him. He was perfectly relaxed. He sighed and stretched, then lay down on the blanket on his back.

"Oh, yes, now this is the life. Wading in the creek, a beautiful girl beside me, and relaxing in the warm sun. You should try it."

"You're being a flatterer again," she said. But she liked it, she admitted to herself. Leslie Stanwood was becoming more and more appealing to her. Why not?

She eased down on the blanket on her back two feet from where he lay. She shaded her eyes and relaxed. "Yes, this is nice, Leslie. The warm sun, the light breeze, and the chatter of the stream. I could go to sleep easily." She closed her eyes.

A moment later her eyes snapped open and she saw Leslie hovering over her. His face was only inches away.

"Abby, you're affecting me strangely, you know that? Maybe I can get over it quickly with one kiss. Would that be all right?"

"No, Leslie. I made that clear before. Most couples don't kiss until they are at least engaged."

He lifted away. "Engaged. Hell, I'm never going to marry anyone. I don't like most women."

Abby lifted up on her elbows. "That's natural. I don't like some women either. But all you have to do is to like, to love, just one woman. The right woman. You'll change your mind one of these days. Not me, but some little lady will come along and knock you right off your feet."

"I don't think so. I've . . . I've had some unfortunate experiences with women."

"You'll forget all that. The good times you'll remember."

She eased down on her back again and closed her eyes. A branch of the big tree shaded her face now. The next thing she knew was Leslie's lips pressing down firmly on hers. She opened her eyes and tried to say no, but his lips were firmly on hers. One hand was on her far side and his chest almost touched her flattened breasts.

Her hands caught the side of his head and she pushed his head away from her face.

"Leslie, I told you no. That wasn't very nice of you to sneak up on me that way."

"Then why did you lay down beside me? Maybe you're not as nice and pure and untouched as you pretend."

She sat up and edged away from him. Right now she knew she had to be careful. He was bigger and stronger than she was. He could rip her clothes off and force himself on her if he wanted to. He didn't seem like the type, but he was a man, with a man's drives. She had to be careful.

"Leslie, let's be reasonable about this. You're a fine young man, but I told you I have a friend in Kansas City who I think is about ready to propose. I'm not going to do anything to jeopardize that. I like you, but just as a friend. Please don't kiss me again."

"Are you afraid what you might do? Are you afraid that you might want to see me naked and leaning over you?"

"Leslie, if you keep talking that way, I'm going to get up from here and walk back to town."

"Except you don't have the slightest idea where we are."

"We're south of town. I walk north on the trail and I'll find it."

"You didn't wear your walking shoes."

"I can walk in my bare feet if I have to." Abby took a deep breath. "Leslie, I'm sorry I reacted so strongly to a quick kiss. You surprised me. It's best not to surprise a girl. If you want to kiss her, tell her enough times and it usually will work. Well, maybe we should get back to town. I have a lot of things to get done in my hotel room."

"I don't think it's time to go back yet. I want to soak up some more of the sun. I haven't been out enough. My skin is too white. Humor me for another half hour and let me get some color in my skin."

"Well, all right. But you have to promise. . . ."

"I won't touch you, small red-haired flower. I promise."

Ten minutes later he kissed her again as she lay on her back, and this time he held both of her hands down so she couldn't push him away.

Spur McCoy stood in the buggy and looked along
Cherry Creek. They had driven ten minutes south
and found nothing. He turned to Terri and saw the
worry on her face.

"There was a place he brought me once when he
was terribly depressed. It was on one of the little
branch streams that runs into Cherry Creek. It's the
next one up here. The place he liked was about four
miles up where the brook was not more than three
or four feet wide. We used to make dams out of the
rocks in the bottom up there."

"Let's try it. We don't want to pass up any spot and
miss them if they're up here."

"He'll be along the streams somewhere, I'm
sure," Terri said. "He always liked the water."

They drove over the open country now, following
the wandering creek to the south and west. After 20
minutes, Terri pointed ahead. It was plain to see that
there was no buggy there.

"Damn! You're sure this was the place?"

"Yes. We came here three or four times. I was
hoping. There are three more spots on up stream.
We better get back to Cherry Creek."

They drove back in silence. Only when they were
on the main trail south along Cherry Creek did Terri
speak again.

"Are you *sure* that Leslie did those terrible
things?"

"No, not absolutely sure, but I certainly want to
talk to him. We have four or five pieces of evidence
that link him to the time and place, including the
twenty-cent pieces. I'm sorry, but I think he's the
one."

Terri's shoulders shook as she cried. He put one

arm around her and they drove along the rough trail. It was not a highway they could make any time on. Some places the horse had to walk because the ruts were so deep.

"If it is Leslie, do you think we'll be in time?"

"No way of knowing. He's taken her out three times before and she said he was a perfect gentleman. Why not this time as well?"

Terri shivered. "I don't know. It's a bad feeling I have. Now that you tell me this about Leslie, I remember how he acted on those days after the killings here in town. He was different. He often complained of headaches. But after the death of that last girl, he said his headache was gone, that he felt fine."

"Has he gone out with other women here in town?"

"Of course. He's been to dances and to charity things. I don't think he ever goes to the bordellos, though. He said once he would never go there."

"After that first time with him, did you two ever get together again?"

"That's too personal, Spur." She threw up her hands. "Oh, hell, why not. No, we didn't. I wanted him to three or four times. I was curious and . . . you know, a silly young girl. But he wouldn't. He said it was terrible enough with Mother. He wouldn't make me feel as bad as he did."

They came to a place where the stream made a large bend, and Spur drove off the trail. For a moment Spur thought he saw buggy or carriage wheel tracks going the same way, but they petered out before he got to the grassy place by the river. There was no one there, and no buggy.

Spur raced the horse back to the main trail and they charged ahead.

"We've got to get there in time," Terri said, her eyes hard, her face stern. "I won't let my brother kill anyone else."

Abby knew that she was helpless. He was over her, kissing her, and she was flat on her back and vulnerable. She didn't fight him, she relaxed. Maybe if she encouraged him. *No!* In a moment of truth she realized that Leslie was the killer they had been hunting for so long. He had to be the one. Suddenly it all fit. So she couldn't encourage him. That was how some of his victims got killed, by giving in to him and making him think they were loose women. She had to chastise him, make him think of her as pristine pure.

When the kiss ended he moved so he laid on top of her. She felt a lump at his crotch and knew he was getting excited. But some of the women he didn't rape before he killed them. Was he confused, mixed up?

She watched him as he hovered over her.

"Leslie, are you going to do this, to rob me of my most precious asset, my virginity?"

He frowned and lifted up. "Virginity? You've never slept with a man?"

"Of course not. That happens after a girl gets married. If a girl sleeps around she gets pregnant, and then she's really ruined. Who would marry a pregnant girl?"

"I can't believe no man has ever ripped your clothes off and chewed on those big breasts of yours."

"Believe it. That happens to me only when I get married. At least that's what I've always dreamed about. Somehow I can't figure out how a man as nice and gentlemanly and courteous as you are would rob a girl of all of her dreams, just to satisfy some spur-of-the-moment passion."

"Huh! You don't know much about men. A stiff prick has no conscience. You ever heard that saying? Hell, when I get it hard and I'm in the mood, I want to poke it in some woman, any woman."

"You can do it in your hand. A man told me once that's what he did when he got frustrated and a girl wouldn't sleep with him. He'd do it with his hand."

"I never do that."

"This same man told me any man who said that was lying to others and to himself."

Leslie eased off her and sat up. Abby lifted up beside him. "If you do it with your hand, can I watch?" she asked.

"You never seen much of a man, have you?"

"Of course not. I'm not married."

"You keep saying that."

"It's true. Most women don't sleep with a man before they get married. I read in a magazine that fewer than five percent of women have sex before marriage."

"I don't believe that."

"Isn't it time we went back to town now?" Abby asked.

"Hell, no." His nostrils flared, his eyes turned cold and angry. "We're not going back now because I don't believe you. Did there for a minute. But a pretty girl like you with all that long red hair and your flirty ways and those big tits—hell, I bet you've been fucked a lot of times. I bet you love getting poked. So we're going to find out."

He reached out before she could stop him and grabbed one breast in each hand.

"Now, we're going to find out just how much little Abby can back up her claim of virginity. Don't! Don't try to get my hands off you or I'll squeeze and twist your pretty tits and it'll hurt like fire. Just relax and let your emotions fly. You love having me hold your tits, don't you, Abby?"

"No, no, I don't. You better let go of me right now or you'll be sorry."

He laughed. "Sorry? How will I be sorry?"

Leslie sat beside her, his legs spread a little. She balled up her right fist and before he noticed what she was doing, she pounded her fist three times into his crotch down where his scrotum hung.

Chapter Twenty-Nine

Spur McCoy watched Terri Stanwood as she stood and scanned the narrowing stream they followed. They had seen no one for three or four miles. No small ranches, no buildings.

"Did he ever come out this far?" Spur asked.

"Oh, yes, but he's not at the double bend. There's one more spot about half a mile on upstream. I don't know what we'll do if he's not there."

They drove again. Spur made better time now since the trail was less traveled and had fewer ruts. He figured they were making about eight miles an hour. A half mile would take . . . how long?

He tried to do the mathematics in his head to keep himself from exploding. Eight miles in an hour. One mile would be one eighth of 60 minutes, about eight minutes. Half of a mile should be what . . . four minutes, maybe five.

"This last place is really hidden. Most people don't know it's there. Even the carriage will be out of sight back in the brush and trees. Just a little farther, then we turn left toward the stream, which wanders along another quarter mile. Yes, right here!"

He turned off the track toward the stream and saw it angling away to the left. There was lots of brush and trees ahead, and the stream made a quarter of a mile half circle and came back to the trail.

They went another hundred yards and a small trail opened to the left again.

"In there, that's it. Turn in here."

Spur saw wheel tracks in the grass and prints of one horse. This could be it!

Leslie Stanwood screeched in pain as the pounding in his testicles filled his whole system with a nearly unbearable agony. He rolled away from Abby, drawing up his legs to lessen the terrible pain of one crushed testicle where it had been smashed between her pounding fist and his pelvic bone.

Abby jumped up at once and ran for the rig. She lifted her skirt, stepped up into the carriage, and looked for the reins. They were tied at one side. Furiously she pulled at the leathers.

She saw Leslie get to his knees and stare at her. Then he fell again, wailing in pain. She got the reins loose. Driving horses had never been her specialty. The horse stood with its nose almost against a wall of trees and brush.

How in the world did she make the creature back up? She had no idea. She slapped the reins on the horse's back, and the animal rumbled in her throat and then turned and looked at Abby. Abby pulled on the reins, and slowly the animal turned and tried to move forward and to the right, but ran into a tree again.

Abby screamed at the horse, but it wouldn't move. She turned to look at Leslie. He was halfway to her. She screamed again, and jumped down and ran into the brush, trying to hide from him.

She crouched behind an oak tree, panting, a tear in her skirt and a scratch across one cheek. She looked for a club, a limb that had broken off. She could find nothing that looked substantial.

A moment later she heard him coming in the brush. He was moving faster now, not back to normal, but coming for her. She scurried through more brush, and was stopped by the creek. She saw a branch there that had been washed downstream. It was three feet long and as thick as her arm.

Yes! She grabbed it, and rushed behind another oak tree that was twice as thick through as she was. Abby held her breath as she waited.

For a moment it was quiet. Then she heard him coming again. She held the stick beside her. Her throat was dry and hurting. She panted to get in enough breath. Her muscles felt as if they were stretched to the limit and needing a rest.

For just a second, she closed her eyes as she leaned against the tree. Then she saw him eight feet away, and she took off through the trees again, not knowing where she found the strength. She ran, flailing at the brush, dodging trees, working away from the stream and clutching desperately the stick she carried.

Again she slid behind a tree, this one a giant fir

tree that towered overhead 100 feet. She panted and tried to listen for her attacker.

He came slower now, but moved directly toward her. She could tell he was close. How close? She peeked around the rough fir bark and saw him 20 feet away. Now he carried a knife in one hand, a long, thin knife. The Chicago ice pick! *Leslie was the killer!*

She screamed. His head came up and he glared at her.

"Bitch! Fucking bitch. You hurt me, but not half as bad as I'm gonna hurt you!" He tried to run, but his legs didn't work that well and he stumbled and fell.

Abby ran from him again. Tears streamed down her cheeks. The bodice of her dress had caught on a branch and tore halfway to her waist. She didn't care. She had to run!

She turned again, not even sure what direction she went now, but when she looked up, Leslie stood directly in front of her, six feet away. He laughed and waved the long knife at her. She held out the branch and swung it, trying to hit him. He laughed at her again and stepped out of reach of the stick.

She swung it again, harder, and it turned her halfway around. That was when he darted in. She got the stick back in time to knock down the knife. It fell from his hand as the club pounded on his right wrist.

Leslie screamed and jumped toward her and grabbed the club. She tried to push him away, but he tore the stick out of her hands and lifted it over his head to use it against her.

A shot blasted in the forested quietness. The slug

had been aimed hurriedly and through brush, and it missed its target by a foot, but it was enough to stop Leslie before he could swing the club.

"Abby! Over this way! Run!"

"Spur!" She recognized his voice and jolted away from the spot and ran with all her energy toward his voice. He crashed through brush at that moment and lifted his sixgun. Leslie saw him at the same time and darted behind a big fir tree.

Spur caught Abby as she ran into his arms.

"Did he hurt you?"

"Scared me to death. He's the killer. He has a Chicago ice pick. He was going to use it on . . ." She stopped and sobbed.

Terri Stanwood ran up and took Abby's hand and led her away.

Spur leaped forward toward where the man had vanished. He stopped at the side of the fir and listened. He could hear movement ahead. He raced that way and stopped again, listening. Leslie was moving toward where they had found the carriage. He might be trying for it.

Spur moved silently toward the sound, gaining every second. Twice more he stopped dead still to listen. The man moved slowly, without much skill, through the tangle of brush and larger trees.

The clearing wasn't much, but as Spur came to the near edge, he saw Leslie at the far side. Not time enough for a shot. Spur raced across the cleared area and paused at the brush.

More sounds ahead. Leslie would be in for a surprise when he got to where he had left the carriage.

Sure now of his destination, Spur took a shorter

route through open places where he could sprint. He came to the spot where the carriage had been, and waited behind a sturdy black oak tree.

Three minutes later, Leslie stumbled out of the brush and looked where the carriage had been.

"Damnit, no!" he bellowed.

Spur snapped off a shot at the man, but the range was too great and the round fell short. It sent Leslie back into the cover and surging toward larger trees.

Spur didn't waste another round. He filled the three empty chambers as he ran so he had six rounds ready. Then he eased into the woods behind the fugitive.

Leslie Stanwood was a better woodsman than Spur had first guessed. For a half hour he eluded Spur, as he moved upstream, working higher and higher into the fringe of mountains, using the thicker timber and brush to cover his movement.

At one time Spur saw him cross an open spot more than a 100 yards ahead of him. Spur ran then, crashing brush and making up the distance quickly. Then he had to listen.

Leslie had turned again. Spur followed the sounds and leaped over a fallen log. Just as he touched the ground on the far side of the log, a three-inch log slammed forward toward him. It had been held by a bent-back young fir tree and he had tripped the triggering vine that held it in place.

Spur slammed his body to the ground, and the deadly log jolted through the air two inches over his head. He got up and charged forward. He could hear Stanwood tearing through the brush ahead of him.

It was a battle of wits, of skills, and of endurance.

Spur knew nothing of the constant pain Stanwood suffered from the crushed testicle. He charged along, waiting for the right time to send a slug into the man's body, killing him if possible, wounding him at the least. The man did not deserve to live, not after all the women he had killed.

At least they had arrived in time to save Abby. How she'd gotten away from him he had no idea. Spur stopped to listen. Ahead there was no sound. He looked forward through the trees and saw a sheer rock wall rising 50 feet from the forest floor. There was no way up it. Stanwood would have to go around one end or the other to narrow ravines to work higher on this mountain.

Which way would he go? Stanwood was probably right-handed, most people were. He would go to the right.

Spur angled in that direction, not waiting to climb up to the bottom of the cliff. He could pick up valuable time that way, if he was right.

A small bare spot ahead was covered with sheet rock and afforded no soil for trees or brush. He was halfway across the 40-foot expanse when he heard a noise. He looked up and saw a dozen boulders smashing downward toward him.

Spur sprinted for the nearest edge of the rock field, but he knew he wouldn't make it in time. Directly ahead of him he saw where the rock plate had reared up and left a two-foot-high ledge.

He dove toward it, and slithered the last three feet below the rock ledge just as a thousand pounds of rocks and boulders and dirt smashed across the rock plate.

Half a dozen boulders had hit the rock and

bounced over him. Two smaller ones the size of a baseball had missed the top of the ledge on their bouncing journey and come down hitting him. One slammed into his shoulder on the ground, and the other hit the heel of his boot. His foot felt fine, but his right shoulder would be sore for a week. He flexed his arm. It still worked.

Slowly he edged up so he could look up the way the man-made boulder slide had come. He saw Leslie peering around a two-foot Douglas fir. There was no chance for a shot. Spur eased back down and played dead. Maybe the young man would think he had killed his pursuer.

Spur listened carefully. As soon as he heard the man running through the woods above him toward the edge of the rock wall, Spur was up and moving.

His shoulder hurt more than he figured it would. He kept his sixgun in leather to rest his right arm.

They paced each other along the wall, both out of sight of each other but not out of hearing. Spur couldn't get close enough for a shot. He heard a roar, and wasn't sure what it was.

Then he rounded some brush and saw where a deer trail skirted the cliff and went upward along a narrow gully toward a higher valley. Hundreds of deer a year must use the path coming down for water.

He saw something move along the trail. Then it stopped and blended in. A minute later it moved again. It was a small brown bear cub no more than three or four months old. It rolled in the grass beside the trail.

Just then Leslie broke out of brush and headed up the deer trail. He didn't see the cub. Spur had a chance for one quick shot, but he held up. Leslie looked back, saw Spur, and raced forward.

A huge sow bear reared up on her hind feet as she came out of the brush along the trail 100 feet above Leslie. She roared in anger, dropped down, and ran with that awkward gait that can reach 20 miles an hour.

She went straight down the trail until she was between her cub and Leslie. Then she stopped, reared up on her hind feet, and bellowed out a roar of defiance and warning.

Leslie had moved 50 feet up the trail along the narrow gully. There was no place to go. The solid granite wall was still on his left. The steep side of the gully was on his right, and the sow bear stood her ground 30 feet in front of him.

He turned and looked back at Spur. The Secret Service agent stood there, with his gun hand down, watching.

"Come on down, Stanwood, and face the music. You'll have more of a chance in court than you will with that furious brown mother bear."

"You'd like that, wouldn't you? Bet you can't prove a thing, McCoy."

"Oh, but we can. We have the partly burned pocket flap to the coat you wore when you butchered Maud. It didn't burn all up in your furnace. We have one witness who can put you with Maud at the saloon and two who can swear you were at the murder scene. Remember that couple you bumped into leaving the Colorado hotel late that night?

"Then we have the hair that Helen Foley pulled out of your head. Doc Partlow's new microscope will show an exact match with hairs from your head.

Of course there are the twenty-cent pieces, and how your mother molested and seduced you until you hated her and all loose women. We've got plenty to hang you six times, Stanwood. Come on down and quit bothering the bear cub."

"You can't prove any of that."

"You know we can, Leslie. Your sister can tell a lot to the sheriff about you and your mother. We've got the handkerchief you dropped and the mallard button off that sport coat of yours. It's easy to see where the spare one was taken out of the lining and sewn back on the middle spot. Give it up."

"It was their fault. They all deserved to die. Women are such sluts. The good ones are good but the bad ones make me sick. Even Abby was ready to rip off her clothes. If I'd been a little slower with her, she'd have been begging me to take her clothes off."

"So you did kill all those women between here and Kansas City?"

"Of course. They all deserved to die. Some of them died hard because they were so vile. Others I let off easy because they made just a few mistakes. But you'll never prove any of this. I can go up the side of the gully here and that she-bear will stay with her cub."

"I wouldn't want to try it. You're betting your life on her instincts to stay with her cub rather than chase a threat. I'd bet on her chasing you."

"I know more about bears than you do, McCoy. Watch." He stared at the bear and roared. Then he turned and walked to the side of the gully about 15 feet away, and began moving up it hand over hand. It was more than a 45-degree angle.

The she-bear didn't waste a second. As soon as

Leslie began moving up the side of the gully, she dropped to all fours and charged.

She ran full speed and jumped at him. One huge black paw swept out and slapped Leslie's legs. There was a scream of pain as the crushing blow broke both his legs and slammed him to the side, where he bounced off the side of the gully and rolled to the bottom 20 feet below.

The sow turned and followed him. She landed on him with her two front feet, and one big paw with the vicious curved claws slashed at Leslie's head.

He screamed as he saw the bear coming at him. His bellow of fear and anger and defeat cut off as his head jolted to the side, his neck broken in three places and his spinal cord separated from his head. He died instantly.

The she-bear slapped his head the other way, then picked up his body in her huge jaws and dragged it back to the trail. She sniffed it, pawed at it three times. When the danger didn't move, she trotted back to where her cub played at the side of the trail with a pine cone.

When he saw the she-bear's attack begin, Spur had faded back into the brush so he could see but not be seen. Now the sow looked his way and sniffed, but the wind was blowing across the bear and toward Spur, so she had no hint of his scent.

She stared at the spot where she had seen the other danger, but it was gone. Slowly she lowered to all four feet and nosed her cub, then growled at it in motherly warning, sending it upward on the deer trail toward the higher meadow.

Spur waited for 20 minutes until he was sure the brown bear was well up the trail. Then he went and checked on Leslie. There had been no hope that he might be alive. His head had been all but torn off his shoulders.

Spur picked up the limp body and carried it down the trail, then through the brush toward the stream below. From there he could see the trail 200 yards beyond. He left the body there and hurried back to where he had left the buggy.

The buggy and the carriage were both there. Terri had found the carriage as he'd told her to do and driven it away from where it was parked so Leslie couldn't get away in it.

Abby saw him first. She looked up and screamed. For the first time, Spur looked down at his shirt and pants and realized that they were streaked with blood.

Abby ran toward him.

"I'm fine, fine," he said as she rushed up. "This isn't any of my blood." Abby put her arms around him as they walked on to the buggy. She couldn't say a word, just watched him as if she were afraid he might get away. He sat down and took a deep breath.

Terri looked at him and he glanced away.

"It was a bear, then," Terri said. "I thought I heard one roaring up on the side of the mountain. The new cubs are coming out about this time and the she-bears can be vicious."

He told them what had happened. "He confessed that he killed the women, said it was their fault for being such sluts."

They watched him. "I'm sorry, Terri, there was nothing I could do. My sixgun wouldn't have stopped that big sow. She must have weighed four hundred pounds."

Terri dried her tears. "Somehow I knew he would never come back down the mountain alive. I just knew."

Spur told the women to wait, and he drove the buggy along the creek to the spot he had left Leslie. He picked him up and put him in the buggy seat, and drove back to the carriage.

Terri came and looked at her brother. She bent and kissed his one cheek that wasn't smashed in. Her tears dripped on his face.

"Leslie, dear brother. Mother never gave you a chance at life. She wanted all of your life and hers too. I guess it's too bad that you never found her these last few months."

Spur tied a lead line to the buggy horse and the other end to the back of the carriage. Then they got in the larger rig and Spur drove slowly back toward town.

There was no rush now, no hurry at all. The murdering maniac would strike no more.

Chapter Thirty

The new day dawned bright and clear, and Spur awoke early. He got up and shaved, then went for a haircut. He wore a new shirt and a fresh pair of town pants as he walked down to the telegraph office to send a wire to his boss.

It was short and pointed. "KILLER CAUGHT HERE. DECEASED. TAKING NEXT TRAIN TO KANSAS CITY. CONTACT ME THERE AT MANOR HOUSE HOTEL."

That done, he settled down to a big breakfast at the Carriage House Cafe. He ordered four eggs over easy, country-fried potatoes, two portions of bacon, and half a dozen hotcakes and hot syrup, apple juice and coffee, toast and jam. He was halfway into the meal when Abby slid onto a chair opposite him.

"Morning," she said with the usual lilt back in her voice.

"I wanted you to sleep in," Spur said. He covered her small hand with his. "How is it this morning?"

"I'm fine. He didn't hurt me. He just grabbed me a little. Then I hit him where he would hurt the most and ran into the woods, like I told you."

"There's no rush. We can stay here a couple of days and let you get settled down."

"No, no. I want to get back to Kansas City and I want to go when you go. I'd like a little protection myself for a change, if it's all right."

"Done. First there are a few things to get cleaned up here. I have to make a report to the sheriff. Then I need to talk to Judge Ambrose."

"I want to come along."

"Fine. First some breakfast. You're looking a little underfed."

A half hour later they talked to the sheriff. He grinned when they came in. "Local newspaper reporter was in. I told him the whole story. First thing he did was wire a story to the *New York Times*. You're going to be famous."

"Just what I need, Sheriff Warner. I hope he mentioned your name a few times."

Warner chuckled. "I saw to that." He shook his head. "A bear, a damn brown bear. I never thought our killer would take his last breath staring at a furious she-bear. I've seen them when they got cubs. Get damn mean and nasty. Chased him up a canyon! Damn!"

"You mentioned that you wanted me to fill out a report on what happened yesterday."

"Yep. Right here. Got some questions for you to answer there and places for you to put in the writing. Same thing I have one of my men fill out on a death."

Spur put down the facts, signed it, and they talked a minute. A bellowing scream echoed through the small jail from the back room. A man charged out, his eyes wide.

"Sheriff, you better come. We got trouble in cell two."

"That's Thurlow Stanwood. What the hell is he up to this time?"

"Not a lot," the deputy said.

Spur motioned for Abby to stay in her chair, and he and the sheriff ran with the deputy through two rooms and into the cell block.

Thurlow Stanwood leaned almost to the floor against the bars of his cell. Then Spur saw the strip of blanket around his throat and tied to the bars over his head. His body weight pulled against the cloth noose and cinched it tightly on his throat.

The jailer opened the door and they pushed Stanwood upright. Already his body was stiff with rigor mortis.

"He's dead, hours ago," Spur said. "Let him back down where he was."

They lowered the body so it hung by the neck again. Now Spur nodded. "He fixed the noose around his neck, then tied his own hands down low here so he couldn't save himself. Then he leaned down until the noose cut off the air to his throat, and in two minutes he would be unconscious and not a chance he could keep from strangling.

"His own body weight strangled him the same way that a bad hangman's noose would have done."

They cut him down and put him on the bunk.

Then Sheriff Warner turned to the two other men in the jail.

"What happened?" he asked. "You better tell me straight or you two guys are going to rot in here without food or water. Now talk."

One of the men shrugged. He was small, wiry, in jail for robbery. "Hell, don't matter none to me. He told us he was gonna do it soon as it got dark last night. He said nobody ever checked after the last call about eight. So he ripped his blanket using his teeth and made his ropes.

"Damned if he didn't tell us exactly how he was gonna do it and it worked. He said good-bye to us, then tied his hands down there and lowered down easy so he wouldn't break the blanket rope. He gagged and wheezed and struggled a little. Then he was dead."

"Why? Did he say why?"

The other man spoke up. He was the town drunk but smart enough. "Sure as hell did. He found out his kid got himself killed by that she-bear, and he found out Leslie was the killer who slaughtered the three women here in town. He couldn't take it. Said he worked hard to leave his kids something. Now it was gone and his kid was dead. He couldn't take the embarrassment and the prison term."

The undertaker came in and carried away the body. Spur talked in the front office a minute with the sheriff, then Spur and Abby went outside. He told her about Stanwood.

"That's terrible. I never thought a man as strong as he was would take his own life."

"Stress and worry like this put a new light on things for some people," Spur said.

"I want to go see Terri," Abby said. "It might be better if I tell her what happened here. She helped me yesterday. I've got to go."

Spur nodded. "You go see her and I'll talk to the judge." They parted, and Spur continued down the street to the courthouse. He found Judge Ambrose in his office before court began. Spur told him about Thurlow Stanwood.

"Too bad, too bad. I've been going over his case. I'd about been ready to go easy on Stanwood. He did this town a lot of good. I figured if he returned the original price of the ranch, plus ten years of interest at four percent, the debt should be paid. I'd put him on probation for five years. Damn. I guess the fact that his son was a crazy murderer was too much for him."

"So what happens now, Judge?"

"Terri inherits. The wife deserted. Terri is the only one left. I'll make the same arrangement with her. Fifteen thousand plus four percent for ten years. With interest compounding it should be around twenty thousand dollars somewhere. That money would go in trust for the heirs if they can be found. If no heirs are found the money reverts to the county after ten years."

"Sounds fair. I'm sure Terri would agree to that. The ranch and mine and lumber business must be worth more than a million dollars."

"At least. So Terri is now an extremely wealthy young lady."

"Thanks, Judge. Is it all right if I tell her the good news?"

"Don't see why not. I'll make it official this morning. Too bad about Stanwood—both of them. I knew Thurlow. Sure, he had some faults, but he was good for this country."

Spur left the courthouse and headed for the Stanwood town place. On the way, he passed the Longly General Store. A sturdily built man with black hair and a wind- and sunburned face was loading up a freight wagon with some supplies. He had a hook nose and steady brown eyes. Spur paused as the man talked with the store owner.

"So, you're loaded up with your goods. You must have talked to the bank."

"Yes, I did. Nice man over there. He loaned me the money and said I could get all I need for two more wagons and the expenses of shearing my sheep. I've hired two young men to train as shearers. I might keep them on as I build my flock."

"Plenty of room in this country for both sheep and cattle," Longly said as Spur walked on past. "How did your wife like that new dress?"

Alfonso Ortega grinned. "Oh, she liked it a great deal. But that night I got almost no sleep at all. She kept thanking me and thanking me until I was worn right down to a nub." Both men laughed. "Now I think I will get her another new dress." The men laughed again and went into the store.

Spur continued to the Stanwood town house, and found the two women sitting on the front porch in rocking chairs staring at the white peaks of the Rocky Mountains far to the west.

He walked up, and they nodded and Terri pointed to another chair. He sat. Spur saw that Terri had been crying.

"Terri, I'm sorry. He was a proud man. Everything just crashed down on top of him all at once."

She nodded. Spur decided not to tell her about the easy way the judge was going to handle the theft of the ranch with her father. She didn't need any more grief.

They sat and rocked for five minutes.

Terri looked at Spur. "Why is life so unfair? Why must I lose my father and my brother all within a matter of hours?"

"I don't know, Terri. Life is never fair and life is never easy. My father used to tell me that. If we use that as a guide, then we can be a little ready for the bad things, and know we have to work hard to make good things happen."

"Would you like to take a ride down along the river?" Abby asked.

Terri looked up quickly. "After what happened to you yesterday?"

Abby shrugged. "It's over, forgotten. Well, not really forgotten, but pushed way back in my memory. I know you love the river. We can go the other direction."

Spur drove the carriage, and they went to the river a short way north of town and watched the water. They parked in the shade, and Terri cried again. Abby held her until she had cried it all out.

She wiped her eyes and sat up and looked at both of them.

"All right, now I'm through crying. We'll go back into town and arrange for a funeral for both Father and Leslie. It will be private with just a quick talk at the gravesite. Then I need to start figuring out what I can do. I'll have to talk with Judge Ambrose to see how this might change things."

"That's good, Terri. Grab life by the throat and try

and make it be at least reasonable. When shall we go back?"

"Right now. Let's get done what has to be done."

It was nearly four that afternoon when the quick funeral was over. Only a few people attended. Most didn't know it was happening, and that was fine with Terri.

It was five before Terri, Abby, and Spur sat in her parlor with coffee and cinnamon rolls.

Terri had a pad of paper and two sharp pencils. "First I have to talk with the judge. I need to find out how long this arrangement will continue. Someone said it could take a year or even two years to find any heirs that might be in New York State. I want to get that cleared up. If I have to move out of the house, I'll do it. I'll try to get a job here in town doing something. If I can't, I have an Uncle John who lives back near Albany, New York. He has a big store, and I'm sure I can work there."

Spur cleared his throat and shook his head. "That won't be necessary, Terri. I had a talk with the judge this morning. He said I could tell you what he decided. As soon as he found out about your father, he told me what he would order.

"First the ranch's value ten years ago was established at fifteen thousand dollars. That amount, with interest at four percent compounded yearly, will be put in a trust fund for any heirs found by the court.

"The rest of the resources—lands, property, cattle, mines, and saw log contracts, and the mill and any retail operations of the Flying S Enterprises— shall remain the property of one Terri Stanwood, to do with as she pleases."

Terri sat there for a moment, a small frown creasing her face. "You're sure about this, Spur? You're not just saying this to cheer me up?"

"It's absolutely true. The judge said such payment would be right and proper, and that the increase in value of the property was the result of your father's industry and genius and hard work, and those qualities could not be discounted. Everything is yours."

Terri cried again.

The cook had fixed a big dinner for them, and they ate and drank wine and talked about the future.

Already Terri was full of plans. She would need a ranch manager, some man she could trust who could run a big outfit.

"And don't forget to look for a husband," Abby said. "Get one who can also run the ranch and the rest of the operation. That's not going to be easy."

"I already found one, but he probably won't take either job," Terri said, looking at Spur. "I'm offering him the general manager's job at six thousand dollars a year, plus an option to marry the owner whenever he wants to."

Her voice dropped and the tease went out, and Spur realized she was serious. Abby watched him. Terri stared at him with an eager expression that was so vulnerable that Spur really wanted to accept her offer.

"Now, Terri, that's a great future, but I've already got a job with a contract. You wouldn't want me to break a contract, would you?"

"Hell, yes!" she said, and they all laughed. The serious moment was over, and they were back to being friends again.

They talked until nearly midnight, and then at last said good-bye. She offered them guest rooms for the night, but they declined and said they would see her tomorrow. There would be a lot of legal papers to sign and she wanted Spur there to look over everything.

"Don't worry, I'll pay you for the work. In fact, I'll overpay you and take you both out to lunch or supper or whatever it is by then."

Back at the hotel Spur took Abby to her room, and she lifted her brows. He kissed her seriously, and she returned the kiss. Then he stepped back.

"Tomorrow we'll get Terri all set, and then the next day head for the train and Cheyenne and then Kansas City. I've heard that the train now has those new compartments, little rooms built along the side of the car that are absolutely private. We can enjoy ourselves all the way into Kansas City."

"Sounds good to me," Abby said. She cocked her head to one side. "You slept with Terri, didn't you?"

Spur groaned. "Damn, how did you know?"

"A woman can tell. It was the way Terri looked at you, the way she touched you, the way I do sometimes. The 'ownership touch' I call it, to warn other females off." She smiled. "I'm not a bit jealous. Terri probably needed some loving coming from that family. Can I ask you another question?"

He kissed her again, then nodded. "Why didn't you accept her offer to manage her ranch and marry her and pick up a quick million-dollar enterprise?"

He pecked a kiss on Abby's nose, and then caressed her breast just for a moment. "I like you better. Besides, do I look like a big businessman?"

She leaned back and stared at him, then grinned.

"McCoy, you can be absolutely anything you want to be." She turned and unlocked her door and pulled him inside.

"Right now I want you to be with me tonight here in my room, and we'll talk about all the fun things we're going to do on that train. I've never made love on a train. That will be wild. But tonight I want it to be sweet and soft and gentle. Do you think you can handle that assignment, Spur McCoy?"

Spur waited as she lit the lamp in her room, and then he locked the door. When he turned, she ran into his arms. "Can I handle this assignment of a sexy bundle with the long red hair and the slender hips that won't stop pounding? Hell, I don't know, but I intend to give it a good try—all night if need be."

It took all night.

REAL WEST

The true life adventures of America's greatest frontiersmen.

THE LIFE OF KIT CARSON by John S.C. Abbott. Christopher "Kit" Carson could shoot a man at twenty paces, trap and hunt better than the most skilled Indian, and follow any trail — even in the dead of winter. His courage and strength as an Indian fighter earned him the rank of brigadier general of the U.S. Army. This is the true story of his remarkable life.

__2968-5 $2.95

THE LIFE OF BUFFALO BILL by William Cody. Strong, proud and courageous, Buffalo Bill Cody helped shape the history of the United States. Told in his own words, the real story of his life and adventures on the untamed frontier is as wild and unforgettable as any tall tale ever written about him.

__2981-2 $2.95

SPEND YOUR LEISURE MOMENTS WITH US.

Hundreds of exciting titles to choose from—something for everyone's taste in fine books: breathtaking historical romance, chilling horror, spine-tingling suspense, taut medical thrillers, involving mysteries, action-packed men's adventure and wild Westerns.

SEND FOR A FREE CATALOGUE TODAY!